"A winning series."   —*The Paperback Forum*

"It's murder most English all the way!"   —*The Literary Times*

INSPECTOR WITHERSPOON ALWAYS TRIUMPHS . . . HOW DOES HE DO IT?

Even the Inspector himself doesn't know—because his secret weapon is as ladylike as she is clever. She's Mrs. Jeffries—the determined, delightful detective who stars in this unique Victorian mystery series. Be sure to read them all.

The Inspector and Mrs. Jeffries
A doctor is found dead in his own office—and Mrs. Jeffries must scour the premises to find the prescription for murder.

Mrs. Jeffries Dusts for Clues
One case is solved and another is opened when the Inspector finds a missing brooch—pinned to a dead woman's gown. But Mrs. Jeffries never cleans a room without dusting under the bed—and never gives up on a case before every loose end is tightly tied.

The Ghost and Mrs. Jeffries
Death is unpredictable . . . but the murder of Mrs. Hodges was foreseen at a spooky séance. The practical-minded housekeeper may not be able to see the future—but she can look into the past and put things in order to solve this haunting crime.

Mrs. Jeffries Takes Stock
A businessman has been murdered—and it could be because he cheated his stockholders. The housekeeper's interest is piqued, and when it comes to catching killers, the smart money's on Mrs. Jeffries.

Mrs. Jeffries on the Ball
A festive Jubilee celebration turns into a fatal affair—and Mrs. Jeffries must find the guilty party.

continued . . .

Mrs. Jeffries on the Trail
Why was Annie Shields out selling flowers late on a foggy night? And more importantly, who killed her while she was doing it?

Mrs. Jeffries Plays the Cook
Mrs. Jeffries finds herself doing double duty: cooking for the Inspector's household and trying to cook a killer's goose.

Mrs. Jeffries and the Missing Alibi
When Inspector Witherspoon becomes the main suspect in a murder, Scotland Yard refuses to let him investigate. But no one said anything about Mrs. Jeffries.

Mrs. Jeffries Stands Corrected
When a local publican is murdered and Inspector Witherspoon botches the investigation, trouble starts to brew for Mrs. Jeffries.

Mrs. Jeffries Takes the Stage
After a theater critic is murdered, Mrs. Jeffries uncovers the victim's secret past: a real-life drama more compelling than any stage play.

Mrs. Jeffries Questions the Answer
Hannah Cameron was not well-liked. But were her friends or family the sort to stab her in the back? Mrs. Jeffries must find out.

Mrs. Jeffries Reveals Her Art
Mrs. Jeffries has to work double-time to find a missing model *and* a killer. And she'll have to get her whole staff involved—before someone else becomes the next subject.

Mrs. Jeffries Takes the Cake
The evidence was all there: a dead body, two dessert plates, and a gun. As if Mr. Ashbury had been sharing cake with his own killer. Now, Mrs. Jeffries will have to dish up some clues.

Mrs. Jeffries Rocks the Boat
Mirabelle had traveled by boat all the way from Australia to visit her sister—only to wind up murdered. Now, Mrs. Jeffries must solve the case—and it's sink or swim.

Mrs. Jeffries Weeds the Plot
Three attempts have been made on Annabeth Gentry's life. Is it due to her recent inheritance, or is it because her bloodhound dug up the body of a murdered thief?

**Visit Emily Brightwell's website at
www.emilybrightwell.com.**

**Also available from Prime Crime:
The first three Mrs. Jeffries Mysteries in one volume
*Mrs. Jeffries Learns the Trade***

MRS. JEFFRIES
and the
Feast of St. Stephen

Emily Brightwell

BERKLEY PRIME CRIME, NEW YORK

THE BERKLEY PUBLISHING GROUP
Published by the Penguin Group
Penguin Group (USA) Inc.
375 Hudson Street, New York, New York 10014, USA
Penguin Group (Canada), 90 Eglinton Avenue East, Suite 700, Toronto, Ontario M4P 2Y3, Canada
(a division of Pearson Penguin Canada Inc.)
Penguin Books Ltd., 80 Strand, London WC2R 0RL, England
Penguin Group Ireland, 25 St. Stephen's Green, Dublin 2, Ireland (a division of Penguin Books Ltd.)
Penguin Group (Australia), 250 Camberwell Road, Camberwell, Victoria 3124, Australia
(a division of Pearson Australia Group Pty. Ltd.)
Penguin Books India Pvt. Ltd., 11 Community Centre, Panchsheel Park, New Delhi—110 017, India
Penguin Group (NZ), 67 Apollo Drive, Rosedale, North Shore 0632, New Zealand
(a division of Pearson New Zealand Ltd.)
Penguin Books (South Africa) (Pty.) Ltd., 24 Sturdee Avenue, Rosebank, Johannesburg 2196,
South Africa

Penguin Books Ltd., Registered Offices: 80 Strand, London WC2R 0RL, England

This is a work of fiction. Names, characters, places, and incidents either are the product of the author's imagination or are used fictitiously, and any resemblance to actual persons, living or dead, business establishments, events, or locales is entirely coincidental. The publisher does not have any control over and does not assume any responsibility for author or third-party websites or their content.

MRS. JEFFRIES AND THE FEAST OF ST. STEPHEN

A Berkley Prime Crime Book / published by arrangement with the author

PRINTING HISTORY
Berkley Prime Crime hardcover edition / October 2007
Berkley Prime Crime mass-market edition / October 2008

Copyright © 2007 by Cheryl Arguile.
Cover illustration by David Stimson.
Cover design by Annette Fiore Defex.

ISBN: 978-0-425-22427-4

BERKLEY® PRIME CRIME
Berkley Prime Crime Books are published by The Berkley Publishing Group,
a division of Penguin Group (USA) Inc.,
375 Hudson Street, New York, New York 10014.
BERKLEY PRIME CRIME and the BERKLEY PRIME CRIME design are trademarks belonging to Penguin Group (USA) Inc.

PRINTED IN THE UNITED STATES OF AMERICA

10 9 8 7 6 5 4 3 2 1

*This book is dedicated to
Richard Arguile
with love and thanks for all the years
of support, encouragement, and help.
I couldn't have done it without you!*

CHAPTER 1

"I do hope you like this, Stephen." Maria Farringdon smiled as she handed the bottle of Bordeaux to her host. "Of course, it's nowhere near as special as that lovely ruby port we received from you yesterday, but our wine merchant assures us this is very good. I do hope you like it."

"Thank you, dear lady." Stephen Whitfield bowed graciously in acknowledgment of the gift. He glanced at the bottle, and his blue eyes widened as he read the label. Blast, she'd managed to outdo him. He'd no doubt that the choice of such an expensive wine had been her idea, not her husband's. Basil was far too well-bred to have gone to such extravagance. This was only to be expected: women from her background always managed to get it wrong. They simply weren't raised to understand the really important social nuances. "But there was no need for you to go to any trouble."

"Nonsense," Basil Farringdon said. "Of course it was necessary. You send us a wonderful bottle of your special port every year. You go to a great deal of trouble."

"Not really," he replied.

"But you do," Basil countered. "You have it shipped all the way from Portugal, and you cork it yourself. It's about time we reciprocated, don't you think." His wide, chubby face creased in a smile. "Maria chose this just for you."

"And it is much appreciated." Stephen forced a chuckle and glanced at her. She was smiling at him, but he could see that the smile hadn't quite reached her eyes. To annoy her, he took her arm and tugged her gently toward a set of double doors farther down the hall. "Let's go into the drawing room. You two are the first to arrive, but I expect the others will be here shortly." He looked over his shoulder. Flagg, his butler, had returned from hanging up the guests' heavy winter wraps and now hovered discreetly at the front door. "I'd like this opened and brought to the drawing room."

"Yes, sir." Flagg took the bottle and disappeared.

Whitfield held himself ramrod straight as he escorted his guests into the drawing room. The moment they stepped inside the cavernous room, Maria Farringdon pulled her arm out of his grasp and moved quickly toward a blue brocade love seat. Basil followed his wife.

Whitfield walked over to a mahogany sideboard near the fireplace. He grinned at Maria, his expression amused. She'd not liked his taking her arm, but she could hardly object, as he was merely playing the solicitous host. "Would you care for an aperitif, or would you rather wait for the Bordeaux?"

"I'd like a sherry." Maria Farringdon returned his smile with an amused one of her own. She couldn't wait for the evening to progress, for the other guests to arrive. Whitfield was in for a big surprise, and it wouldn't be one that he was expecting, either. He was so conceited, she thought. He really thought himself a great catch. She studied him dispassionately as he lifted the crystal stopper off the top of a decanter. He was a tall, thin man with steel gray hair, a bristling mustache, and a lean, hawkish face that some women considered very handsome. He'd been a widower for years now, and every widow in London had set her cap for him at one time or another. Maria had never understood why; he wasn't that rich, and he certainly wasn't very charming.

She eased her thin backside flush against the back of the seat and braced her feet firmly on the floor. Brocade was a very slippery material, and she wasn't taking any chances of sliding off. She arranged the skirt of her green silk dress and leaned back, preparing to enjoy the spectacle. This was going to be priceless, absolutely priceless. Who would have thought the old fool would actually open it in front of her!

"I'll have sherry as well," Basil Farringdon said as he sat down in the armchair next to the sofa. "Are there many others coming this evening?" he asked.

"It's just a small dinner party," Stephen replied. "Henry will be here—I knew you'd want to see him—and Eliza's invited as well. She's bringing an acquaintance of hers and, of course, my sister-in-law, Rosalind, will be joining us."

Maria glanced at her husband, and their eyes met. They'd both heard the rumors about Eliza Graham's "acquaintance." Apparently Stephen was the only person in London who was still in the dark.

"Ah, excellent." Stephen looked up from his task as the drawing room door opened and two people, a man and a woman, stepped inside. "You're finally here."

"We're not late, Stephen." The woman smiled as she spoke, but there was just the barest hint of irritation in her tone. Eliza Graham was forty-seven and well past her youth, yet her hair was still a lustrous dark brown and her skin smooth and unlined. Her elegant wine red evening gown rustled softly as she and her companion swept into the room. "The traffic was dreadful, and it took ages for Hugh to find a cab. It appears that everyone has decided to stay in town for the Christmas season."

"Now, now, dear." Hugh Langdon let go of her arm. "It didn't take all that long. It just seemed a long time because it's so very cold outside. But at least it has finally stopped raining."

"Does everyone know Hugh?" Eliza stopped and looked around at the other guests.

"I'm afraid I haven't had the pleasure." Basil, who'd risen to his feet when they entered the room, crossed the small space separating them, with his hand extended. "I'm Basil Farringdon, and this is my wife, Maria."

"Sorry, thought you all knew each other," Stephen mumbled from the background. "This is Hugh Langdon."

Hugh shook hands and then bowed to Maria. "I'm very pleased to meet you both."

Maria smiled politely and inclined her head in acknowledgment of the introduction. She was quite surprised by the man's appearance. He looked so very average, so very ordinary, not at all like she'd imagined. According to the gossip she'd heard, he was supposedly quite a Lothario and had a string of brokenhearted women in his past. But if she was any judge, Langdon had to be pushing sixty. His hair, though still more brown than gray, was receding from his forehead; he was barely an inch or so taller than average; and beneath his beautifully tailored navy blue evening coat, he had a distinct potbelly. But then again, when you were as rich as Langdon, you didn't need to worry overly much about your appearance.

Maria glanced at Stephen just as Langdon and Eliza sat down together on the settee opposite her. She saw Stephen's eyes narrow, and a flush crept up his sharp cheekbones. Oh, yes, indeed, tonight was going to be great fun!

"It's going to be cold tonight," Wiggins, the footman, said as he came into the kitchen. He was a good-looking young man with brown hair, round apple cheeks, and a very cheerful disposition.

"It's been cold all week," Mrs. Goodge, the portly, gray-haired cook, said. She put a platter of pork chops on the table.

"Gracious, that's a lot of pork," Mrs. Jeffries, the housekeeper, commented as she slipped into her spot at the head of the table. "I'm surprised that any of us is even hungry after that lovely tea we had at Mrs. Maynard's." The household was eating much later than they usually did because they'd gone to a Christmas tea at their neighbors'.

"There are two extra chops," the cook replied. "The inspector is having dinner at Lady Cannonberry's tonight, but he didn't let me know till I'd already started the chops, so the lad here"—she indicated Wiggins with a nod in his direction—"can eat hearty if he's a mind to."

As there was always plenty of food for the servants in the household of Inspector Gerald Witherspoon, the comment wasn't taken seriously.

"Betsy's the one that needs to eat hearty," Wiggins said, tossing a fast glance in the maid's direction. "She's gettin' as thin as a lamppost."

"I've only lost a pound or two," Betsy muttered. She pushed a lock of blond hair, which had slipped out of her cap, back behind her ear. She knew the others were worried about her, but she was fine, just fine. She wished they'd stop fretting over her. The past six months had been the most miserable of her life, but she was getting over it. "I haven't lost that much weight."

"Yes, you 'ave," Wiggins argued. "And when he gets back and sees how peaked you look, he'll 'ave a fit."

They all knew who "he" was.

"Wiggins, that's Betsy's personal business." Mrs. Goodge cast an anxious glance in the maid's direction.

"It's alright, Mrs. Goodge," Betsy said. "Wiggins is just concerned, that's all. Not to worry, though: I'll eat plenty tonight." She reached for the bowl of boiled potatoes that was next to the chops. "And it won't be because I'm worried about what *he'll* think, either. It'll be because I'm hungry enough to eat a horse." It would be a cold day in the pits of hell before she'd ever be concerned about him again, she told herself as she slapped a huge spoonful of potatoes onto her plate. Besides, one of the painful truths she'd learned this past six months was that time did heal all wounds. Two weeks ago, she'd realized she was looking forward to Christmas. The crowds of shoppers on High Street, the smell of Mrs. Goodge's baking, the decorations in some of the more posh shops—she'd found herself liking all of it. She'd even smiled at a young man getting off the omnibus yesterday. Her heart was definitely on the mend, and what's more, she'd never let it get broken like that again!

Mrs. Jeffries glanced at the cook. Both women were relieved to see Betsy showing a bit of appetite; in truth, the girl had gotten so thin that they were concerned for her health. The housekeeper put a slice of bread onto her own plate and reached for the butter pot. The maid had seemed better lately, but she still wasn't her old self. Perhaps it would be best to avoid personal subjects and instead keep the conversation to Inspector Witherspoon's police business.

That always cheered everyone up. "Constable Barnes mentioned that the Collinger case is going to trial next week." She stuck her knife in the pot and scooped out a good chunk of creamy butter. "The inspector will be testifying, of course. I believe he's a bit nervous about it."

"Can't think why," Mrs. Goodge replied. "He's testified lots of times, and he always gets it right."

Witherspoon's latest case, the apprehension of a man who'd murdered an elderly woman during the course of a robbery, had involved very little investigation on any of their parts. Harold Collinger, the killer, had left a trail of evidence so obvious that a two-year-old could have followed it. He'd not only been found with the victim's belongings in his possession, but he'd bragged to his mates down at the pub about doing in the poor woman. Within two days after the discovery of the body, Collinger had been arrested and had confessed.

"Yes, but testifying still makes him a bit uncomfortable," Mrs. Jeffries commented. Inspector Witherspoon had solved more homicides than anyone in the history of the Metropolitan Police Force. He wasn't quite sure how he'd managed to catch so many killers; it just seemed to happen. And he didn't know why he'd suddenly become such a good detective. How could he, when his entire household went to so much trouble to make sure he was kept firmly in the dark? Gerald Witherspoon, one of nature's true gentlemen, had a great deal of help on each and every one of his cases.

When he "caught a case," as Wiggins so colorfully put it, his household leapt into action: they snooped around the crime scene, they found out what they could about the suspects, and most of all, they learned as much information as possible about the victim. A few trusted friends knew of their activities, but for the most part, they worked hard to be discreet. Each member of the household had their own area of expertise.

Mrs. Goodge was excellent at finding out background information, and she never even had to leave the house to do it; she had a steady stream of delivery boys, gas men, fruit vendors, and tinkers tramping through her kitchen. She plied them with treats and tea as she learned every morsel of gossip there was to be had about both victims and suspects. The elderly cook had served some of the richest families in all England, so if her local sources were no good, she used her connections to her former colleagues to find out what she needed to know.

Betsy was very good at getting facts out of shopkeepers, while Wiggins was quite handy at persuading maids or footmen to reveal all sorts of useful clues. Both of them had become rather skilled at following people as well.

"It wasn't much of a case, was it?" Betsy sighed heavily. "We knew right away who'd done it." She'd been bitterly disappointed when the case had been solved so quickly; she'd been hoping that having a good murder to sink her teeth into might prove a welcome distraction. But instead that stupid killer had confessed, and she'd had nothing to do but her household tasks. It wasn't fair. It had been the first murder they'd had since *he'd* left, and it had turned out to be about as interesting as the boiled potatoes she was trying to choke down.

"Yes, well, it was one of the inspector's less complex murders," the housekeeper replied. She stifled a surge of irritation. Smythe, Betsy's fiancé, had been gone for six months, and despite Betsy's protests that she was fine, the girl could still slide into a good bout of self-pity. It was time for her to buck up and act like a grown woman. For goodness' sake, there were people starving on these very streets of London, people who would love that food heaped on the girl's plate. "Besides, I'm not sure any of us were up to a complicated murder."

"Why wouldn't we be up to it?" Betsy protested. "I was prepared to do my part, and so was Wiggins . . ." She broke off as a loud knocking came from the back door.

"I'll see who it is." Wiggins leapt to his feet and started for the hall. Fred, the household's mongrel dog, who'd been sleeping peacefully on a rug near the warm stove, jumped up and trailed after the footman.

"Cor blimey!" they heard Wiggins exclaim. "Look what the cat's dragged home! What are you knockin' for? You shoulda just walked right in."

"I wasn't sure of my welcome," said a familiar voice.

Betsy got to her feet and stared into the darkened hallway. She'd gone deathly pale. Mrs. Jeffries and Mrs. Goodge stood up as well. The cook looked at the housekeeper, her expression anxious. Both of them glanced at Betsy, but she didn't notice; her entire attention was focused on the footsteps coming down the hall.

Wiggins, followed by a tall, dark-haired man wearing a long, heavy gray coat, came into the kitchen. Dampness glistened on the man's thick black hair. A blue and gray woven scarf hung around his neck, and he pulled off a pair of leather gloves as he walked. His face was red from the cold, and there was a hint of shadow on his high cheekbones and his chin.

"Look who I found," the footman said gleefully. "Isn't it wonderful? He made it home in time for Christmas."

"Hello, Smythe. Welcome home," Mrs. Jeffries said softly.

"Maria, are you all right?" Basil Farringdon whispered in his wife's ear as they walked into the brilliantly lighted dining room for dinner. "You've been staring at Stephen for the last hour."

"That's because he's putting on such a good show," she replied softly. "Did you see his face when he took us all into the morning room to show off that ridiculous Christmas tree? I thought he was going to have an apoplexy attack when Mrs. Graham didn't give it more than a glance."

"Shh . . . He'll hear you." Basil looked over his shoulder at their host. Despite the fact that the butler announced that dinner was served, Whitfield hadn't moved toward the dining room.

"Don't be silly," she whispered. "Right now the only thing he's interested in doing is pouring that Bordeaux down his throat. Honestly, he acts as if he's afraid someone's going to steal it away, and he's glaring at Mr. Langdon like he's worried the man's going to run off with his silver."

Whitfield was standing in the open door of the morning room. A Christmas tree blazing with candles and colored ornaments of painted glass, wood, and clay stood in front of the marble fireplace. Two uniformed footmen, one with a bucket of sand at his feet and one with a bucket of water, stood on either side of the mantel. Whitfield held a glass of wine in one hand while with his other he pointed at the evergreen boughs decorating the mantelpiece behind the tree. He was saying something, but the others in the room were paying no attention to him. Eliza Graham was standing in front of the tree, laughing at some quip of Hugh Langdon's; Henry Becker, another guest, was laughing as well. Rosalind Murray, Whitfield's sister-in-law, was in the corner of the dining room, gesturing for the butler to begin pouring the wine for the first course.

"More like he's worried Langdon's going to run off with Mrs. Graham." Basil chuckled softly, caught himself, and composed his features so that no one could possibly accuse him of actually enjoying himself. For goodness' sake, this was a social obligation, and he must act appropriately.

Whitfield, with one last glare at his guests, turned on his heel and stumbled into the dining room. The others followed suit.

Farringdon waited till everyone had approached the table; then he pulled out the ornate Queen Anne dining chair, seated his wife, and took his own seat.

Hugh Langdon seated Eliza Graham and took the chair next to her. Stephen was at the head of the table with Maria on his right and Eliza Graham on his left. Henry Becker was next to Maria. Basil was beside Rosalind Murray.

"It's nice to see you again, Mrs. Murray," Basil said politely.

"It's good to see you, Mr. Farringdon," she replied. She was a tall blond woman in her late fifties. Her complexion was pale, her eyes were blue, and the gray in her hair was quickly overtaking the blond. She wore a lavender silk high-necked evening gown and an anxious smile.

The dining room door opened, and the servants began serving the first course.

"Will you be staying in town for Christmas?" Maria asked Rosalind. She felt very sorry for the poor woman, especially tonight. Eliza Graham's bright beauty made the pale Rosalind look even blander than usual.

"Oh yes, we've no plans to leave town." Rosalind smiled faintly.

"We're thinking of going to Scotland," Hugh interjected. "But Eliza's afraid we'll be trapped up there by bad weather."

Stephen glared at Hugh and gestured for Flagg. He nodded at the glass of white wine next to his soup bowl. "I don't want that." He raised the glass of Bordeaux he'd brought with him to the table. "I want this."

"But the first course is a fish soup," Rosalind protested. "It won't go with Bordeaux."

Whitfield ignored her. "Bring me the bottle. It's in the drawing room," he ordered Flagg. Rosalind gave an almost imperceptible shrug and turned her attention back to the guests.

"I thought we agreed you'd be here for Christmas Eve dinner," Whitfield said accusingly to Eliza. "And for Boxing Day as well."

"Those plans were very tentative," Eliza replied softly. She cast a quick, nervous smile at Langdon.

"Ah, yes, Boxing Day. It's actually the Feast of St. Stephen," Henry Becker said to no one in particular. "He was quite an interesting saint. I believe he was stoned to death, or perhaps he was drawn and quartered."

Rosalind frowned at Stephen. "If we're having a full dinner for Christmas Eve, Stephen, you'd best let me know so that I can make arrangements with the cook. The servants have plans as well, you know."

"The servants will do as they are told," he snapped.

Maria Farringdon glanced at her husband, her expression amused. Basil gave her a stern look, then quickly picked up his wineglass to hide his own smile. His good wife was enjoying herself far too much, and truth to tell, so was he. Gracious, this might end in fisticuffs before the evening was out.

"I say, Stephen, this is very good wine." Henry Becker, who was totally oblivious to the undercurrents of tension around the table, put his glass down and smiled at his host. He was a slight man with a narrow chest and a full head of graying hair. A widower of many years, he'd been to school with Stephen and Basil, and desired nothing more than some congenial company, a good dinner, and some decent wine.

"It's French," Stephen replied. He took another long sip from his own drink and then nodded at Flagg, who'd come in with the Bordeaux, to refill his glass. "Mr. Langdon, do you like French wine?"

"It depends," Langdon replied. He put down his soup spoon and turned his attention to his host. "Some French wine is excellent, but some of it isn't worth drinking."

"Or perhaps some people simply can't appreciate a fine wine." Whitfield paused and took a deep breath. "Not everyone has a refined palate."

Maria Farringdon snickered and tried to cover the noise with a discreet cough. Basil gave her a warning look, but none of the other guests appeared to notice her outburst.

"And some people will drink any old rubbish as long as it has a fancy label on it," Langdon replied with an amused smile.

Stephen stared at him for a long moment. "I've an announcement I'd like to make."

"An announcement," Eliza interjected. "What sort of announcement?"

"Why, surely you know." Stephen took another deep breath, wheezing a bit as though he was having trouble getting air. "It's something we've been discussing for several months now."

"Perhaps this isn't the right time," Eliza said with a nervous glance at Hugh. "We ought to discuss the matter further. Nothing has been settled as yet. I told you I needed a bit more time to think the matter over."

"Nonsense." Whitfield coughed. "You've had plenty of time."

Langdon looked first at his host and then at Eliza, but he said nothing. He leaned back in his chair and folded his arms over his chest.

"What kind of announcement is it?" Henry asked eagerly.

"A very pleasant one." Stephen could barely choke out the words. His face had turned bright red, and his shoulders slumped forward.

"Stephen, you've gone a funny color." Basil stared at him in concern.

"You're very flushed," Rosalind said. "You've turned red. Have you got a fever?"

Eliza stared at him. "You don't look well at all. I think perhaps you've had too much excitement."

"Are you alright, sir?" Langdon unfolded his arms and leaned toward his host, his expression concerned.

But their host wasn't alright. Suddenly his eyes widened, his mouth gaped open, and he sat bolt upright. "Ye gods, you've all turned blue."

"Turned blue," Langdon repeated. "Is this some sort of absurd joke?"

Rosalind had risen from her chair. "Stephen, for goodness' sake, what is wrong with you?"

But Stephen didn't seem to hear her. His shoulders began to shake, his hands clenched into fists, and his face contorted as though he was in pain. He clutched at his chest. "The light, the light, what's wrong with the light?" he cried. Then he slumped forward and plunged face-first into his soup bowl.

Eliza screamed, Henry blinked in surprise, Maria's jaw dropped, and Hugh Langdon was frozen by shock. Basil rushed to his host, grabbed him by the hair, and yanked his face out of the soup bowl. "Get a doctor," he yelled.

"There's one just across the road," Rosalind Murray said. "Run and fetch Mrs. Winston's new lodger. He's a doctor," she ordered Flagg. "Do it quickly. Mr. Whitfield has taken ill."

"I'm afraid it's too late," Dr. Bosworth said as he straightened up. He turned toward the people crowding around the foot of the dead man's bed. "He's gone."

"I'm Rosalind Murray." A woman stepped away from the others and came toward him. "Stephen was my brother-in-law. I'm sorry we didn't have a chance to introduce ourselves properly, but we were in a hurry to get help for Stephen. I'm so sorry to have called you out when you're not even our doctor, but I remembered my neighbor mentioning that she'd rented rooms to a physician, so when Stephen collapsed, all I could think of was getting you here." She glanced at the body on the bed. "What happened to him? Was it a heart attack?"

Bosworth hesitated a moment. "I'm not sure. Can you tell me what he was doing before he collapsed?"

"We were having dinner." She waved at the crowd around the foot of Stephen's bed. "As you can see, we've guests." She looked at them. "Perhaps you'd all be more comfortable in the drawing room, now that we know Stephen is beyond all hope."

"Are you certain there's nothing we can do to help?" a short, rather chubby fellow asked.

"Not really." Rosalind smiled wanly. "Honestly, perhaps it would be best if you all simply went home. This can't be very pleasant."

There was a general murmur of agreement, and with much shuffling of feet and muttering among themselves, the group headed for the door.

"Just a moment," Bosworth called. There was something very wrong here; he could feel it. But these were wealthy, influential people, so he had to be careful.

The little cluster of guests stopped and stared at him expectantly.

"What's wrong, Doctor?" Rosalind asked. "Why can't they leave?"

"I'd like one of you to tell me exactly what happened before Mr. Whitfield died."

"I can give you that information. There's no need to detain our guests," Rosalind said coolly.

"I'm Maria Farringdon. Stephen said we were all turning blue," a small, slender woman with gray hair supplied. "Then he clutched his chest and fell into his soup bowl. That's when Mrs. Murray yelled for the butler to go get you."

"So he was still alive at that point?" Bosworth pressed. "And you're sure about what he said?"

"Honestly, Doctor, I don't think it's seemly for us to be standing by poor Stephen's bedside, having a discussion of his last moments," Rosalind snapped. "At least let's go into the drawing room."

"Of course I'm sure," Maria replied. "We all heard him quite clearly."

"His face contorted just before he went into the soup," the man standing next to Maria Farringdon volunteered. "Don't forget that."

"And he said there was something wrong with the light," another fellow, this one holding the arm of an attractive older woman, added. "I thought it a very odd remark."

"Doctor, can we please go into the drawing room?" Rosalind Murray pleaded. "This is very unseemly."

"Yes, of course," Bosworth agreed. "But do make sure

that no one eats or drinks anything, and I do mean anything."

She stared at him in disbelief. "Doctor, have you gone mad? What on earth are you talking about?"

"I think you'd better call the police," Bosworth replied calmly. "As a matter of fact, I'm going to insist upon it."

"The police!" She gaped at him. "Why do we need the police? Didn't Stephen have a stroke or a heart attack?"

Bosworth could hear the others muttering and exclaiming in surprise, but he ignored them and instead looked back at the body on the bed. "There will have to be an autopsy. Mr. Whitfield may well have had a heart attack, but if he did, it wasn't brought on by anything natural."

"What does that mean?" Rosalind Murray cried. "I don't understand any of this."

"It means I think Mr. Whitfield was poisoned," Bosworth announced. "That's why I don't want anyone eating or drinking anything."

Betsy and Smythe stared at each other across the length of the kitchen. "Hello, Betsy," he said.

"Hello, Smythe," she replied. She wasn't sure what to do or even what she felt. She'd planned and thought about this moment for so long, but now that it was here, she was completely in the dark. She'd practiced dozens of mean, cutting things to say to him when he got back, thought often of how she was going to turn up her nose and pretend he meant nothing to her. But now that he was right here in front of her, she couldn't do it. Despite the fact that he'd left her at the altar (at least in her mind), she found she could do nothing but stand like a silly ninny and drink in the sight of him. "How was your trip?"

"It was fine," he muttered. He felt frozen to the spot.

"Take off your coat and sit down, Smythe," Mrs. Jeffries said briskly. "We're just about ready to eat, and I'm sure you're hungry." She could see that both of them had been struck dumb by the sight of each other. Good. It meant they still loved each other, and she was wise enough to know that where there was love, there was hope that things could be put right.

"Alright." Without taking his eyes off Betsy, Smythe slipped out of his heavy coat, slapped it onto the coat tree in the corner, and made his way to the table.

Mrs. Goodge had already gone to the cupboard for another place setting. She stopped at the cutlery drawer and took out a knife and fork. She put everything down at his usual place at the table next to Betsy and then went back to her own chair. "It's good to have you back, Smythe," she said. "We've missed you."

"I've missed all of you," he replied as he sat down next to his fiancée. "But most of all, I've missed you," he said softly to the woman sitting beside him.

Betsy found she couldn't say anything.

"I'm back to stay," he tried. He wished she'd say something. "And I'll never leave you again."

Still, she simply stared at him.

"Cor blimey, Betsy, aren't you goin' to speak to 'im?" Wiggins exclaimed.

"Wiggins, be quiet," the cook hissed. Though she rather agreed with the lad, this was getting embarrassing. Mind you, she did understand Betsy's point of view. Canceling all those wedding plans hadn't been very pleasant for the poor girl. Even though the household knew that Smythe was coming back, everyone else in the neighborhood had assumed that he'd jilted her and made a run for it. Being the object of pity hadn't been easy for Betsy.

"Say something, Betsy," Smythe pleaded. His worst fears were being realized. He'd been prepared for tears or accusations or even a good screaming match, but this dead silence was devastating. It meant she felt nothing. That she'd locked him out of her heart for good.

"What do you want me to say?" she replied calmly. "Welcome home. Mrs. Jeffries, can you please pass the pork chops?"

Smythe gaped at her for a moment. He glanced at the others, noting that their faces reflected the same shock that he felt sure was mirrored in his own expression. "Is that it, then? Pass the bloomin' pork chops?"

"We've got extra," Wiggins supplied helpfully. "The inspector went to Lady Cannonberry's for dinner, so you can 'ave his chops."

Smythe ignored him. "I've been gone for six months," he cried, "and that's all you've got to say to me? For God's sake, woman, I've spent months slogging about the outback, lookin' for a crazy old man." He couldn't believe she was reacting like this. He'd spent practically every waking moment over the past six months thinking about her, telling himself he'd do whatever it took to fix things between them. He knew he'd done the unforgivable, but it couldn't be helped. He'd owed a debt of honor, and now that he'd paid it, he wanted to get on with his life. But she was acting as if he'd only stepped out to have a drink.

Blast a Spaniard, he'd never understand women. He'd sent letter after letter and received nothing in return. But he'd not minded: he'd told himself that she was hurt and upset, and that he could make it right when he got home.

"That was your choice," Betsy said simply. "May I have the butter pot, please?" she said to Mrs. Goodge.

"Betsy," Mrs. Jeffries said softly. "Perhaps you and Smythe would like to go upstairs and have a discussion in private."

"There's nothing to discuss." Betsy grinned. Now that he was back, she intended to enjoy herself a bit. He owed her for the humiliation of being left at the altar (so to speak) and for the misery of the past six months. She fully intended to forgive him—after all, she loved him more than she loved her own life—but she damned well intended that he suffer a bit before they could patch up their differences.

Smythe's jaw was partially open in shock as he stared at his beloved. But he was saved by a loud knock on the front door from having to think of the right thing to say. He got to his feet. Old habits die hard, and he didn't want the women going to the door after dark.

But Wiggins rose first. "I'll get it. You two keep on talking."

"There's nothing to talk about." Betsy reached for a slice of bread and slathered it with butter. She smiled at Smythe. "You'd better hope that the inspector will give you your old position back—that is, if you're interested in working."

Smythe had been the inspector's coachman before he'd gone to Australia.

Mrs. Jeffries sighed inwardly. She wasn't sure whether she was relieved or annoyed. Smythe was home, and Betsy was obviously going to lead him on a merry chase. She hoped the girl didn't go too far. The coachman adored her, but he had his pride. But then again, Betsy had been the one who'd stayed here and faced all the questions about their "postponed" wedding, so Mrs. Jeffries could understand the lass wanting a bit of her own back.

"I think things are going to be very interesting," Mrs. Goodge muttered in a voice low enough that only the housekeeper could hear her. "But at least we don't have a murder to cope with, so the two of them should be able to work out their differences."

Mrs. Jeffries nodded. She could hear Wiggins speaking to someone upstairs. The voice was very faint, but she thought she recognized it. She heard the front door slam shut, and then Wiggins' footsteps pounding along the hallway and down the back stairs.

"That was Constable Barnes at the door," Wiggins cried as he flew into the kitchen. "I sent him over to Lady Cannonberry's to fetch the inspector."

Everyone went still. There was only one reason that Witherspoon would be called out at this time of the evening.

"We've got us a murder," Wiggins continued. "Leastways, that's what the constable said. Should Smythe and I have a go at followin' them?"

The housekeeper nodded. In the past she'd learned it was wise to send the men along to get a firsthand report, whatever the situation might be.

Smythe, with one final glare at his beloved, was already on his feet. He reached across the table and grabbed a pork chop and a slice of bread. "I'm hungry, so I'll take this to eat on the way."

"We can catch 'em on Holland Park Road," Wiggins said as he hurried toward the coat tree for his cap and jacket.

"Be careful," Mrs. Jeffries warned. "Don't let anyone see you."

"And mind you take your scarf and gloves," Mrs. Goodge said to the footman. "It's cold out there, and I'll not have you catching a chill."

"It's not fair!" Betsy exclaimed. "I've been sitting here twiddlin' my ruddy thumbs for six months, and the minute *he* walks in the back door, we get us a murder."

Wisely, Smythe refrained from saying the words that popped into his head.

* * *

Bosworth had a very difficult time convincing the constable to call in his superiors. It was only because he was a police surgeon, albeit in a different district, that the man was persuaded to nip back to the station and call for a detective.

"Dr. Bosworth, have we met before?" Gerald Witherspoon asked politely.

"Yes, actually, we have. On one of your previous cases, I did the postmortem." Bosworth could hardly admit that he'd been to the inspector's house a dozen different times and that he was well acquainted with the inspector's entire household. They frequently asked his advice about the murders Witherspoon investigated.

"Ah, yes, I thought you looked familiar." The inspector nodded. "This is Constable Barnes."

Barnes reached over to shake hands. He was an older man with a craggy face and a headful of iron gray hair. As he was well aware of Bosworth's connection to the household of Upper Edmonton Gardens, his eyes were twinkling with amusement. "It's nice to see you again, Doctor."

"It's nice to see you, too, Constable." Bosworth shook his hand. "I do hope I've not called you both out on a wild-goose chase."

"What happened here, Doctor?" Witherspoon asked.

They were standing in the foyer. Bosworth pointed down the hall. "The owner of this house, Mr. Stephen Whitfield, was suddenly taken ill this evening while dining with friends. I live just across the road; I've just taken rooms with Mrs. Winston. But that's neither here nor there. They sent for me when he took ill, but by the time I arrived, he was dead. I think he's been poisoned."

"Poisoned?" Witherspoon repeated.

"That's correct," Bosworth replied. "The other dinner

guests are in there." He nodded toward the closed door of the drawing room. "The servants have all gone back downstairs. The victim's sister—in-law lives here as well. She's very upset, which is quite understandable. But she's raising a bit of a fuss. When the local constable said this was your district, I insisted they send for you."

"I see," the inspector said slowly.

"And knowing your methods as I do, I guessed you'd want to see the body before it was moved any farther." Bosworth turned and started down the hallway. "It's just down here, Inspector."

Witherspoon and Barnes followed after him. They climbed a short flight of stairs to the first floor. A uniformed constable stood by the door. "Good evening." He nodded respectfully. "I've not let anyone in, sir."

"Very good, Constable," Witherspoon said as they stepped into the dead man's room.

Bosworth went to the bedside. "As you can see, the body shows no signs of foul play." He pointed at the corpse. The late Stephen Whitfield stared straight up at the corniced ceiling.

"What led you to believe he'd been murdered?" the inspector asked. He took a deep breath and stepped closer to the bed. He was quite squeamish about corpses, but with no sign of foul play, at least this one wasn't likely to be covered in blood or have other bits of tissue popping out from every orifice. He forced himself to look at the body and then almost sighed aloud with relief.

Except for the open eyes, the fellow might as well have been having a nap.

"I'm not sure," Bosworth mused. "I sensed something was wrong even before I asked the dinner guests what had happened, but of course you're not interested in my private

intuition. It was when they told me what he'd said before
he collapsed that I began to suspect poison."

"What did he say?" Barnes asked. Actually, he was quite
interested in Bosworth's private intuition. Policemen liked
facts, but as every good copper knew, you didn't ignore feelings or instincts. Especially not from someone as experi-
enced as Bosworth.

"He said that everyone was turning blue and that there
was something wrong with the light. He said it quite
clearly before he collapsed."

"And that led you to the conclusion that he'd been poisoned?" Witherspoon pressed. Drat, he had a feeling this
was going to be a nasty one. Why couldn't the fellow have
just keeled over with a heart attack?

"Yes, I think he ingested a massive dose of foxglove. Seeing blue is one of the symptoms. But we'll know more when
the postmortem is done."

"Are you an expert on this?" Barnes asked. "I mean,
surely, isn't seeing odd things symptomatic with the man's
just having a heart attack? When my uncle died, he claimed
he saw fairies dancing on the fireplace mantel. No offense
meant, sir, but we do need reasonable grounds to do a postmortem on a body."

"And this is obviously a man of some means and importance," the inspector added. Like Barnes, he didn't want to
start a murder investigation unless they had genuine reasons
to think the death was a homicide and not an act of God.

Bosworth smiled grimly. "Actually, I am a bit of an authority, though I'm more familiar with death by firearms. I
spent several years practicing in the United States, in Cali-
fornia. When I was working in San Francisco, we had a case
of a landlady who murdered her tenants. They were mostly
seamen or miners. She robbed them, you see. None of them

was rich, but they usually came into the city just after they'd been paid. This woman had a beautiful garden with the most amazing flowers you've ever seen. She had some spectacularly lovely foxglove flowers. Usually her victims were dead by the time they reached us, but once, I managed to get there before the poor miner actually expired. He kept screaming that everyone had turned blue and that the light had gone strange. When we did the autopsy, we found enough digitalis in his system to kill an elephant. Digitalis comes from foxglove."

"Did you exhume the other bodies?" Barnes asked curiously.

"Only one, and it was full of foxglove as well. The leaves last quite a long time in the stomach."

"And Mr. Whitfield appeared to have the very same symptoms." Witherspoon nodded.

"That's correct," Bosworth replied. "I have a feeling we're going to find lots of foxglove when we open up Mr. Stephen Whitfield."

CHAPTER 2

Inspector Witherspoon and Constable Barnes had taken a hansom to Redcliffe Road in West Brompton. Smythe and Wiggins had rounded the corner just as the two policemen disappeared through the front door of the five-story white stone house. They'd looked about for a suitable place to keep watch, and Smythe had spotted a servants' entrance in a darkened house across the road. So far, their luck had held, and none of the constables going in and out of the murder house had caught so much as a glimpse of them.

"Cor blimey, my feet 'ave gone numb," Wiggins muttered softly. When they stuck their heads up from the stairwell, they had a good view of everything, but most of the time they had to stay hunkered down out of sight. The stone steps were cold, and as the night wore on, it was getting colder and colder.

"Wiggle yer toes," Smythe advised. He glanced at the

footman. They were lying on the staircase, keeping their heads just below ground level to avoid being seen. They'd been there well over an hour now, and it was blooming miserable. Both of them kept shifting positions in a vain effort to get comfortable or stay warm.

Smythe moved his big frame into a sitting position on the second stair from the bottom, low enough so that he'd not be seen. Wiggins eased down onto the step above him, cupped his gloved hands around his face, and blew gently. "Cor blimey, I don't know 'ow much longer I can sit 'ere. The chill is seepin' right through my trousers."

"If something doesn't happen soon, we'll go back to Upper Edmonton Gardens," Smythe said. He wondered whether he dared bring up Betsy. He was desperate to know whether she'd said anything about him, about whether she wanted him to come back or whether she still cared about him.

Wiggins stopped his blowing and said, "She still loves you. She's got skinny as a lamppost waitin' for you to come back."

"She never answered my letters," Smythe muttered. Blast a Spaniard, had the lad turned into a mind reader? He wanted to talk about Betsy, but now that her name had come up, he was embarrassed.

"She was angry, Smythe," Wiggins said softly. "And 'urt. When the weddin' was called off . . ."

"It wasn't called off. It was postponed," Smythe hissed.

"Alright, postponed," Wiggins agreed, "but you were the one that left. Betsy 'ad to stay 'ere and answer all the questions. It were 'ard for her. All them pryin' comments and pityin' looks she got. She almost run off, you know, but Mrs. Jeffries stopped her from goin'. Neither of 'em know that I know about it, so don't say anything."

"What happened?" Smythe asked softly. He wasn't sure

he really wanted to know. The very idea of Upper Edmonton Gardens without Betsy was too awful to bear.

Wiggins stretched and took a quick look at the house across the road before he spoke. "It were right after you left. We'd been called in to supper, but I'd 'ad to run back upstairs for something. On the way back down, I happened to glance out the window on the top landing, and I saw Betsy standing there in the garden, starin' at the 'ouse. She 'ad on her hat and gloves, and her carpetbag was lying at her feet. I felt awful when I saw her just standing there lookin' so miserable. She's like a sister to me, you know, and I wasn't sure what to do. Just then, Mrs. Jeffries stepped out from behind the bushes and they started talking. They didn't speak for very long. Then Mrs. Jeffries went back to the house. I remember holding my breath, waitin' to see what Betsy was goin' to do. But then she picked up her carpetbag and came on inside. I was so relieved. I hated the thought of her goin', of her leavin' and all of us breakin' apart."

Smythe sighed heavily. He knew exactly what the lad meant. Everyone in Witherspoon's household had ended up there for a variety of reasons, but over the years, the bonds they'd formed had become real and important. They'd become family.

Suddenly they heard the door of the house across the road open. Wiggins stuck his head up. "Someone's comin' out." Moving cautiously, lest they make noise and give themselves away, they flattened themselves back onto the staircase and, lying close together, peeked over the top just in time to see two people, a man and a woman, step outside.

The couple wore formal evening clothes and the man held the woman's arm as they descended the stairs and came out onto the pavement. They paused for a moment, speaking quietly together, before moving off toward Fulham Road.

"I'm goin' to follow 'em and see if I can 'ear what they're sayin,'" Wiggins muttered. But just as he started to get up, the door opened again and another couple came outside. He froze.

Neither he nor Smythe so much as moved a muscle until the footsteps of the second couple had faded as they walked away. "Maybe I should go to the local pub and see who lives in that house," Smythe whispered. "You'll not get the chance to follow anyone, not if people keep comin' out that front door."

Moving cautiously, Wiggins stretched up for another quick look. The first couple had reached the corner, and the man was waving his top hat, probably trying to get a hansom. The second couple had gone the opposite way. The door of the house stayed shut. "Maybe I can follow them." He pointed at the second couple, who were just disappearing around the corner.

"Nah, they've got too much of a head start," Smythe replied. "There's a hansom stand up that way—by the time you reach the corner, they'll be gone. Did you see that pub on the Fulham Road?'

"The one next to the bank?" Wiggins asked.

"That's it." Smythe nodded. "When the inspector and Constable Barnes come out, you come meet me at that pub. We're not 'aving much luck just hidin' here in the dark. At least at the pub we might be able to learn who lives there." Smythe stared across the road. "It's not very well lighted, is it? You'd think a posh neighborhood like this would have better street lighting, and you'd think the house would have decent-sized door lamps. Er, uh, what's the number? I can't read it from this distance."

"It's number nineteen," Wiggins replied, "and we're on Redcliffe Road."

"I know that," Smythe said irritably. "I just couldn't see the number, that's all."

Wiggins could see the number quite clearly. But he held his tongue. Failing eyesight happened to people as they got older, and he didn't think Smythe would take kindly to any reminders that he wasn't as young as he used to be.

"I'm not sure it was a wise idea to let everyone leave," Witherspoon murmured. "But we'd no grounds to force them to remain here. We're not absolutely sure it was even murder."

"We've got their names and addresses, sir," Barnes said patiently. "And they did make statements."

A constable stuck his head into the drawing room. "The wagon is here, sir, and the lads are ready to take him away as soon as you give the command. Are we waiting for the police surgeon?"

"You can take him away," Witherspoon replied. "Dr. Bosworth has volunteered to write the report and do the postmortem. Send word to the station that I've seconded him to our district for this case."

The constable nodded respectfully and left, closing the drawing room door behind him. Witherspoon hoped no one would raise a fuss about his actions. But Dr. Bosworth was a police surgeon, and it seemed foolish to call in someone else just because Bosworth was assigned to another district. "Do you think Dr. Jolyon will object?" he asked Barnes. Dr. Hiram Jolyon was the surgeon assigned to this district.

Barnes shook his head. "Jolyon's a sensible sort. He'll understand that, given the circumstances, it was logical to keep Dr. Bosworth on the case. Besides, I expect he'll appreciate not having to come out on a cold winter night."

The drawing room door was suddenly flung open so hard that it slammed against the doorstop with enough force to rattle the windows. Rosalind Murray flew into the room and charged straight for the two policemen. "This is outrageous!" she cried. "What do you think you're doing?"

"I'm sorry, ma'am," Witherspoon replied. "But we're only doing what is necessary."

"There are police constables in our kitchen." She stopped in front of Witherspoon. Her cheeks were red and her expression furious. "They are taking away food, grabbing every wine bottle in sight, and upsetting the servants. Cook is in tears, and the scullery maids are hiding in the dry larder. What is the meaning of this?"

"I know this is most distressing," Witherspoon said politely. "But we must take as evidence all the food and drink that was served tonight."

"For goodness' sakes, the only one who died was Stephen," Rosalind snapped. "So I hardly think he's been poisoned."

"Nevertheless, we can't risk losing any evidence," the inspector insisted. But what she said was true. No one else had died or even become ill. "Er, was there any one food or beverage that only Mr. Whitfield consumed?"

Rosalind exhaled, unclenched the hand that had been balled into a fist, and closed her eyes for a brief moment as she got herself under control. "He was the only one who drank the Bordeaux that Mrs. Farringdon brought. The bottle is in the dining room." She turned and hurried to the door.

The two policemen were right behind her.

A constable standing at the dining table and pouring the fish soup into a jar stopped and looked up as they burst into the room.

"Carry on with what you were doing, Constable," the inspector said kindly.

"Yes, sir." He went back to pouring the soup.

"Here it is." Rosalind picked up the Bordeaux from the silver tray on the sideboard and handed it to Witherspoon. "Mr. and Mrs. Farringdon brought this to Stephen as a Christmas gift. He insisted it be opened, but he was the only one who drank it. The rest of us had sherry for an aperitif and white wine with our dinner."

Witherspoon noted that the bottle was three-quarters empty. "The Farringdons gave this to Mr. Whitfield tonight?"

Rosalind's eyes widened as she realized the implication behind the question. "I've just said so, Inspector. But if you are implying that either of them had anything to do with Stephen's death, you're mistaken. Basil Farringdon and Stephen were at school together. They've known one another all their lives."

"Our questions aren't meant to implicate anyone," Witherspoon replied. "We're simply trying to ascertain the facts." He was dreadfully tired and quite hungry. He and Ruth had only just started their meal when Barnes had come to fetch him. "Did any of the other guests bring Mr. Whitfield a present?"

"No. The Farringdons brought one only because Stephen took them a bottle of his special ruby port a few days ago. He imports a cask directly from the vineyard and corks it up himself."

"Had he given a bottle of port to any of the other guests?" Barnes asked.

She thought for a moment. "I think he might have given one to Henry Becker. It's a custom he started a few years ago, but he only did it for his old school friends."

"I see," Witherspoon murmured. He'd no idea whether this was useful information.

They could hear bumps and squeaks outside the door as a gurney was wheeled down the hallway.

The color drained out of Rosalind's face. "Oh, dear God, this is dreadful. What are they going to do with Stephen?"

"They're going to take him to a hospital and do a post-mortem," Witherspoon said gently. "I'm so sorry. Please don't let it distress you, ma'am. But we must find out if Mr. Whitfield was poisoned and, if he was, if that poison was administered accidentally or on purpose."

"Did Mr. Whitfield have any enemies?" Barnes asked. He thought he might as well start asking the obvious questions. Despite Witherspoon's misgivings, Barnes knew enough about Dr. Bosworth to trust both the man's medical expertise and the fellow's instincts.

"He had no more enemies than anyone else." She winced as the gurney's wheels scraped hard against the stairs.

"What was his occupation?" Witherspoon asked, hoping to distract her from the thuds overhead as the gurney continued its journey to the dead man's bedroom.

"He was an English gentleman," she replied. "In other words, Inspector, he lived off his income and did very little . . ." She broke off and glanced up at the ceiling as the wheels squeaked to a halt in the room upstairs.

"He had no occupation, correct?" Witherspoon clarified. Drat, that meant he wouldn't have business enemies.

"In his youth, he spent a few years running the family estate, but the estate was sold when he married my sister." She turned her attention back to Witherspoon.

"I see." The inspector desperately tried to think of more questions, but his mind had gone completely blank.

They heard a series of knocks and then a low thud from overhead. A moment later, the wheels began squeaking again as the gurney began the trip down.

Rosalind shuddered. "Inspector, is this going to take much longer?"

"No, ma'am, they are almost finished."

They were bringing the body down the stairs. He could hear bumping and scraping against the banister. "I'm sure this evening has been horrible for you," he said to her. "I'm terribly sorry for your loss."

"Stephen wasn't a blood relative, but he was my brother-in-law and I have lived in his household for almost ten years. I've known him since we were children." She looked past Witherspoon, in the direction of the front door.

They could hear the lads moving about in the foyer, opening the front door, and then the ever-present squeak of wheels. Witherspoon made a mental note to have a word with the duty sergeant and ask who was in charge of maintaining the equipment. They really must get that contraption oiled.

Rosalind closed her eyes briefly. "Is there anything else?"

Witherspoon shook his head. "Dr. Bosworth is doing the postmortem tonight, so we'll be in touch tomorrow. If you'd like, I can ask the local constables to keep a special watch over the house."

"That won't be necessary, Inspector." She opened the door and stepped into the hallway. "I'm sure Stephen's death will turn out to be a heart attack or some sort of accident. Now, if you don't mind, I'm going to go upstairs and lie down. This has been an exhausting ordeal."

"Good night, Mrs. Murray. We'll try to be as unobtrusive as possible when we leave."

"Good night, Inspector." Rosalind Murray turned and went toward the stairway.

Witherspoon was reasonably sure that if the victim had been poisoned, it was probably through the wine. But they couldn't be certain, so it took another hour to finish up in the kitchen. An enormous amount of food had been prepared for the dinner party, and finding suitable containers to carry it all off was impossible, so they had to send back to the station for an evidence box. As they left the house, Witherspoon instructed the local constable on patrol to keep an eye on the house.

"What do you think, sir?" Barnes asked as they turned in the direction of the Fulham Road.

"I've no idea what to think," Witherspoon admitted. "Let's hope this Dr. Bosworth knows his business."

"Oh, I think we're safe in that regard, sir," Barnes said softly. He was well aware of Bosworth's help on previous cases, just as he was aware that Witherspoon's entire household had been assisting him from the very beginning. None of them had told him of their involvement; he'd figured it out on his own. "There's a hansom, sir. I'll just go wave it over."

"What are we going to tell the inspector about Smythe?" Mrs. Goodge whispered as soon as Betsy had gone upstairs to make sure the heat was on in Smythe's room.

"We'll tell him the truth—that Smythe finished his business in Australia and came home because he wanted to get here before Christmas," Mrs. Jeffries replied.

When the coachman had left, they'd told Witherspoon that he'd been called away on urgent business. Witherspoon, being the decent man he was, had agreed that the coachman should have his position back when he returned to England. Not that Smythe needed the position—he didn't. He was as rich as sin, but that, like so many other things in Mrs. Jeffries' life, was a secret. Only she—and Betsy, of course—knew about his wealth. It was Smythe's secret to keep, and he'd let the others know in his own good time.

"That's a good idea. It's always best to stay close to the

truth if at all possible." Mrs. Goodge sank down onto her chair. "And Betsy's being a right little madam about him coming back. Mind you, I'm not sure I blame her. Canceling all those wedding plans was so humiliating for the lass. But I've never seen her act so cold."

"But she still loves him." Mrs. Jeffries grinned. "That's obvious."

"How is it obvious?" Mrs. Goodge reached down to lift Samson, her huge orange tabby cat, onto her lap. Samson, as was his nature, glared at Mrs. Jeffries and then curled up in a ball on the cook's lap. Wiggins had rescued both Fred and Samson at different times. Fred was exceedingly grateful to have a good home. Samson wasn't. The only person he liked was the cook.

Mrs. Jeffries laughed. "If she didn't love him, she'd have treated him like her long-lost brother. Instead she's as cool as an autumn evening and treating him as casually as if he'd just been gone for an hour or two. That can only mean one thing; she's going to forgive him, but she's going to make him dance a bit before she'll give him as much as a smile."

Mrs. Goodge didn't look convinced. "Are you sure about this? I'm the first to admit, I don't know much about affairs of the heart. We both know that cooks take the 'Mrs.' as a courtesy title whether we've been married or not. I, for one, never had a husband and never wanted one, either. But you have. Did you ever do such a thing to your man?"

"Well, certainly not very often," Mrs. Jeffries admitted. "But even I, on occasion, had my little ways to get my own back. That's all Betsy's doing—getting a bit of her own back."

"But it wasn't Smythe's fault that he had to go," the cook protested. She petted Samson's broad back, and he started to purr.

"No, and Betsy knows that," the housekeeper replied. "But he could have taken her with him, and he didn't."

"He was goin' to the bush."

"Betsy told me she wouldn't have cared. What hurt her the most was that he didn't even ask her to go. He simply said he had a debt of honor, and out the door he went. She was the one who had to face all the neighbors and all our friends. She was the one who had to tell them the wedding had been 'postponed,' and then watch how everyone tried to pretend that was just fine when it was obvious they all believed she'd been jilted."

"But, still, she's been miserable without him," Mrs. Goodge pointed out.

"And he without her, I'm sure. But this is something they must work out for themselves." She got up and began to pace the room. Fred, who was keeping a wary eye on the cat, jumped up from his spot in front of the warm stove and began to pace alongside her.

Betsy, a sack of flour nestled in the crook of one arm and a bowl of brown eggs in the other, came back into the kitchen. "The sugar cone has gone hard as a rock," she said as she made her way to the worktable near the sink. "But it should be fine if you let Wiggins have a go at it with the hammer." She placed the eggs next to the slab of white marble that Mrs. Goodge used for baking, and put the flour down beside the bowl.

"Thank you, Betsy," the cook said softly. Without even being asked, Betsy had brought Mrs. Goodge's ingredients from the dry larder to the kitchen. The maid had done it because she knew it was hard for the cook to move about so easily when her rheumatism was acting up. Betsy understood that, now that they had a murder, Mrs. Goodge had to get her baking done early so she could feed her sources. The lass was too caring and kind, Mrs. Goodge thought sourly. It made it impossible to stay irritated at her!

"Should I make more tea?" Betsy asked. "We'll want to stay up so we can hear all the details."

"That's a very good idea," Mrs. Jeffries murmured. "It's almost midnight and no one is back yet. We may need to split up. I'll take the inspector, and you two see what the lads have found out."

Betsy nodded. "I'll use the big pot. As cold as it is, everyone's going to want something to warm themselves up."

Everyone returned within minutes of one another. Smythe and Wiggins were coming through the back door just as Mrs. Jeffries heard the inspector come in the front. She grabbed a tray they had at the ready and headed up the stairs.

"Mrs. Jeffries, you shouldn't have waited up," Witherspoon said as he hung up his bowler hat. "It's dreadfully late, and you must be exhausted."

"Not as exhausted as you must be, sir," she replied. "It's so cold out tonight. I wanted to make sure you had something hot to warm you up. I thought perhaps you might be hungry, so Mrs. Goodge made some roast beef sandwiches as well. Shall we go into the drawing room?" She didn't want him running up to bed before she had a chance to find out what he'd learned.

"Bless you both for being so thoughtful. I'm famished." He slipped out of his overcoat and hung it on the peg under his hat. Witherspoon hadn't been raised with wealth, so consequently he treated his servants like human beings and was exceedingly grateful when they did anything over and above their normal duties.

As they went down the hall to the drawing room, Mrs. Jeffries said, "I've some other news as well, sir. Smythe has returned." She put the tray down on a table by the door and poured his tea.

"Smythe is back—that's excellent news." He sank into his favorite chair. "It's been difficult for Betsy since he's been gone. What a wonderful Christmas present that must be for her. I'm sure she's delighted he's finally home."

"He took care of his business, sir." Mrs. Jeffries put the inspector's tea on the table next to him, picked up her own cup, and sat down on the settee.

"He's a good man." Witherspoon blew surreptitiously on the hot drink. "Imagine going all the way to Australia to help out an old friend who was in trouble. Well, I'm glad he's back, to be sure. Let him know that as of tomorrow, he's a member of the household again, and he's to have his full wages for this month."

"I'm sure he'll be very pleased to hear that," she replied. As she knew, Smythe donated half his salary to the poor box at St. John's Church and the other half to an orphans' home in the East End. She was certain they'd be happy he was back as well. "I do hope that Lady Cannonberry wasn't too upset by your dinner being interrupted."

He put down his tea and helped himself to a sandwich. "Considering we'd only just sat down to eat when Constable Barnes arrived, she was exceedingly gracious about the matter." He took a quick bite of his food.

"I suppose it must have been sheer luck that the constable was at the station when the call came in," she commented. "Usually he's home in the evenings."

"It was. He'd stayed late at the station to have a Christmas drink with one of his friends. His wife is out of town for a few days." Witherspoon swallowed his food. "The doctor called to the scene when the victim took ill was familiar with my previous cases. He specifically sent the first constable who arrived back to the station to fetch me. Barnes and Constable Kerry were just going out for their drink when the lad reported back, so his evening was interrupted, too—not that Constable Barnes would ever complain, of course. This roast beef is wonderful."

"Who was the doctor?" Mrs. Jeffries asked cautiously. She didn't want to get her hopes up just yet.

"A Dr. Bosworth. He's one of our police surgeons, but he's not assigned to my district. He just happened to have rented rooms across from the victim's house, so he was sent for when the poor man fell ill." Witherspoon took another bite of his sandwich.

Mrs. Jeffries' spirits soared. For once, they'd have almost direct access to evidence from the postmortem. She couldn't believe their luck. "Your methods have become very well-known, sir. I'm sure Dr. Bosworth has heard a great deal about you."

"He's worked on one of my cases," Witherspoon said. "But I can't recall which one it was."

He'd actually worked on virtually all of the inspector's cases, but only one of them in an official capacity. "If this isn't his district, is he the one doing the postmortem?" She held her breath.

"Indeed he is. He's doing it tonight." Witherspoon took another sip of tea.

"And he was the one that thought there might be foul play involved?"

"He's fairly sure the fellow was poisoned."

Mrs. Jeffries raised her eyebrows. "He was able to make a diagnosis so quickly?"

"It was something the victim said before he died that led the doctor to think so." He told her the circumstances leading to Bosworth's suspicions. "So you see, even if it turns out the man was poisoned, we've still no evidence it was murder. It could be accidental."

"Even if it was foxglove that killed him?" she queried gently. She didn't want the inspector clinging to false hope. She trusted Bosworth's instincts. The good doctor had seen too many corpses not to have developed a heightened ability to know when something was wrong. This was a murder, not an accident.

Witherspoon sighed deeply. "I know I'm probably deluding myself, but it is Christmas, and you know what happens at this time of year, especially if the victim is a member of the upper class."

"And I take it that the deceased is one of them?" She smiled sympathetically. She knew exactly what was bothering her inspector.

"Oh, yes—at least, he appears to be a wealthy man. The house is huge, and he has no occupation. According to his sister-in-law, he's an English gentleman, and you know what that means."

"They'll put pressure on you to solve this case as soon as possible. They'll want an arrest by Christmas," she murmured.

He nodded in agreement. "There's no real reason why this season should be any different from any other time of the year, but somehow it always is. Perhaps we'll get lucky, and by tomorrow morning we'll find out that the doctor was mistaken and poor Mr. Whitfield died of a perfectly natural heart attack or stroke."

"Perhaps you will, sir," she said politely, though she didn't for a moment believe it to be true.

Witherspoon helped himself to the last sandwich. "Gracious, I was hungry. I do hope poor Constable Barnes had something at home he could eat. It appears there are quite a

number of people who didn't finish their meals tonight." He
told her about the interrupted dinner party at the Whitfield
house.

She questioned him cautiously. By the time she poured
the last of the tea, she'd found out the names of the other
guests and the information they'd given in their statements.
"So it was Mr. and Mrs. Farringdon who'd brought the Bordeaux Whitfield drank?"

"That's correct." Witherspoon covered his mouth as he
yawned. "And the Bordeaux was the only thing that he alone
consumed. So I had that taken into evidence along with
everything else that had been served. I do hope that, if it is
poison that killed Whitfield, it was in the Bordeaux. Otherwise, by tomorrow morning, we may have another half-
dozen corpses."

Downstairs, Smythe and Wiggins were doing some report-
ing of their own.

"There were half a dozen people that come out of the
'ouse," Wiggins said around a mouthful of food. "But I
daren't follow any of 'em, 'cause that ruddy front door kept
opening and I'd no idea 'ow many more of them was coming
down those steps. So I just stayed hid until I saw the inspector and Constable Barnes leave. Then I went and met up
with Smythe."

"At the pub?" Betsy asked archly. "How very convenient."

"It's not like there's much else open at that time of
night," Smythe replied harshly. "And I was only there for a
few minutes before they called last orders."

"So you found out nothing?" she asked.

Mrs. Goodge sighed inwardly and hoped this wasn't a
sign of things to come. "Smythe, why don't you tell us in
your own words what's what?" she asked.

"Thank you, Mrs. Goodge. As it happens, I did find out a bit. The man who died was Stephen Whitfield. The news had already made it to the pub, but no one had any details. I did find out that Whitfield was a widower in his late sixties, rich as sin and courtin' a woman a good twenty years younger."

"I wonder if she was one of the people who come out of the house. They must 'ave been 'aving a dinner party, because they were all in evenin' clothes." Wiggins frowned thoughtfully. "None of them women come out alone, and there was only one of 'em that looked to be youngish. But she was with another bloke."

"I'm sure we'll get the names of the guests from the inspector," the cook said. She'd noticed that Betsy had gone completely silent. That wasn't good, either. "Mrs. Jeffries is upstairs with him now."

Just then they heard her footsteps coming down the back stairs, and a moment later she hurried into the kitchen, carrying a tray of dirty dishes. "Good, you're all still up."

"We want to find out what happened," Betsy said. "Was it a murder?"

"Dr. Bosworth certainly seems to think so." Mrs. Jeffries put the tray down on the counter.

"Our Dr. Bosworth?" Mrs. Goodge asked. "Did it happen in his district?"

Everyone in the household knew that Bosworth had been appointed a police surgeon. It had helped their investigations enormously.

"It wasn't in his district—it was in the inspector's. But Dr. Bosworth had taken rooms just across the street from the victim's house. He was sent for when the man collapsed." She took her usual spot at the head of the table and told them what she'd learned from the inspector.

Tired as they all were, they listened carefully, occasionally asking a question or making a comment. When the housekeeper finished, she leaned back in her chair. "We've the names of the other guests at the dinner party, and we know the man died under suspicious circumstances, but before we go on the hunt, perhaps we'd better wait until we hear whether Dr. Bosworth finds any poison in the man's stomach."

"But we might not find that out until late tomorrow," Betsy protested. "I think we ought to take Dr. Bosworth at his word and start right away."

"What if it's not murder?" Wiggins asked reasonably. "We'd 'ave wasted a lot of time and energy findin' out about people who've done no wrong. That doesn't seem right."

"And just because these people were at the dinner party, that doesn't mean anything, especially if he was poisoned," Mrs. Goodge pointed out. "A poisoner doesn't have to see his victim die. It's not like doin' the deed with a knife or gun. If Stephen Whitfield was poisoned, the killer might have put it in something he ate or drank days before he actually died. Poisons don't always act right away."

"That's true," Betsy agreed. But she wanted to be out of the house. She wanted to be walking the streets and chatting with merchants and grocery clerks so that she wouldn't have to deal with her current problem. "But I don't think it would hurt anything to find out a few bits and pieces about the people who were there last night. Maybe the killer wanted to watch him die and was sitting right there at the dinner table."

"You think one of the Farringdons murdered him?" Mrs. Jeffries asked curiously. It wasn't like Betsy to leap to any sort of conclusions at this stage of the investigation.

"I've no idea. But Whitfield was the only one drinking the Bordeaux wine, and he's the only one who is dead."

"So far," Mrs. Jeffries murmured. "As Mrs. Goodge has pointed out, some poisons don't act right away. The poison might have been in something else, and he simply got a larger, stronger dose than the others."

"I don't think so," Wiggins said. "No one else that come out of the house looked the least bit ill. Betsy's on to something 'ere. The wine was opened as soon as the Farringdons arrived, but Whitfield were the only one drinkin' it. Then it set open for a good while as the guests milled about the place."

"Which means that anyone might have dropped something into it, especially if it looked like Whitfield was the only one drinking it," Smythe said. "Which would mean the killer was definitely wantin' him dead."

"That's right." Betsy grinned triumphantly, then caught herself and composed her features. She didn't want him getting any special smiles. Not yet, at any rate. "So I think we ought to get right on the case. As Mrs. Jeffries said, our inspector is going to have all sorts of pressure on him to get this murder solved before Christmas."

"What about Luty and Hatcher?" Wiggins asked. "Are we goin' to bring them into it before we know for certain?"

Luty Belle Crookshank and her butler, Hatchet, were friends of the household. Luty was a wealthy, eccentric American who'd been a witness in one of their earliest cases. She'd then come to them with a problem of her own to be solved, and ever since, she and her butler had insisted on helping. Unfortunately, due to Luty's illness and her need to travel to America to confer with her American bankers and lawyers, they'd missed several of the inspector's cases, so now they were adamant about being included right from the beginning.

"I think that would be best," Mrs. Jeffries replied. "Right, then. I take it we're all agreed that we ought to proceed with the investigation."

Everyone nodded their assent.

Betsy got up and headed for the stairs. She didn't want to be alone with Smythe. "I best get upstairs. I want to get my chores done bright and early so I can get out and about."

"I'll do a batch of bakin' to feed my sources." The cook got to her feet. "The worst that can happen is, we'll have extra if it turns out not to be a murder, but this time of year, a bit of extra sweets could come in handy."

"Smythe, can you and Wiggins lock up, please?" Mrs. Jeffries said as she followed the maid out to the hall. She understood that Betsy wasn't ready to be alone with her fiancé as yet, and wanted to make it easy on the lass. "Oh, and Wiggins, can you nip over to Luty's as soon as you get up? We'll want them here for our morning meeting."

"I do hope this doesn't turn out to be a waste of your time," Mrs. Jeffries said as she took her place at the table the next morning.

"When will we know for certain whether or not it's murder?" Luty Belle Crookshank asked eagerly. The elderly, gray-haired American wore a maroon day dress with white lace around the collar and cuffs. On her lap was a gray fur muff, and there was a better-than-even chance that inside that muff was a gun: a Colt .45 that Luty called a Peacemaker.

"Wiggins is going to run down to the station to take the inspector's watch to him." Mrs. Jeffries held up the gold pocket watch. She'd lifted it out of Witherspoon's coat earlier that morning. "Dr. Bosworth was doing the postmortem last night, so he ought to have had a report written and sent over to the station by midmorning."

"So when young Wiggins brings the inspector his forgotten pocket watch, he ought to be able to ascertain whether or not the victim was poisoned," Hatchet said. He was a tall, robust man with a headful of white hair, a smooth complexion, and a devotion to Luty Belle that went beyond just serving as a butler. He was also articulate, well educated, and very clever, with his own network of resources gleaned from a past that he didn't care to talk about.

"But the postmortem will only tell us if it's poison, not whether it's murder," Smythe said. He was in a sour mood. He'd tried his best to get Betsy alone so they could talk about their situation, but he'd been stymied at every turn. Last night she'd gone upstairs with Mrs. Jeffries, and this morning he'd waited for ages on the landing for her to come out of her room, only to discover that she was down in the kitchen and had been for hours. He knew she was deliberately keeping him at bay, and it was beginning to make him angry.

"Of course it'll be murder," Mrs. Goodge said. "The man didn't deliberately dose himself with foxglove."

"It could have been that the foxglove was meant for someone else," Betsy pointed out.

"I, for one, am going to proceed as though it's murder and that Stephen Whitfield was the intended victim," the cook said stoutly. "I've got some nice buns rising in the dry larder, a seed cake in the oven, and a set of jam tarts ready to go in as soon as the cake is done."

"Do you have anyone coming through today?" Mrs. Jeffries asked.

"The laundry lad will be here, and there's a butcher's order due to arrive," the cook replied. "But I've sent notes to several of my friends, and I'm sure one of them will be here for early-afternoon tea, so we mustn't have our afternoon meeting until at least half past four. I've got the names of everyone who was at the dinner party, so someone coming through this kitchen ought to know something useful about one of them." Mrs. Goodge understood the value of gossip.

"And I'm off to talk to the local shopkeepers," Betsy announced as she got up. "By now, the fact that Whitfield died should be common knowledge."

"Stephen Whitfield." Luty repeated the name, her expression thoughtful. "I know I've heard that name before."

"He's probably an acquaintance of one of your friends," Hatchet said. "Actually, if no one objects, I think I'll see what I can learn about the Farringdons. They were the ones who brought the Bordeaux."

"And you've heard their names before, haven't you?" Luty charged. She and Hatchet were very competitive when they were on a case. Each of them reveled in finding out more information than the other.

"I may have heard them mentioned in casual conversations," Hatchet admitted. He knew the Farringdons' butler, but he'd die before he'd own up to it in front of Luty.

Luty snorted. "You've got something up your sleeve, but then again"—she grinned—"so do I."

"Excellent. It seems we've all something to do to keep busy until this afternoon." Mrs. Jeffries looked at Smythe. "Would you like to take today to rest? You've had a hard, long journey."

He shook his head and got up. "I'm fine, Mrs. Jeffries. I've got some business of me own to take care of this morning, but I'll be able to get on the hunt by the afternoon." He shot Betsy a quick glance. She was concentrating on doing the buttons on her coat and didn't look up.

"Should I go to the Whitfield 'ouse after I've seen the inspector?" Wiggins asked. "I'll be careful."

"Yes, that's a good idea," the housekeeper said as she got up. "And I'll see if I can get a word or two out of the good doctor. Mind you, if he was up all night doing the post-mortem, he might go home instead of to St. Thomas's Hospital."

"Oh dear, it looks as if Dr. Bosworth was correct." Witherspoon frowned and shook his head as he read from the post-mortem report open on the desk. He and Constable Barnes were in the enquiries room in the police station on Kings Road. They'd met here instead of at the Ladbroke Grove station because it was closer to the victim's home. As both stations were in Witherspoon's district, it didn't matter which one they used as a base. "It was a massive dose of poison that killed the poor fellow."

"Foxglove?" Barnes asked.

Witherspoon squinted at the writing on the page. "So it appears." He sighed and got to his feet. "Perhaps we'd better go and break the news to his sister-in-law." He reached into his coat pocket for his watch. "Oh dear, I think I've forgotten my watch."

"That's all right, sir. I've got mine," Barnes replied just as a constable appeared in the doorway. Wiggins stood right behind him.

"This lad says he's from the inspector's household," the constable explained.

"He is." Barnes grinned. He knew exactly why Wiggins was here. "Come in, young Wiggins, and tell us what brings you down here."

"Good morning, Constable Barnes." Wiggins took off his flat cap and bobbed his head respectfully.

"Gracious, Wiggins, is everything alright at home?" Witherspoon was surprised by the apprehension that had gripped him when he'd seen the footman. He'd been on his own for most of his adult life, but in the past few years he'd become very attached to his household, and one of them showing up unexpectedly might be bad news indeed.

"Everything's fine, sir." Wiggins pulled the inspector's watch out of his pocket and handed it to Witherspoon. "You forgot your watch, sir, so Mrs. Jeffries sent me down to make sure you got it. We thought you might need it."

Relief swept through the inspector. "Thank you, Wiggins. That was very thoughtful of you."

"It's a good thing you arrived when you did," Barnes said. "The inspector and I were just on our way out."

"Goin' back to Ladbroke Grove, were you?" Wiggins asked.

"Actually, we're on our way back to the Whitfield residence," Witherspoon said as he tucked his watch into his waistcoat pocket. "The postmortem shows that the poor fellow was poisoned."

"Ah, what a shame, especially at this time of the year." Wiggins popped his cap onto his head and edged toward the door. He'd found out what he needed. They had them a murder.

CHAPTER 3

Wiggins kept his distance from the two policemen. He'd
toyed with the idea of going back to Upper Edmonton Gardens and telling them it was definitely a poisoning, but
then he'd realized the only person there would be Mrs.
Goodge. She'd more or less already decided it was murder,
anyway, and what's more, he knew she wouldn't appreciate
being interrupted while she was trying to wheedle information out of her sources. So he'd decided to find out what he
could from the servants in the Whitfield household. Surely
someone would stick his or her nose out today.

He rounded the corner onto Redcliffe Road just as the
inspector and Barnes went into the Whitfield house. Wiggins hesitated for a brief moment, then crossed the road, all
the while keeping his eye out for a good hiding spot. He
considered returning to the same stairwell that he and
Smythe had used the night before, but in broad daylight

he'd be easily seen. Instead he kept on walking, slowing his pace while he surveyed his surroundings. But today his luck wasn't good. At this time of the morning, there were too many people coming and going for him to be able to duck behind a convenient bush.

This isn't workin', Wiggins thought as he rounded the corner onto Fulham Road. I've come too far afield. In London, two hundred feet could take you out of one neighborhood and into another. He turned on his heel and started back the way he'd come.

"Cor blimey," he muttered as he got to the corner of Redcliffe Road. "Looks like my luck is changin' for the better." A maid was coming up the servants' staircase of number nineteen. She was dressed in a short gray jacket and a brown skirt. Her blond hair was tucked up under a brown bonnet. Wiggins slowed his pace, waiting to see which way she'd go. She paused on the pavement, pulled on a pair of gloves, and then headed straight for him.

"Excuse me, miss, but did you just come out of that house?" Wiggins pointed at the Whitfield residence. He noticed she wasn't a very pretty girl. She had a large, crooked nose and blotchy skin.

For a split second, he was certain she was going to walk right past him, but she finally stopped. She stared at him, the expression in her hazel eyes wary. "Why do ya want to know?"

"Beg pardon for bothering you, miss." He swept off his cap and bobbed his head respectfully. "But I was lookin' for my cousin, and I was told she works in that house."

"What's her name?" the girl asked.

"Joan Smithson," he replied. "I'm hopin' she can help me find a position. I've just come up from Kent, and I'm in need of work."

The girl shrugged and continued on her way. "Then you're out of luck, lad. There's no one by that name where I work."

He fell into step with her and noted that she didn't quicken her pace in an effort to get rid of him. "I was afraid of that." He sighed heavily. "I was told she was in this neighborhood, but no one was sure of her address."

"Close family, are ya?" The girl laughed.

"The truth is, I've only seen my cousin once and wouldn't know her if I passed her on the street." He was pleased that she was still talking to him. "I'm just so desperate for work, I thought I'd try and find her. I don't suppose there's any positions goin' where you work, is there? I'm a fully trained footman."

"No, there's nothing." She pursed her lips. "What's more, there's a good chance that most of us will be out of work ourselves. God, I don't want to go back to that miserable factory job in Leeds. But I may not have a choice."

"You mean your entire household is getting sacked?" He took her elbow as they came to the corner. "That's awful."

She gave him a sharp glance but didn't jerk her arm away. "We're not getting the boot," she said as they stepped off the sidewalk onto the road. "But our master died suddenly, and no one knows what's goin' to happen."

"You mean your mistress won't keep you on? By the way, my name is Harry Carter. What's yours?" He felt guilty lying to the girl, but he'd learned that it was dangerous to give his real name. It wouldn't do for Inspector Witherspoon to accidentally overhear a young maid mentioning him while the inspector was questioning people at the Whitfield house. But nonetheless, he still felt bad because he had to lie to her.

"I'm Rosemary Keller." She bobbed her head.

"I'm pleased to meet you, Miss Keller," he said politely.

"Call me Rosie." She gave him a smile. "It's my day out today."

"You get a whole day out?" Wiggins was determined to keep the information flowing. "No wonder you don't want to lose your position. Most households only give their servants an afternoon out every week."

"That's all we get as well," she explained hastily. "But I missed my afternoon out last week, so Mrs. Murray said I should take a whole day this week."

"What 'appened last week?" he asked. The comings and goings of a housemaid probably had nothing to do with Whitfield's murder, but it was keeping her chatting and she might eventually say something useful.

"The footman quit, so Marie and I—that's the other housemaid—had to help Mr. Whitfield deliver his port to his friends. It took ages, and we were supposed to be back by lunch so I could have my afternoon out, but our hansom got stuck on Oxford Street and it was half past two before we got back to the house. Mrs. Murray promised me I could have the entire day out today if I'd stay and help clean up the mess down in the dry larder. That's where Mr. Whitfield did the corkin', you see. He'd got one of them wine corkers from Germany. But he did make a terrible mess. He broke two bottles and spilled half the cask of port all over the floor before he got it right. We had to scrub the whole room with sand and soap to get the stink out. I can't abide the smell of liquor, can you?"

"I don't drink," he replied. This was a lie, as he did enjoy a beer from time to time. But he'd learned from past experience that people were more likely to confide in you about all sorts of things if they thought you agreed with them. "Er, if your footman quit, isn't his position vacant?"

"It was up until the master died." She snorted derisively. "But like I said, we're all wonderin' if we're goin' to be shown the door. No one, not even Cook or the butler, seems to know what's goin' to happen next, not with the way Mr. Whitfield died."

He gave her what he hoped was a sympathetic smile. She was getting to the heart of the matter now, and he hoped she wasn't on her way to the countryside to visit family. "Not knowin' is 'ard, isn't it? Uh, if you don't mind my askin', where are you goin' now?" Wiggins prayed she wasn't on her way to a railway station to catch a train.

"Hyde Park," she replied. "I love it there. Even in the winter it's nice to walk about and breathe some fresh air. Then I'm goin' to have tea at the Lyons on Oxford Street." She broke off and smiled self-consciously. "That sounds awful, I know, especially with the master newly dead."

"No, it doesn't," he assured her. "You've a right to 'ave some time to yourself, especially if you've been workin' for days on end. Do you mind if I walk with you a bit of the way?" He was fairly sure she wouldn't. He had a feeling the girl was rather lonely. "I might as well go back to my lodgin' house, and it's on the other side of the park."

"I don't mind." She shrugged.

"I'm sorry you're worried about losin' your position," he said softly. "Uh, what was so odd about the way your Mr. Whitfield died?"

She looked around as though she was making sure no one was near enough to overhear her words. "He was murdered," she whispered. "We've had the police round. They were there last night, and just before I left, they came back. They're questioning everyone, but I didn't want to miss my day out again, so I slipped out of the house when the constable took Marie off to the butler's pantry to ask her some questions."

"Murder!" Wiggins widened his eyes in pretend surprise. "Goodness, how awful."

"It's been terrible."

His hand was still on her arm, and he felt her tremble. For a moment he felt lower than a worm. The poor girl was genuinely distressed by what had happened in her household, and he was leading her on just to get information from her. Then he told himself that he was helping to catch a killer. But that made him feel only a little less miserable.

Then she sighed. "But worse things happen at sea, as my old gran always says," she continued chattily. "And I am getting my day out."

He stopped feeling quite so remorseful. "But even if your master was murdered, won't someone inherit his house, and won't they need a staff?"

"Mr. Whitfield didn't have any close relations except for Mrs. Murray, and she's just a sister-in-law. None of us has any idea who gets his estate. Mind you, he's rich as old King Midas, so whoever gets it all will be havin' a nice Christmas." She giggled. "It won't be Mrs. Murray, either, not from what I overheard the other day."

He took her elbow again as they reached another busy street corner. "What was it that you overheard?" he asked.

"Mrs. Murray, I know this is difficult, but we must ask questions," Witherspoon said. He and Constable Barnes were back in the drawing room of the Whitfield house. The room was substantially different from the way it had been the previous evening. Instead of the huge wreath that had hung over the fireplace, there was now a picture draped in black crepe. Witherspoon assumed the painting was a portrait of the deceased. The candles, the holly, and the evergreen boughs with their bright red ribbons had all been removed as well.

Black crepe was also draped over the tops of the curtains at the windows and over the gold gilt frames of the other paintings on the walls. He wondered how the household had managed to find so much black crepe in such a short period of time. Did they keep it stored in the attic in case someone died? Had they borrowed it from a neighbor? He remembered crepe-hanging from his childhood, but in recent years the custom had died out.

Unlike the room, Rosalind Murray was not draped in black. She wore a high-necked gray dress with green trim on the cuffs and collar.

"I understand that, Inspector, but I've no idea what you expect me to say." She sank down onto the sofa. "I simply can't believe that someone would want to murder Stephen. Are you certain it wasn't an accident?"

"Mrs. Murray, we think the poison was in Mr. Whitfield's wine," Barnes said. "Unless you can think of a reasonable explanation as to how a rather large dose of foxglove accidentally ended up there, then I'm afraid we're going to have to assume it was added deliberately."

"Which would make it murder," she said dully. "I do understand."

"Could you tell us again what happened last night?" Witherspoon asked. "Why was Mr. Whitfield the only person drinking the Bordeaux?" He thought this a very good question.

"Because civilized people don't guzzle Bordeaux before dinner." She sighed. "I'm sorry. I shouldn't have made that comment. Stephen had a perfect right to drink what he liked, but generally before dinner, one has an aperitif, not a full-bodied wine like Bordeaux. The rest of us had sherry. There was going to be wine with dinner, so I've no idea why Stephen made such a spectacle of himself. But the moment he saw the label, he poured it down his throat like a drunk in a gin mill."

"And it was the Farringdons who brought the Bordeaux, correct?" Witherspoon probed.

"I've already told you they were the ones who brought it," she said wearily.

Witherspoon nodded. "Yes, of course you did. I simply wanted to ensure I'd understood you correctly. Can you describe the sequence of events after the wine had been opened?"

"I'm not sure I understand what you're asking." She frowned. "When the Farringdons arrived, I was still upstairs. I assume they handed the bottle to Stephen and he gave it to Flagg, who opened it in the butler's pantry and then brought it back into the drawing room to be served."

Witherspoon smiled slightly. "What I meant to ask was what happened to the wine after it was opened. My understanding was that dinner wasn't served until after eight o'clock and that the guests went into the morning room to look at Mr. Whitfield's Christmas tree. Where was the wine when the guests were moving about?"

"Oh, now I see what you mean." Her pale brows furrowed as she thought about the question. "Let me see, I believe the first time I saw the bottle, it was sitting on a silver tray next to the decanter of sherry in the drawing room." She shook her head. "The next time I recall seeing it was when Stephen asked Flagg to bring it into the dining room."

"So the bottle remained in the drawing room the entire time the guests were milling about and looking at the holiday decorations," Witherspoon pressed. He had a feeling that understanding who may or may not have had access to that wine bottle might be the key to solving this case.

"I think so," she replied.

"Do you recall whether anyone went into the drawing room after you'd all gone into the morning room?" Barnes asked.

She shook her head, dislodging a tendril of hair that fell across her cheek. "At one time or another, everyone left the morning room. Mr. Langdon went back in at one point, and Henry went in because he wanted to have a look out the window to see if it was snowing. I believe Basil left as well. I was in and out several times myself."

"For what reason?" Witherspoon asked. Gracious, when he was a guest in someone's home, he sat politely in the drawing room. What was wrong with these people? Everyone dashing about from room to room was going to make this very difficult, very difficult indeed. Drat.

"For any number of reasons," she snapped. "But if you want a list, I'll be happy to oblige. I checked with Cook to ensure the roast beef wasn't overdone, I asked Flagg to bring up another bottle of sherry to the drawing room, and I had Marie take away a linen serviette."

"In other words, you were down in the kitchen or in the butler's pantry when you weren't in the morning room," Barnes said. "Did you go into the drawing room?"

"Of course I did. I've just told you, I asked Flagg to bring up another bottle of sherry. I'd gone into the drawing room specifically to see how much sherry was left in the decanter."

"When you were in the drawing room, did anyone else come in?" Witherspoon asked softly.

"No, but I was only there for a moment or two."

"After you left the drawing room," Barnes continued, "where did you go first, the kitchen or the butler's pantry?"

Like Witherspoon, he knew it was important to get an idea of where everyone was in that crucial hour before the ill-fated dinner.

"I went to see Flagg in the pantry first, and then I went into the kitchen," she replied.

"About how long were you downstairs?" the inspector asked.

"I didn't note the time, Inspector." She crossed her arms over her chest. "But it was probably no more than ten minutes."

"When did you ask the maid to replace the serviette?" the constable inquired. He could tell by her stony expression that she resented this line of questioning.

"Just before we went into the dining room to sit down for dinner." She uncrossed her arms and sat up straighter. "I'd gone in to do a final check that the table was properly set, and noticed that one of the serviettes had a tear in the lace edging. I sent Marie down to the linen cupboard to get another one."

Witherspoon glanced in the direction of the dining room. "Was the dining room door open? I mean, could you see into the morning room?"

"No, you could not. Flagg opened the connecting doors when he announced that dinner was served. I didn't want the guests seeing the preparations."

"We'd like to confirm that with your butler," Barnes murmured. "And we'll need to speak to the other servants as well."

"Speak to whomever you like." She waved her hand dismissively.

"Did Mr. Whitfield have any enemies?' Witherspoon asked. He always felt a bit foolish with this question. Obviously the poor fellow had an enemy; someone had murdered him.

"Not particularly," she replied.

"Had he had any disputes with neighbors or sacked any servants?" Barnes pressed. He didn't see how a neighbor or a disgruntled former employee could poison a bottle of wine, but stranger things had happened, and a good copper covered all the possibilities.

"Stephen most certainly didn't argue with our neighbors, and he didn't run the household—I did. I've never sacked a servant. We've always been very lucky in our staff," she replied.

"How long have you been in the household?" Witherspoon asked.

"Ten years. My sister was Mr. Whitfield's late wife. When my husband died, Stephen invited me to come live with him, as we were both widowed." She looked down at the carpet and then back up to the two policemen. "He needed someone to run his household, and I was alone, so it seemed an ideal solution to both our circumstances."

Witherspoon nodded sympathetically. "I understand there were five dinner guests and the two of you."

"That's correct. There were the Farringdons, Henry Becker, Mrs. Graham, and Mr. Langdon. The dinner had been planned for quite a while. Stephen wasn't overly sociable, but he did like to have the occasional dinner party," she explained.

"Was Mr. Whitfield worried or anxious about anything lately—his health, or his finances?" Witherspoon asked. This was always a very delicate matter, but it had to be addressed. The possibility that the victim had deliberately poisoned himself had to be investigated, and the only way to do that was by asking uncomfortable questions. The inspector had noticed that relatives tended to get upset at the very hint of such a thing. Most people would rather deal with a murderer in their midst than consider that a loved one had taken his own life.

"He wasn't worried about anything," she insisted. "Stephen was looking forward to life. He was making plans for the future, he was enjoying himself, and he'd no financial or health worries whatsoever. He was a bit irritated when Mrs. Graham brought Mr. Langdon along last night, but that certainly didn't stop him from announcing his plans."

"What sort of plans?" Barnes looked up from his little brown notebook.

"He was going to Italy in the spring." She smiled bitterly. "I think he was going to invite Mrs. Graham to accompany him. But you'll have to ask her that. Stephen didn't confide all his plans to me."

"Then how did you know he was planning a trip?" Witherspoon asked.

"He's been buying travel guides, Inspector. One doesn't usually purchase a *Baedeker's* for central and northern Italy unless one is planning to go there." She sniffed disdainfully.

"Did he show you these guides?" Barnes asked.

"Of course not, but he left them lying about where anyone could see them," she replied.

"Did you ask him anything about his plans for a trip?" Witherspoon queried further.

"Yes, but all he said was that he was thinking of going in the spring. He said his plans weren't definite as yet, but I knew he was lying. He'd already been in touch with his bank to secure letters of credit for the journey."

"Was he in the habit of being secretive?" the inspector asked hopefully.

She sighed heavily and pursed her lips. "I wouldn't say he was secretive, but he didn't like being questioned. He was far too much of a gentleman to make a fuss about it, but he had a way of discouraging one from asking too much of him."

"How did you know about the letters of credit?" Barnes was careful to keep his tone matter-of-fact.

"I saw the instructions he sent to his banker, Constable. He accidentally dropped the letter on the floor of his study, and I picked it up when I went in to find a book. Naturally, I read it." She stared at Barnes defiantly. "But it hardly mattered whether I'd read the instructions or not. Just before he died, Stephen was getting ready to tell all of us about the trip. He actually said he had an announcement to make, but he collapsed before he could say anything more."

Betsy was determined to keep her mind on the task ahead of her. She took a deep breath, banished the mental image of her former fiancé looking at her with those big brown eyes of his, and then pulled open the door of the grocer's shop and stepped inside.

As she'd planned, she was the only customer, so the young man behind the counter gave her his full attention as she approached. Betsy gave him a dazzling smile.

"Good morning, miss, may I help you?" he asked politely. He didn't return her smile.

"I'd like an ounce of cinnamon, please, and a pound of flour," Betsy said. Mrs. Goodge had given her a short list of provisions before Betsy had left that morning.

"Certainly, miss." He turned around to a row of jars on a shelf behind the counter and pulled down a glass container.

"I was wondering if you knew a family named Whitfield in this neighborhood?" she asked. She held up a cream-colored envelope that she'd borrowed from the inspector's study. "I've got a note from my employer for a Mr. Stephen Whitfield, but I've lost the address."

The clerk took the lid off the jar and set it down next to a set of scales on the far end of the counter. "Whitfield, Whitfield . . . the name sounds familiar, but I've no idea where someone of that name might live." He poured a tiny amount of the spice onto the metal basket on one end of the scale.

Betsy forced herself to smile. This wasn't going as she'd planned. Whitfield's name was supposed to magically open the fellow's mouth so that all sorts of useful information tumbled out. "That's alright. I don't know why he didn't simply write the address on the envelope, but instead he put it on a slip of paper and tucked it into my shopping basket. Unfortunately I've lost it." Maybe the address ploy wasn't such a good idea.

He finished measuring her spice, tipped it onto a small square of paper, and then folded it into a snug little package. He turned and went down the length of the counter to a shelf at the other end and pulled down a small sack of flour. He did all of this in total silence.

"Does anyone else work here in your shop?" Betsy asked. "Perhaps someone else would be able to help me."

He shook his head and put the flour next to the packet of cinnamon. "There's only me here."

"Oh dear, I've no idea what to do next." Betsy watched him carefully as he added up what she owed on a slip of brown paper next to the cash box. Playing the damsel in distress usually worked: He might not know Whitfield by name, but this trick usually got her turned in the direction of someone who did know the locals. There was always at least one shopkeeper in every neighborhood who knew everything and everyone. She smiled expectantly, sure he would tell her where she ought to go next.

"Will that be all, miss?" he asked coolly.

Betsy's smile disappeared. "Yes, thank you." She paid for the provisions, tucked them into her basket, and hurried out of the shop. She hoped her luck got better at the next place.

"Who was the first of the dinner guests to arrive?" Barnes asked. He was in the butler's pantry with Flagg. They were sitting opposite each other at a rickety table.

"Mr. and Mrs. Farringdon," Flagg replied.

"And what time did they arrive?"

"It had just gone a few minutes past seven." Flagg picked a nonexistent piece of lint off his jacket sleeve. "Dinner was to be served at eight, but Mr. Whitfield had asked the guests to come early to enjoy the Christmas decorations."

Barnes nodded in encouragement. It was always useful when people volunteered more information than they'd been asked. "I understand the Farringdons brought a bottle of Bordeaux with them. Did you immediately take charge of it?"

"Mr. Whitfield wanted it opened right away, so after I hung up Mr. Farringdon's cloak and Mrs. Farringdon's jacket, I brought the bottle down here, opened it, put it on a silver tray, and took it back upstairs."

"Did you serve the wine?"

"No, he served himself," Flagg replied. "Mr. Whitfield didn't like servants hovering about the room when he had guests. So I put the wine down and went back to my position in the front hall. That way I could be close if he needed me but also available to answer the door as well."

"Were you able to hear if Mr. Whitfield offered any of the Bordeaux to the Farringdons?"

"I'm not sure." Flagg's broad face creased in a worried frown. "Right after the Farringdons arrived, Mrs. Graham

and Mr. Langdon knocked on the front door and I was busy
with them. It took Mrs. Graham ages to get out of her coat
and gloves."

Barnes was disappointed. It would have been interesting
to find out what the Farringdons might have said when the
Bordeaux was offered to them. "When the other guests went
inside the drawing room, did you hear if Mr. Whitfield offered them the Bordeaux?"

Flagg stared at him blankly. "Of course I heard. I was
standing just out in the hallway. He offered everyone a glass
of wine, but they all wanted sherry."

Barnes had no idea whether this line of inquiry was useful, but the inspector had said he wanted a complete ac-
counting of where the bottle had been, from the moment it
arrived in the house until it was taken into evidence.

"By that time, Mr. Becker had arrived, but he only wore
a topcoat so it took just a few seconds to put it on the coat
tree," Flagg continued.

"When did Mrs. Murray go into the drawing room?"
Barnes asked.

"I don't know. I don't recall seeing her come down the
stairs. But that doesn't mean much: she nips about quietly
and could easily have slipped in when I was putting the
coats away," Flagg replied.

"When did Mr. Whitfield and his guests leave the drawing room?"

Flagg looked puzzled. "You mean for dinner?'

"I understand that Mr. Whitfield had one of those 'Christmas trees' done up," Barnes explained. "Didn't he take his
guests in to see it?"

"Oh, that." Flagg snorted softly. "As soon as everyone had
their drink, he took them into the morning room. It was just
a pine tree with some painted glass and clay ornaments,

some ribbons, and those wretched candles. That caused a bit of a to-do, I'll tell you. One of the footmen actually quit over them silly candles, told me right to my face that he wasn't going to stand there for hours on end and then walked straight out of the house without so much as a by-your-leave. But Mr. Whitfield didn't care what sort of trouble the ruddy tree caused. He thought Mrs. Graham would find the tree amusing, and that was all that mattered to him."

"And did she find it amusing?" the constable pressed.

Flagg shrugged. "I wouldn't know about that, sir."

Barnes decided to leave that line of questioning for another time. "When did your footman leave?"

"It was the day before the dinner party, sir," Flagg explained. "And truth to tell, it wasn't a surprise. Some lads just aren't cut out for service, and Jacob Prine was one of them. He's a nice enough lad, but he hated working as a servant. Twice I cuffed him for talking back to Cook. Full of himself, he was."

"So he just quit and walked out?" Barnes queried. "Where did he go?"

"His uncle owns two very successful pubs, one in Hammersmith and one in Chiswick. He went there. He'd been champing at the bit to get out of here." Flagg leaned across the table. "Actually, I think the boy was a bit scared of the tree. He didn't like fire, and I don't think he wanted to be near all them blazing candles. I didn't much blame him, either."

Barnes wrote down the name in his notebook. Even though the boy had left the day before the murder, it wouldn't hurt to verify his movements. "Where is he likely to have gone? Hammersmith or Chiswick?"

"He'll be at Hammersmith. The Lineman's Tow is the name of the pub."

Barnes decided that they now had a pretty good idea of who might have had access to the open Bordeaux. Apparently everyone could have slipped in and doctored it with foxglove. But he wasn't through asking questions. He closed his notebook and looked at Flagg. "What sort of person was Mr. Whitfield?"

Flagg was taken aback. "I'm afraid I don't understand your question. It's hardly my place to . . ."

"You're not stupid, Mr. Flagg. Your employer has been murdered, so that means someone wanted him dead. It's our job to find out who that someone might be, and you'll do the late Mr. Whitfield a great service if you're simply honest with me. What sort of man was he?"

Flagg stared at Barnes for a long moment. "He wasn't any worse than most men of his class."

"What does that mean?'

"He wasn't a kind man by any means, but he was fair and he treated us decently." Flagg sighed. "Mind you, we didn't like the way he'd treated Mrs. Murray recently. She deserved better."

"What did he do to her?"

"Ever since he became acquainted with Mrs. Graham, he's pushed Mrs. Murray aside." Flagg sniffed disapprovingly. "Hardly the act of a gentleman."

"Isn't Mrs. Murray his sister-in-law?" Barnes said, taking care to keep his tone casual.

"Oh, yes, but up until he met Mrs. Graham, everyone assumed that Mr. Whitfield and Mrs. Murray would eventually marry. He always promised he'd take care of her, and frankly, unless he settled an allowance on her, I don't think he could have taken care of her and still been married to Mrs. Graham."

"Mr. Whitfield was going to marry Mrs. Graham?"

Barnes asked. He wanted to make sure he understood exactly what the man was telling him. "He actually told you this?"

"Not directly." Flagg chuckled. "He was hardly in the habit of discussing his personal business with me, but one does have eyes and ears. Two weeks ago he sent for his solicitor, and then he made an appointment with a jeweler."

"And those actions led you to believe he was going to propose to Mrs. Graham?"

"Those, and the fact that Cook overheard Mrs. Murray and Mr. Whitfield having words on the subject," Flagg replied. "Of course, Cook wouldn't say precisely what she overheard. She does that, you know—pretends that she doesn't like gossip—but she's no better than anyone else." He leaned across the table again. "But she told me that Mrs. Murray and Mr. Whitfield had some very strong words after the solicitor was here last week. Mrs. Murray is a lady; she never raises her voice. But Cook claims she was screaming her head off last week."

"You look dreadfully tired, Dr. Bosworth," Mrs. Jeffries said as she took a chair opposite him. He was sitting behind his desk, his pale skin even paler after a night of hard work. His red hair was mussed and tufts of it were standing on end. There was a faint air of disinfectant about his person. "I'm sorry. I shouldn't have come. This could have waited till later."

"Don't be sorry. I was expecting you'd be here this morning." Bosworth covered his mouth with his hand to hide a yawn. "That's one of the reasons I came to my office—I was fairly sure this would be where you'd look for me. You're here about Stephen Whitfield."

"I am. Was it poison?"

"It was. He had enough foxglove in his stomach to kill an elephant. That's one of the reasons that death occurred so rapidly—he ingested a massive dose," he replied. "Luckily, as the postmortem was done so quickly, the contents of the stomach were still fresh, and I found an enormous amount of crushed leaves."

"And you're certain it was foxglove?" she asked. She wanted to be sure about this fact. Foxglove was a poison anyone would be able to obtain. It grew all over the countryside, especially in the woodlands. If Whitfield had died of some other kind of poison, it might limit the number of people who could reasonably acquire a large enough supply to kill someone.

"I'm sure." He smiled. "I've seen it before."

"And it was in the Bordeaux?"

He nodded. "Correct."

"You had the wine tested?"

"I didn't need to have it tested. I simply poured a bit out, and the foxglove was floating in the wine as clear as day. It's a wonder no one noticed the leaves in the liquid. They were certainly big enough to be seen."

She thought about that for a moment. "That is very odd. If the leaves were that visible, the killer was taking a terrible risk. If Whitfield had noticed them, he probably wouldn't have drunk the wine."

"Perhaps." Bosworth shrugged. "But perhaps not. The bottle itself is a very dark color, so the leaves couldn't have been seen unless one held it up to a lamp or took it out in strong sunlight for a good look."

"But once the wine was poured into a glass, the leaves should have been spotted," she argued.

"Only if the person drinking the wine bothered to look." Bosworth leaned back in his chair. "Mrs. Jeffries, there are a number of people who are . . . Well, I'm not sure how to put it, but their need for alcoholic beverages is so great, they simply pour down their throats whatever is handed to them. Stephen Whitfield might have been one of those people."

"You mean an alcoholic?" Mrs. Jeffries had heard the word before but wasn't precisely sure this was the correct context. "But aren't those simply people who lie about in gin palaces and end up in the streets?"

"That's generally what happens if you're poor. If you've money, you can avoid ending up in those circumstances," he said. "Take my word for it—it's not just the poor that suffer from this affliction. There are just as many of the wealthy who have the same compulsion to drink; they simply have the means to hide it better. I'm not saying that this has anything to do with Whitfield's murder. I am saying that a craving for alcohol could be the reason he didn't bother to so much as glance at the contents of his cup."

"I see." She nodded in understanding. "Dr. Bosworth, wouldn't a massive dose like that have changed the taste of the wine?"

"Of course it would, but as we just noted, if he was a person with a craving for alcohol, he wouldn't have cared what it tasted like. He'd have been concerned only with getting it down his throat."

"But what if he wasn't one of those sort of people, one of those alcoholics? What if he had no craving? Wouldn't he have noticed that the wine tasted peculiar?"

Bosworth thought for a moment before he spoke. "He certainly should have noticed—unless, of course, he had a limited sense of taste. That could well be the case. He wasn't a young man."

"I'm not young, either, but I can tell if something tastes odd."

"Can you?" He grinned. "Remember, the man was drinking a full-bodied French red wine, which has a strong flavor in and of itself. He may well have thought it was supposed to taste as it did, or he might not have had any sense of taste at all. I've half a dozen patients who can't taste food or drink. It's quite a common affliction."

"Really?"

"Yes. The sense of taste is closely allied with the sense of smell. An infection in the sinuses, a blow to the head, a high fever—any or all of those conditions can leave one without the ability to taste or smell much of anything."

"That could explain why Whitfield didn't notice that the wine tasted unusual," she murmured. "Would the foxglove have changed the taste all that much?'

"I've no idea. Most of the people who have ever put the stuff in their mouths are dead. But I expect it would. Most poisons do have a strong taste. Perhaps it's Mother Nature's way of trying to keep us from ingesting things that are likely to kill us."

"With a large dose like the one he had, wouldn't it be obvious that Whitfield had been poisoned and not died of natural causes?" she asked.

Bosworth shook his head. "Unless they'd had some experience with foxglove poisoning, most physicians would assume he'd died of a heart attack. I only thought to look for poisioning because before Whitfield collapsed, he claimed everyone had turned blue. But if he'd collapsed without speaking, considering his age and his general health, even I would have thought it was his heart."

"Then he was lucky you were the one they fetched to attend him," she said with a smile. "Otherwise the killer would have gotten away with it."

"Your killer may still get away with it," Bosworth warned.

"Proving this kind of poisoning won't be easy. Just about anyone in England who can go for a walk in the countryside has access to foxglove."

"But it doesn't grow in the dead of winter."

"It doesn't have to," he replied. "The poison was in the leaves. Your killer probably gathered them this past summer, dried them out, and crushed them to be put in the wine. The poison would still be very, very potent." He raised his hand to try to hide another yawn.

But Mrs. Jeffries was having none of that. She got to her feet. "You must go home and rest. I've taken up too much of your time."

"I'm glad to help," Bosworth replied as he got up. "Do let me know what happens. I do like learning who the culprit is before it comes out in the newspapers."

"If this case is as difficult as I think it might be," she replied, "you may have a long wait."

CHAPTER 4

Smythe pushed his way into the Dirty Duck Pub and hoped that his old source would be open for business. He took a deep breath, inhaling the mingled scents of beer, tobacco, wood smoke, and river. This was one of the things he'd missed the most when he was gone: the smell of home, of London. Seamen, dockworkers, street vendors, day laborers, and locals crowded the bar and filled the benches along the wall; but considering the number of people in the room, it was relatively quiet. The pub might be on the quayside, but Blimpey Groggins, the man he'd come to see and the probable owner of this establishment, kept the rowdies and troublemakers out of the place.

Smythe eased past a bread seller, taking care not to bump her basket. He craned his neck to look past a burly teamster and saw that Blimpey was sitting at his usual table near the fireplace. He was talking with two other men. Smythe hung back a moment. Blimpey looked to be conducting business, and he wouldn't appreciate being interrupted. One of the men wore an old-fashioned black business suit, a silver and maroon cravat, and a shirt so white that it almost hurt your eyes. He appeared to be a banker. The other fellow had on a ragged gray jacket and paint-stained trousers.

Blimpey Groggins had started out in life as a thief. Breaking and entering was his specialty. But he was possessed of a superb memory and soon realized that as he had no stomach for either prison or violence, he could make far more money buying and selling information. He had sources in the Old Bailey, the magistrate courts, the financial centers in the City, the steamship lines, and the insurance companies. He also had an excellent relationship with every thief, con artist, and crook in southern England. His clients ranged from insurance companies wanting to know whether a suspicious fire had been deliberately set, to petty thieves looking for character references on which fence was the most reliable.

But Blimpey had standards. He wouldn't trade in information that caused physical harm to a woman or a child. Smythe had used him a number of times and had found his information very dependable.

The man in the dark suit stood, picked up his top hat from the table, nodded, and left. A moment later, the day laborer rose and walked away as well.

Fearing he wasn't the only one waiting for Blimpey, Smythe pushed his way through the crowd and slipped onto the stool opposite his quarry. "Hello, Blimpey."

"Well, look what the cat dragged in. Welcome back, Smythe." Blimpey grinned. "You're a sight for sore eyes. I was wonderin' if you were goin' to stay away forever." Blimpey was a short, rotund man with ginger-colored hair, a ruddy complexion, and a broad face. Even though he could afford a

Bond Street tailor, Blimpey was dressed in his usual outfit of a brown checked suit that had seen better days and a white shirt that was fading to gray. A long red scarf was twined about his neck, and on his head was a dirty porkpie hat.

"Australia's a long ways off, and it takes time to get there and back." Smythe laughed. He was delighted that there was someone who was glad to see him. "My business took a bit longer than I thought. I'm back to stay, though."

"Good. I'll buy you a pint, then." Blimpey waved at the barmaid, held up his glass, and pointed at Smythe.

"That's nice of ya." Smythe sighed heavily. "You're one of the first friendly faces I've seen since I got back." The others at the household had been happy to see him, but they'd all let him know how much he'd hurt Betsy. None of them seemed to take into account how miserable he'd been the whole time he'd been gone.

"I heard you 'ad to postpone your weddin'. I'll bet that didn't make your lady very happy." Blimpey smiled sympathetically.

"From the way some people are actin', it might be permanent," he muttered darkly. He had no doubt that Blimpey knew every little detail of what had happened and why he'd had to go to Australia.

"Are you back at the inspector's?" Blimpey drew back so that the barmaid had room to put the drinks down on the small tabletop. "Thanks, luv."

"I am." Smythe nodded his thanks as well. "But if Betsy and I don't work out our differences properly, I'm not sure I'll stay." The moment the words were out of his mouth, he knew they were true. He couldn't bear to be in the same house with her and know that she'd lost all feeling for him, that she didn't love him.

"You'll work it all out," Blimpey said. "She's just hurt

and angry over bein' left that way. It was right humiliatin' for her, you know. My Nell yammered at me about it for a good two weeks after you was gone."

Nell was Blimpey's wife, and as Smythe had had a hand in helping the two of them reach the altar, Blimpey felt it was his duty to give Smythe a bit of assistance with his lady love.

"What was I supposed to do?" Smythe cried. "I had to go and help. The old bastard had saved my life. I'd not have anything to my name if he'd not taken me in and shown me how to survive. I owed him. I couldn't let him just hide out in the bush, not at his age."

"You found him, then?"

" 'Course I did, and hired him a good solicitor. It was plain as the nose on yer face that he was innocent, so the charges were dropped once I let the lawyer take over." Smythe sighed heavily. "Stupid old git, he never shoulda run. But the idea of prison scared him so bad, he took off into the bush, even though he'd not done it."

"And you come back to face a very angry fiancée." Blimpey grinned. "Like I said, Betsy loves you. She'll come around. Don't give up, and don't even think of leavin'. Just let her have her way for now. Let her get a bit of her own back. After all, she was the one that was here in London with all them pityin' stares."

Smythe was getting tired of hearing about how hard Betsy had had it while he was gone. Did people think that tramping out into the bush was a picnic? But he held his tongue.

"You didn't just drop by to ask after my health," Blimpey continued. "What else do ya need?"

"Information." Smythe sipped his beer.

"I heard your inspector caught that toff's murder, the poisonin'."

Smythe stared at him incredulously. "How did you find

out he was poisoned? We've not even had that confirmed ourselves yet."

"Don't be daft, man. It's my job to find out these things. My sources told me about it ten minutes after the post-mortem report was delivered to the police. Stephen Whitfield was poisoned, all right, and from the amount he had in his stomach, it wasn't an accident."

"Cor blimey, that was bloomin' fast." Smythe laughed. He suddenly felt better, as though everything was going to be all right. "We need to find out who might have wanted Whitfield dead."

"There's always plenty about that want a rich man dead," Blimpey replied. "But I'm guessin' you'd like a bit more information so you can narrow it down a bit."

Smythe nodded. "We think the poison might 'ave been in a bottle of Bordeaux that was brought by one of the other guests."

"That's what the police surgeon said as well," Blimpey replied.

"Did you read the ruddy thing?"

Blimpey shook his head. "Nah, but I knew you were back, and I knew it was the inspector's case, so I knew you'd be along today. I thought you'd appreciate havin' a few pertinent details."

"I do," Smythe said quickly. "Was there anything else in the report I ought to know about?"

"No, just the fact that he was poisoned and that the poison was in the wine he'd drunk earlier. How come your inspector doesn't just arrest the person who gave Whitfield the Bordeaux? Doesn't he think that person is the most likely killer?" Blimpey asked.

"There might have been plenty of time for any of the other guests to have tampered with the bottle."

"Who were the other guests?" Blimpey took a quick sip of his pint.

Smythe repeated the names he'd gotten from Mrs. Jeffries at their meeting early this morning. "Do you know anything about any of them?"

"Not much. Hugh Langdon's got a reputation as a bit of a cad, and Basil Farringdon's family is one of the oldest in England. But like most of that class, they have plenty of breeding but wouldn't 'ave had near as much money if he'd not married a bit more."

"So Mrs. Farringdon was the one with the cash?" Smythe took another drink of his beer.

"That's the rumor, but don't take it to the bank just yet, lad," Blimpey replied. "This is only gossip I'm repeatin', not facts. Give me a couple of days and I'll have more than just idle chat to pass on."

"Good, I knew I could rely on you." He drained the remainder of his pint and stood up. "I'll be back in a day or two."

"You goin' off to do some snoopin' on your own?" Blimpey asked casually.

"I thought I'd make the rounds of the pubs in Whitfield's neighborhood and see what I could pick up."

"Try the Crow's Roost. It's just off the Fulham Road," Blimpey suggested. "It's the cheapest pub in that neighborhood and caters mostly to servants and workin' people. Stand a few rounds, and I've no doubt you'll loosen plenty of tongues."

The Farringdons lived on Connaught Street in Mayfair. Witherspoon and Barnes stood on the pavement and stared at the elegant five-story house. The ground-floor level was white stone and the upper floors red brick. The inspector stepped onto the short stone walkway and walked up to the front door. To his right, a flight of steps led down to a tradesmen's entrance. From his vantage point behind the inspector, Barnes could see a kitchen maid peering out the lower window. When his eyes met hers, she dropped the curtain and stepped back. Good. Their presence would be causing plenty of talk in the kitchen now, and that always helped an investigation.

Witherspoon knocked on the door. A few moments later, a woman wearing housekeeper's black peered out at them. "Yes?"

"We'd like to see Mr. and Mrs. Farringdon," Witherspoon said politely.

"They should be expecting us," Barnes added.

The housekeeper glanced over her shoulder and then looked back at them. "Mr. and Mrs. Farringdon are not receiving this morning,"

"This isn't a social call," Witherspoon said bluntly. "It is imperative we speak with them right away."

She hesitated and then opened the door wider. "Come in. I'll tell Mr. Farringdon you are here and that you insist upon speaking to him."

As they waited, Witherspoon took a look around. A home could tell you a lot about the people who lived in it, and what this home said was that the Farringdons were very, very rich.

The foyer was painted a lush peacock blue, the polished wood floor was covered with an ornate Oriental rug, and the staircase was at least eight feet wide. Next to the stairs was a round claw-foot table covered with a gold fringed shawl and holding a tall blue and white vase with brilliantly colored feathers. Opposite that was a huge oblong mirror set in an intricately carved rosewood frame.

"Looks like they've got plenty of money," Barnes muttered.

"So it would seem," Witherspoon replied. He turned his attention toward the hall as they heard footsteps. It was Basil Farringdon, and he didn't look happy.

"My housekeeper said you insisted on barging in," he said. "This is not a convenient time."

"Murder is rarely convenient for any of us," Witherspoon retorted softly.

Farringdon stopped, and his eyes widened. "Murder! Ye gods, what on earth are you talking about?"

"He's talking about murder, sir," Barnes said. "Surely you expected to see us again."

"I most certainly did not," he retorted.

Barnes eyed him skeptically. "Last night your host died in very unusual circumstances. We did tell you'd we'd be in touch, yet you seem surprised at our presence."

The constable had decided to get this part of the interview over quickly. They didn't have time to play about, and he'd found that the fastest way to get the upper crust to cooperate was to be as blunt and rude as they were.

"Of course I'm surprised," Farringdon snapped. "I thought Stephen had a heart attack."

"But it wasn't a heart attack," Witherspoon said. "And we must ask you a few more questions."

"Why? I've already made a statement." Farringdon had recovered some of his bluster. "That ought to suffice."

"I'm afraid it doesn't sir," Witherspoon said. "Mr. Whitfield was murdered."

"Are you certain?" Farringdon demanded. "Despite that young pup of a doctor's insistence on fetching the police, I assumed Stephen died of natural causes."

"Mr. Whitfield's death wasn't natural," the inspector

replied. Gracious, how many ways did they have to repeat this?

Farringdon frowned. "Our sort of people don't get themselves murdered, Inspector. Are you certain it wasn't a heart attack or a stroke?"

Barnes had had enough. "It was murder," he said. His knees were hurting, and it was so warm in here that he could feel sweat beading on the back of his neck.

Farringdon hesitated and then turned and started back the way he'd just come. "Come along to my study, then. It's this way."

"May I have a word with Mrs. Farringdon, sir?" Barnes asked as they followed him down the hallway. "It will take up less of your time that way."

It would also avoid the two of them being interviewed together and verifying each other's statements.

"My wife isn't home," Farringdon replied.

"Is she expected back soon?" Barnes pressed.

"She's shopping, Constable, and as she's no social engagements for today, it might be hours before she comes home." Farringdon pushed through a partly opened door, and the two policemen trailed after him into his study.

Witherspoon squinted as he stepped into the gloomy room. Heavy green curtains were drawn across the windows, blocking the morning light, and the only source of illumination was two small lamps on the desk in the far corner. The walls were painted a pale gray, with dark wood wainscoting along the lower half. Two straight-backed chairs were in front of the desk. A green leather wing chair and a matching sofa were along the far wall.

Farringdon sat down behind the desk and nodded toward the chairs. "You may sit."

"Thank you," Witherspoon replied as he and Barnes sat

where their host had indicated. "Mr. Farringdon, we understand you and your wife bought a bottle of Bordeaux wine for Mr. Whitfield. Is that correct?"

Farringdon's eyebrows rose. "That is correct. It was a little Christmas gift."

"Where did you acquire the Bordeaux?" Barnes asked.

Farringdon uncrossed his arms and straightened up. "Presumably it came from our wine merchant. But my wife, not me, is in charge of the household, so you'll need to ask her."

"What's the name of your wine merchant?" Barnes took out his notebook and flipped it open.

"Kerringtons and Stuart," he supplied. "They're in Oxford Street."

"How long had you and Mr. Whitfield known one another?" Witherspoon asked.

Farringdon sighed heavily, as though he was bored. "I don't see what on earth this has to do with his death . . ."

Witherspoon interrupted. "Nevertheless, it's important that you answer all our questions."

Farringdon drew back slightly, as though he was surprised. "All right, then, we've known each other since we were children. Stephen and I were in the same house at school, and we went up to Oxford together."

"So you'd been friends almost all of your lives." The inspector was trying to get him to speak a bit more freely. He'd found that once people began talking, they would frequently reveal all sorts of interesting information.

"I suppose you could say that." Farringdon shrugged. "Of course, once we were both married, we didn't see one another quite as often."

"But you went to his house for a holiday dinner, isn't that correct?" Barnes said. "And you bought him a gift."

"Only because for the past three years he's been sending us a gift," Farringdon replied. "He gives a nice bottle of his special port."

"Did Mr. Whitfield make his own port?" Witherspoon unbuttoned his heavy overcoat. He wished he'd taken it off, as it was hideously warm in the room.

"Gracious, no." Farringdon laughed. "Stephen could no more brew his own wine or spirits than he could captain a ship around the Horn. He had his wine merchant import a cask of port directly from the vineyards of Portugal. He corked it himself and sent us all a bottle."

"And he's been doing this for the past three years?" Barnes asked.

"That's correct. This year, since we were invited to dinner, Maria insisted we take him a bottle of really good Bordeaux." Farringdon leaned forward. "Stephen considered himself a bit of a connoisseur of both food and wine, but my wife was certain he'd no sense of taste. He and Mrs. Murray came to our autumn ball, and Stephen kept muttering that there was something wrong with the champagne cups and that they tasted off. Of course there wasn't, but Maria fretted over it for days."

Witherspoon smiled slightly. "Were you present when the bottle was actually opened?"

Farringdon thought for a moment. "No, I believe the butler took it off to the pantry to do that. Why are you so interested in that bottle of Bordeaux?"

Barnes wondered what took the fellow so long to ask. "Because the poison that killed Mr. Whitfield was in the bottle you brought."

Farringdon's eyes widened. "That's absurd. That bottle came directly from our wine merchants, and it wasn't open when we handed it to the butler."

"We're not accusing you or your wife of anything," Witherspoon soothed him.

"That's not how the question sounded to me," he snapped. "I take great umbrage at your implication. There was nothing wrong with the wine we brought."

"We're not implying anything." Witherspoon wondered how many times in every murder investigation he ended up saying those words. "We're simply trying to understand the sequence of events as they happened."

"We're trying to establish whether or not the bottle was left unattended at any given moment," Barnes interjected.

Farringdon relaxed a bit. "It was. It was sitting right there in the drawing room, where anyone could have tampered with it."

"Excellent, sir, that's precisely the sort of information we need." Witherspoon nodded encouragingly. "When the butler brought the Bordeaux into the drawing room, were all the other guests present?"

"I think so." He frowned slightly and rubbed his chin. "No, wait, I think that Henry was there, but Mrs. Graham and Mr. Langdon arrived at just about the same time Flagg brought the bottle in. Then Mrs. Murray came in . . . Yes, that's right. She was the last to come into the drawing room."

Witherspoon made a mental note to ask Flagg whether he'd put down the tray holding the bottle while he answered the door to let Mrs. Graham and Mr. Langdon into the house. He'd also have had to take their outer garments to the cloakroom, leaving the open bottle in either the hall or the foyer. "What happened after all the guests had arrived? Did everyone stay in the drawing room?"

"We had an aperitif, of course. Stephen offered everyone the wine, but the rest of us had sherry. We sat about and chatted for a few minutes, made pleasant conversation; then Stephen led us all into the morning room to see his Christmas tree. It was quite spectacular. It was one of the first I've ever seen in a private home, though I'm told they're becoming popular in some circles these days." Farringdon chuckled. "I'd thought it was households with children that would like that sort of thing, but then again, Stephen was a great admirer of the late Prince Albert, so I expect he felt he was honoring his memory by having the tree. He knew His Highness, you know. Stephen's mother was from Coburg and was a distant cousin to the late prince consort."

"And you all went in together to see this Christmas tree?" Witherspoon pressed. "No one stayed behind in the drawing room?"

"Everyone went," Farringdon said firmly. "Stephen was adamant that we all go. He ushered us into the morning room as if we were a herd of sheep. I don't really blame him: he'd gone to a great deal of trouble and I expect he wanted us to enjoy the sight. As I said, the tree was lovely. Very bright and colorful. Of course there was a footman on duty to ensure that the candles didn't catch anything on fire. I expect the lad blew the candles out when poor Stephen was taken ill. The household did go into a bit of an uproar."

"Did everyone stay in the morning room together?" Witherspoon asked.

"Everyone stayed for a few moments. Then, of course, there was the usual milling-about that happens at social occasions."

"Can you be a bit more specific, sir?" The inspector wanted to get some idea of who had been where at any given moment.

"I don't think so, Inspector. I wasn't really paying attention to everyone's comings and goings."

"Try, sir. It's very important," Barnes urged.

Farringdon frowned in concentration. "Gracious, I don't know that I can recall the exact sequence of who went in and out."

"It was only last night, sir," Witherspoon pressed, his tone just a tad impatient.

"Well, at one point, Mrs. Murray excused herself to have a word with the cook," Farringdon said slowly. "I remember that because she mentioned it to Maria when she excused herself."

"Excellent, that's very good," the inspector encouraged him.

"And Mr. Langdon asked if he could help himself to another sherry, so I know that he went into the drawing room. Henry went to the water closet, and I believe Mrs. Graham excused herself to go and fetch another handkerchief from her evening wrap. Oh dear, I honestly don't remember anymore. We were all milling about and chatting. The door opened and closed half a dozen times."

"Did you or Mrs. Farringdon leave the morning room during this period?" Witherspoon was careful to keep his tone very casual as he asked the question.

Farringdon shook his head. "No, we were both there the whole time. We didn't leave the morning room until the butler announced that dinner was being served."

"How long were you in the house before everyone went in to dinner?" Barnes asked. He thought it might be useful to know how long Stephen Whitfield had been drinking poisoned wine.

"We arrived at seven and dinner was served at eight." Farringdon smiled triumphantly. "I do remember that, because the hall clock had just gonged the hour when we went into the dining room."

"And Mr. Whitfield had been drinking the Bordeaux for all that time?" The constable clarified. "He didn't drink sherry or have any other kind of aperitif?"

"Stephen had nothing but the wine. He was drinking steadily the whole time. He must have had three-quarters of the bottle before we even went in to dinner."

Luty Belle charged into the kitchen, unbuttoning her fur-trimmed cloak as she walked. "Sorry we're late, but it ain't my fault." She flopped into her usual spot next to Wiggins. "Blame him." She pointed to her tall, stately, white-haired butler, Hatchet. "If he hadn't insisted we stop and make small talk with Lord Dinsworthy . . ."

"Don't be absurd, madam. You were quite willing to make that stop when you thought Lord Dinsworthy might have some useful information about one of the principals in the case," Hatchet retorted. He pulled out a chair on the other side of the footman and sat down. "You only began making a fuss when you realized that Lord Dinsworthy had absolutely nothing useful to tell us. You were rude to the poor man."

She snorted and slipped her cloak off her shoulders, letting it fall onto the back of her chair. "He was makin' us late, and if you don't make a clean getaway, the man will talk you to death."

"We've only just sat down," Mrs. Jeffries said cheerfully. "And Betsy isn't back yet, either. So we'll give her a few minutes."

Luty and Hatchet had been present at their morning meeting and had gone out to do their investigating with the same set of facts as everyone else. Because of her wealth, Luty had enormous resources in the financial community, while Hatchet had a network of resources of his own.

"She should be here on time," Smythe muttered. He couldn't decide whether to be angry with her or to throw himself at her feet and beg for forgiveness. He'd careened back and forth all day between the two courses of action, and he was dead tired. On top of that, when he'd gone to Howard's stables to see the inspector's horses, Bow and Arrow, they'd acted like they didn't know who he was, either! This was turning into a right miserable homecoming.

"Sometimes you can't 'elp bein' a bit late." Wiggins' mouth watered as he looked at the table. "Cor blimey, Mrs. Goodge, you've outdone yourself. Look at all this; freshly made brown bread, red currant jam, and a madeira cake."

"Why thank you, Wiggins," the cook replied.

"I'm sure Betsy will be here any moment," Mrs. Jeffries said just as they heard the back door open. Betsy, her face flushed with excitement, hurried into the room a moment later. "I'm sorry to be late, but the omnibus took ages getting across the bridge."

"We've not started yet," Mrs. Goodge assured her quickly.

"But as you're here now, we'll get started," Mrs. Jeffries said. "Who would like to begin?" She noticed that Smythe was staring at the tabletop and that Betsy was keeping her gaze on the buttons of her jacket as she undid them.

"If it's all the same to everyone, I'll go ahead and start," Mrs. Goodge volunteered. Considering the way Betsy and Smythe were avoiding even looking at one another, she thought it best to settle right down to business. She paused briefly to see whether anyone objected, and then plunged ahead. "I had a nice chat with one of my sources today, and I did find out a bit about our victim. Stephen Whitfield's been a widower for over ten years. The gossip I heard is that his sister-in-law, Rosalind Murray, has had her eye on becoming the second Mrs. Whitfield for quite some time now."

Betsy muttered something, but since her chair was scraping the floor, no one except Smythe could actually hear what she said. He wasn't sure, but he thought it sounded like "silly cow," a reference, no doubt, to any woman wanting to marry. He snorted faintly to let Betsy know he was aware of her attitude, and then kept his attention firmly fixed on the cook.

"Why'd she wait ten years?" Wiggins asked as he helped himself to a slice of bread. "I mean, if 'e's been a widower all that time. Poor lady wasn't gettin' any younger."

"My source wasn't certain, but she'd heard rumors that Mrs. Murray would lose an allowance from her husband's family if she remarried."

"So what?" Betsy asked. "If they really loved each other, *nothing* should have kept them apart." She glanced at her fiancé. Smythe narrowed his eyes, but said nothing. "Besides, wasn't Whitfield wealthy?" she continued.

"He's supposed to be." Mrs. Goodge shrugged. "But then again, I also heard that Rosalind Murray was considered quite an adventuress when she was a young woman. She went to India with her brother and only came home because her mother became ill."

"You found out quite a bit about Mrs. Murray," Luty said admiringly.

"She's the only one I heard anything useful about," the cook replied. "And I doubt the facts that the woman was an adventuress in her youth and is good at math are very helpful to our case. Supposedly she used to explain the stock market to her father. But none of my sources knew anything about the Farringdons or the other guests."

"Mine did." Luty chuckled. "I got an earful from my neighbor. Her sister lives in Chelsea, right across the road from Eliza Graham. Mrs. Graham's first husband died three years ago."

"How did he die?" Mrs. Jeffries asked quickly. Their previous investigations had taught them that background details about the suspects in a case were very important.

"Lydia didn't know." Luty shrugged. "But I reckon it won't be too hard to find out something like that. I'll try and track it down before our next meetin'. But let me tell ya what I did find out. Accordin' to all the gossip, Eliza Graham is a sociable sort of person, if you get my meanin'. She didn't wear widow's weeds for the full year after her husband died, and she started goin' out in society, too. That sure caused a few tongues to wag."

"What are widow's weeds?" Wiggins asked.

"Black clothing," the cook explained. "The Americans call mourning clothes 'widow's weeds.'"

"That's right." Luty nodded. "The only other gossip I heard about the woman was that she needs a rich husband. The family of the late Mr. Graham made sure she didn't get much when he died. That's about all I found out today. But I've got several sources lined up to visit tomorrow, so I ought to have something for our afternoon meeting."

"You've done an excellent job, Luty," Mrs. Jeffries said. She turned her attention to Hatchet. "Would you like to go next?"

"Thank you. I would, actually. Unfortunately my day wasn't terribly productive. The source I had hoped to speak with is currently indisposed with a bad cold." Hatchet hoped the Farringdon butler wasn't the malingering type. "The only information I managed to obtain is that Stephen Whitfield spends several weeks every summer at the Thompson Hotel in Dover." He smiled apologetically. "Apparently he's very fond of the gardens, which my sources assure me are rather spectacular."

"At least you found out something," Betsy said. "My day was miserable. I didn't find one shopkeeper that knew anything about Whitfield. Honestly, you'd think the man didn't buy food or drink or anything else. What did the household live on? Air?"

"Maybe Whitfield didn't buy from the local shops," Smythe speculated. He resisted the urge to reach for her hand under the table. "Maybe he buys his provisions elsewhere. There's lots of shopping areas in that part of London."

"I know," she replied glumly. "But people usually shop close to home, so that's where I started. There's another street of shops about half a mile away. Maybe I'll have better luck there tomorrow. Oh, wait a minute—I tell a lie. I did find out something. Whitfield did buy his vegetables at the local greengrocer's, and I found out he didn't care for beets. That's right useful information, isn't it?"

Everyone laughed. Then Mrs. Jeffries said, "Don't worry, Betsy. Tomorrow will be better. I didn't find out all that much myself. But Dr. Bosworth confirmed that Whitfield had been poisoned." She told them the rest of the details she'd learned from the good doctor. "So at least we know we're on the right track, so to speak," she concluded. "It was most definitely foxglove."

"Cor blimey." Wiggins shook his head. "Anyone who takes a stroll in the country could find that plant, then, couldn't they? The government ought to do something about that. Why, it's a wonder that hundreds of people don't end up poisoned."

"That wouldn't do any good, Wiggins," Luty said quickly. "Even if they ripped up every foxglove plant in the country, there are dozens of other things that are just as deadly. Yew trees, hemlock, horsetail, nightshade—and those are just the ones I can name off the top of my head. If the government tried to get rid of everything that could kill a person, there wouldn't be much countryside left!"

"Don't put anything in your mouth when you're walking in the country. That's my motto," Mrs. Goodge said wisely. "I learned that when I was just a girl."

"In America, we've got even more stuff that can kill ya," Luty added enthusiastically. "Oleander, locoweed, castor beans, mistletoe, rhododendrons, pokeweed, morning glory . . ."

"We've got mistletoe and morning glory here, too," Wiggins interrupted eagerly.

"Obviously there is no shortage of poisonous plants on either side of the Atlantic," Mrs. Jeffries interjected. "But we must get on with our meeting. The inspector might be home soon, and it's important that we hear everyone's report." She looked at Wiggins. "Would you like to go next?"

"I 'ad a bit of luck today," he began. "I met up with a maid from the Whitfield house, and she told me the servants was all scared they'd be lookin' for other positions now that the master was dead."

"Wouldn't the person who inherits the Whitfield house need a staff?" Betsy asked.

"Yeah, but none of them know who is inheritin' the house," the footman replied. "And that's why they're all worried. Up until recently, the servants thought that everything would go to Mrs. Murray, seein' as she's his only relation. But Rosie—that's the maid—she told me that a few weeks back, Whitfield made an appointment to see his solicitor and change his will. He and Mrs. Murray had a huge row about it. They was screamin' at each other so loudly the entire household heard 'em."

"What were they saying?" Mrs. Jeffries prompted.

"Rosie says Mrs. Murray was yelling that she'd given him the best years of her life and she wasn't going to be pushed aside now, and he was screamin' that he was the master and he'd do as he pleased. Then Rosie said it went all quiet-like, but you could hear Mrs. Murray crying. Mr. Whitfield started talkin' nicer to her then . . ."

Mrs. Jeffries interrupted. "Where were they when they were having this conversation? I mean, where in the house? Was it somewhere close enough for Rosie to actually overhear them, or is she just taking a guess on what was said when the shouting ended?"

Wiggins grinned broadly. "I wondered about that, too, but Rosie did overhear 'em. She and one of the tweenies crept up and put their ears to his study door. But it's a ruddy thick door, and all they could hear was him sayin' somethin' like, 'There's only so much I can do with my money, you know that.' Anyways, they'd no idea what those words meant, and frankly I can't figure it out, either."

"It could mean most of his estate is entailed," Hatchet murmured. "But if that's the case, why would he even bother calling in his solicitor?"

"Maybe only the house is entailed," Wiggins suggested. "He might 'ave made investments and such that aren't part of the entailment. Besides, he doesn't have any close relations, so even if his property is entailed, maybe there's no one to get it if it doesn't go to Mrs. Murray."

"In which case I believe the estate goes to the crown," Mrs. Jeffries replied. "But before we come to any conclusions about Whitfield's estate, let's try to find out the facts. Rosie could easily have misinterpreted the argument that happened between Mrs. Murray and Whitfield."

"I might be able to find out a few bits and pieces about Whitfield's estate by our meetin' tomorrow," Luty offered. "I ain't promisin' anything for certain—sometimes it takes a day or two to shake any information out of them close-mouthed lawyers—but I can try."

"Anything you can find out would be very useful, Luty." Mrs. Jeffries turned back to the footman. "Is that all you heard?"

"The only other thing I found out is that the servants all like Mrs. Murray," Wiggins said. "And I hope she isn't the killer. Rosie said she's a right decent sort. She doesn't take advantage of the servants. She let Rosie have a whole day out because she missed her afternoon off last week. She'd been 'elpin' Mr. Whitfield deliver his fancy port to all his friends. Then, when they got back to the house, there was such a mess in the kitchen from where he'd been corkin' the liquor, she had to help clean it up."

"Just because Mrs. Murray is kind to servants doesn't mean she didn't kill him," Betsy said. "But I understand how you feel. We always want the killer to be someone mean and nasty. But it doesn't always happen that way, does it? Even decent-seeming people can turn out to be murderers."

"I still 'ope it isn't Mrs. Murray," Wiggins said.

"If everyone else is finished, I'll go next," Smythe said. "I didn't learn much today, but my source did confirm that Whitfield had been poisoned. He also said that Hugh Langdon has a reputation as a cad, and that Basil Farringdon is from an old aristocratic family but it's his wife that has the cash."

"You mean he married her for her money?" Mrs. Goodge snorted. "There's a surprise."

Smythe grinned. "Don't be so cynical, Mrs. Goodge.

Maybe she married him for his position. I also found out that Henry Becker played whist with Whitfield on Thursday nights. Becker almost always lost."

"Doesn't it take four people for whist?" Mrs. Jeffries asked.

The coachman nodded. "Two other men played as well. One is named Thornton and one is named Rogers."

"You'd have to be a pretty sore loser to murder someone over a whist game," Luty muttered. "But I've seen people get real fed up with always gettin' whipped. It's not much of a motive, but you never know."

"It does seem an unlikely motive," Mrs. Jeffries agreed. "But, as you said, one never knows. We'll have to have a close look at Henry Becker."

"We'd have done so in any case," Hatchet commented. "He was at the dinner party."

"Tomorrow I'm going to make the round of the pubs near the Whitfield house and see what I can pick up," Smythe said.

"That's a very good idea," Mrs. Jeffries said. "And as Hatchet has reminded us, we need to find out what we can about all the guests that were at the Whitfield house."

"I'll have a go at seeing what I can learn about Eliza Graham," Luty volunteered. "I was goin' to find out how her husband died anyways."

"Don't forget that you're going to try and find out what you can about Whitfield's estate," Mrs. Jeffries reminded her. Information about who inherited from the dead man would be very useful.

"I didn't forget," Luty replied. "I can do both."

"And I'll see what my sources know about Henry Becker," Hatchet added. "And perhaps I can manage to learn a thing or two about Hugh Langdon."

"I'll suss out the Farringdons' neighborhood," Wiggins

said. "Maybe I'll get lucky again and find another house-maid that likes to chat."

"Excellent." Mrs. Jeffries glanced toward the window over the sink. Her sharp ears had picked up the sound of a hansom stopping out front. "That might be the inspector."

Before she could complete the sentence, the others were on the move and getting up. Hatchet grabbed Luty's cloak from the back of her chair and draped it across her shoulders. "We'll stop in tomorrow morning to find out what you've learned from the inspector. Put on your gloves, madam," he ordered as he shoved her toward the back door. "It's cold outside."

Luty grinned and waved as she disappeared down the hallway. Betsy was right on their heels, but she veered off into the dry larder. Wiggins went up the back stairs to finish polishing the sconces on the second-floor landing, and Smythe muttered that he wanted to make a quick trip to Howard's to check on Bow and Arrow.

Mrs. Jeffries looked at the cook. "How long will it be before the inspector's dinner is ready to be served?"

"You've a good hour." Mrs. Goodge grinned. "It'll take that long for the pudding to finish. There's plenty of time for you to find out everything he's done today."

CHAPTER 5

Mrs. Jeffries spent the following morning sorting the contents of the upstairs linen closet. She'd learned a great deal while the inspector had eaten his dinner, and now she needed to think about everything he'd told her. Sometimes keeping her hands busy helped to free up her mind. She'd shared the information with the others this morning during their brief meeting, and everyone except for Mrs. Goodge had gone off to hunt for clues.

Mrs. Jeffries pulled a stack of sheets out of the closet and laid them on the top of the old tea trolley she used for household tasks. This case was still very much a puzzle. From what she'd heard from the inspector, Basil and Maria Farringdon could become suspects, but so far they'd no motive for wanting Whitfield dead. She leaned down and pulled her dusting rag from the second shelf of the trolley, straightened up, and swept the cloth around the inside of the cupboard. She paused as she remembered a tidbit she'd heard from the inspector. Maria Farringdon had been insulted by Whitfield about her champagne cups. But that was hardly a motive for murder, unless the killer was completely unbalanced. Thus far, they'd no evidence that Maria Farringdon was insane.

Rosalind Murray was still very much in the running as a suspect, since she'd had a screaming argument with Whitfield. But as for what it had been about—well, they were still in the dark over that issue. Experience had shown Mrs. Jeffries that information obtained by eavesdropping through heavy doors could easily be misinterpreted. Mrs. Jeffries grunted as she stretched to reach the far corner of the shelf with her cloth.

What about Eliza Graham? Where did she fit into this strange story? On the surface, it appeared that she was now pushing Mrs. Murray aside in Whitfield's affections. Perhaps that might be another reason for taking a second look at Rosalind Murray. The old adages often proved true: Hell hath no fury like a woman scorned. But then again, Mrs. Graham had brought Hugh Langdon with her to dinner that night. Mrs. Jeffries had no idea what bearing that might have on the case. Perhaps it meant nothing, and Langdon simply happened to be in the wrong place at the wrong time. Such occurrences happened frequently. Or perhaps there was more to his being there than it appeared.

She stepped back and surveyed the inside of the dark cupboard as best she could. It would do. She laid the rag down and put the sheets back into the closet. Reaching into the bowl of dewberry wood chips on the top of the trolley, she picked up a handful and tossed them onto the stack of sheets.

She moved to the next shelf and pulled out the pillowcases.

She glanced at the bowl of dewberry chips. There were only half a dozen left. Betsy had told her that this was the last of them. She frowned as she thought of the maid. Betsy was still keeping her distance from Smythe. At breakfast this morning, she'd spoken barely two words to him. Mrs. Jeffries wondered just how much of that sort of behavior he was going to tolerate.

Smythe loved the girl dearly, but he was a proud man. At some point he was going to get tired of waiting for her to forgive him. She hoped that Betsy would come to her senses soon. Smythe's decision to go, honorable and noble as it had been, had hurt her deeply. But he was back now, and that which had been broken could be mended. The human heart was far more malleable than most people realized. Betsy would get over this, and if she didn't, she'd lose a very good man. Men like Smythe didn't grow on trees. Mrs. Jeffries wondered if it might be wise to drop a hint or two in Betsy's direction; then she realized it was really none of her business. The two of them had to work this out for themselves. She sighed heavily. She knew that there was nothing certain in this life but change; yet the thought of Smythe's leaving permanently and their little band's being broken up prematurely filled her with despair. That was one change that didn't have to happen if Smythe and Betsy would sit down like adults and talk to each other.

She finished the dusting, replaced the pillowcases, and tossed in the last of the wood chips. Mrs. Jeffries took off her apron, draped it over the trolley, and then pushed the trolley into the spare room at the end of the hallway. The house was in good order. It was time for her to get out and about.

Mr. Henry Becker lived in a six-story brick house on a short road off the Marylebone High Street. A tall, austere butler opened the door and immediately ushered them inside. "Mr. Becker has been expecting you," the butler said as he led them to the drawing room. "He'd like you to make yourselves comfortable. I'll tell him you're here."

Witherspoon raised his eyebrows. "That's a surprise," he said as soon as the servant had left.

"It is indeed, sir. People of this class usually behave as if they're doing us a favor by even opening the door." Barnes glanced around the opulently furnished room. The ceiling was a good twelve feet high, with an enormous crystal chandelier smack in the middle. A grand piano was in one corner, and a gold gilt harp stood next to it. Gold brocade curtains hung from the three tall windows, and the floor was covered with a green and gold fleur-de-lys-patterned carpet. The same pattern was duplicated in the white and gold wallpaper. Vases of ivy and holly stood on top of all the cabinets and tabletops. Evergreen boughs tied with huge red velvet ribbons lay across the top of the mantelpiece, and tall silver candlesticks, also festooned with red ribbons, stood on each end. "Mr. Becker didn't stint himself on his Christmas decorations."

"Indeed he didn't. The gentleman also appears to enjoy bright colors," Witherspoon murmured as he looked at the Empire-style furniture upholstered in silver, gray, and gold brocade.

The door opened and Henry Becker hurried into the room, a welcoming smile on his face. "Oh, good, you're here. I've been waiting for you." He nodded politely at Witherspoon and Barnes. "I told my man to have you make yourselves comfortable. Do please take a seat. Would either of you care for tea, or perhaps you would prefer coffee?" He gestured toward the sofa, yanked on the bellpull by the door, and then plopped down on a tall wingback chair.

"Thank you, tea would be very nice," Witherspoon replied. He and Barnes sat down. He waited until the constable had taken out his notebook before he started to speak. "I appreciate your seeing us, Mr. Becker. I know a visit from the police, especially at this time of the year, isn't very pleasant."

"Nonsense. I find it exciting. I've been looking forward to it." Becker turned his head as his butler stepped into the room. "Bring us some tea, please." As soon as the servant left, he turned his attention back to the two policemen. "I must tell you, I was beginning to wonder if you were ever going to come and see me. I'd actually thought perhaps I ought to go alone and see you chaps, but then you turned up, so all is well."

Witherspoon had never encountered such an eager witness. The fellow was obviously rich, and at first glance he appeared quite ordinary: average height, darkish hair with a good deal of gray in it, and very average features. But his eyes sparkled with enthusiasm, and he'd smiled almost continuously since he'd entered the room.

Perhaps Mr. Becker smiled a bit too much.

The inspector stared at him for a moment before he replied. "I'm sorry if it appeared we weren't interested in your statement, Mr. Becker, but we had to wait for the results of the postmortem to confirm that a crime had actually been committed."

Becker's smile faded, and he pursed his lips. "Yes, I suppose you do have to wait for official confirmation of some sort, don't you?"

"We do, sir." The inspector eased back in his seat.

"I quite understand, Inspector. Of course you had to find out if old Stephen had been poisoned or simply keeled over from natural causes." Becker sighed. "I suppose I ought to be careful in what I say. Stephen wasn't really that old; we were the same age. We were at school together. Still, I shouldn't be surprised that it happened."

"Why weren't you surprised, sir?" Barnes asked.

Becker smiled again, though this time his expression was wistful, not eager. "We always lose schoolmates at this time of the year, so I suppose I've been deluding myself and I really am getting old. I just don't feel any differently than I did when I was a lad."

"That's most unfortunate, sir," Witherspoon replied. "Losing old friends is always painful, especially at this festive season."

"It most certainly is." Becker broke off as the butler returned with their tea. "Put it down on the table, Manley. I'll pour."

"Yes, sir." The servant put the tray down next to Becker and then withdrew, closing the door quietly behind him as he left the room.

Becker picked up the silver pot and poured tea into the three cups. "Do you take sugar, Inspector?"

"Two lumps, please."

"And you, Constable?"

"Three lumps, sir," Barnes replied.

"As I was saying"—Becker handed Witherspoon his tea—"Christmas used to be my favorite time of the year, but now it looks as if I'm going to another funeral come January." He handed Barnes his tea. "Luckily, it's so cold out that one doesn't have to worry about decomposition, does one?"

The inspector glanced at Barnes, and the constable gave a barely perceptible shrug. He, too, thought Becker's conversation more than a little strange.

"They never have the funerals until after the holidays, so I suppose they must store the corpses someplace," Becker continued. "Do they use cellars or some sort of cold storage?"

"I'm not certain," Witherspoon replied.

"There are several places where bodies are kept," Barnes said. "Now that Mr. Whitfield's postmortem is completed, the body will be released to a funeral parlor or an undertaker's establishment. His family will make that decision."

"He didn't really have any family except for Rosalind, and she's only a sister-in-law. Does that count?" Becker asked curiously.

"I don't know," Witherspoon replied. "I imagine his solicitor has all the particulars about his burial."

"I doubt it. I expect Stephen thought he'd live forever," Becker said cheerfully. "His own death is the sort of subject he wouldn't like to think about. Poor Rosalind will probably get stuck making the arrangements."

"Er, uh, Mr. Becker, you said you were at school with Mr. Whitfield," Witherspoon began.

"Right, we were at Eton together. Whitfield and I were in the same house." Becker grinned broadly. "Stephen didn't like school very much, but, then, neither did I."

"Was Basil Farringdon also in your house?" The inspector took a sip of his tea.

"He was. He was quite good at sports, as I recall."

"And you've all been friends ever since?" Barnes asked. He studied Becker closely, wondering whether the man had a firm grip on all his faculties. In his long years as a policeman, he'd sometimes arrested people who had obviously committed the crime in question, but he'd sensed that, though those people appeared rational, they really weren't. There were simply some poor souls who completely lost their hold on this world and slipped into another one. But

Barnes' job was to keep the peace, and though he often felt very sorry for these unfortunate folk, they couldn't be allowed to run around engaging in murder or mayhem. He thought that Becker had the same sort of look in his eyes, almost as if he wasn't quite all there. Still, the man was rich as sin and probably had a ruddy platoon of lawyers at his beck and call, so they'd better take his statement seriously.

"More or less," Becker answered. "We lost touch for a few years when I was traveling, but once I was back in the country, we renewed our acquaintance." He took a sip of his tea. "Actually, now that I think of it, we lost touch for longer than that. I was back in London for ages before I ran into Stephen. Yes, that's right—his wife had just died. We happened to come across each other at a dinner party. I suppose that was when we sort of reacquainted ourselves."

"How long ago was this?" Witherspoon took another sip of tea. It really was excellent.

Becker thought for a moment. "Let me see. His wife died about ten or eleven years ago—yes, that's right." He gave a short bark of a laugh. "Shortly after that, Rosalind moved in to be his housekeeper. That set a few tongues wagging, I can tell you."

"Yes, I'm sure it did," Witherspoon replied. He found this all very interesting, but as it had happened more than a decade ago, he didn't see how old gossip could have any relevance to who might have wanted to murder Whitfield now. "What time did you arrive at the Whitfield house the night of the death?"

"A few minutes past seven," Becker replied. "My hansom pulled up just as the Farringdons were going inside."

"And what time was dinner served?" Barnes asked. They already had that information, but he wanted to confirm as much of Basil Farringdon's statement as possible.

"Eight o'clock. We had drinks first, and then Stephen ushered us into the morning room to have a look at his Christmas tree. It was rather lovely." He broke off and looked around the room. "I'm thinking of having one here next year. I think that corner over by the fireplace would be perfect. Mind you, one does need a footman on duty to make sure the candles don't burn the house down, but we've plenty of footmen here and most of them don't appear to be doing much of anything."

"Yes, I'm sure that would be just the right spot for it," the inspector murmured. "Er, uh, what happened then?"

Becker dragged his gaze away from the proposed spot for next year's Christmas tree and looked at the two policemen. "What happened when?"

"When you were in the morning room looking at the tree," Witherspoon prompted. "What happened at that point in the evening?"

Becker looked confused. "We all stood around and chatted and admired Stephen's tree."

"Perhaps I'm not making myself clear." Witherspoon smiled grimly. "What we need to know is the sequence of events throughout the evening. Could you describe everything that happened from the time you arrived until the moment Mr. Whitfield collapsed?"

Becker's expression brightened. "Of course, of course, that's precisely what you'd need to know. Now give me a moment to think, Inspector. I do want to get this right."

They sipped their tea in silence for a few minutes while Becker gathered his thoughts. Finally he said, "I came in just after the Farringdons, and I must admit I was a bit annoyed."

"Why was that, sir?" Barnes asked. He still couldn't decide whether Becker was just a lonely man who took any and all opportunities to chat, or whether he was a tad unbalanced.

"They'd brought a gift and I hadn't," he admitted. "It was slightly awkward for a few minutes. Stephen was waving about this bottle of Bordeaux, telling me they'd brought it for him, while I stood there empty-handed. Stephen had given me one of his bottles of port. Dreadful stuff—I can't abide it—but I could hardly refuse to take it. Last year I gave it to my next-door neighbor. But he's dead now, so I am rather stuck with the stuff. I suppose it'll sit in my wine cellar till I give it to one of my servants or find some other poor soul to foist it on."

Wiggins dropped to his knee and pretended to tie his shoe. He was directly across the road from the Farringdon house and he wanted to get the lay of the land, so to speak. He kept his eye on the staircase to the left of the front door— the stairs leading down to the kitchen, the ones the servants used.

"How long does it take to tie a bloomin' shoelace? Get a move on. You're blocking the pavement," a woman's voice said from behind him.

He leapt up and whirled about, coming face-to-face with a middle-aged woman carrying a shopping basket over her arm. "Sorry, ma'am." He doffed his cap respectfully and moved out of her way. "There was a knot in the lace."

She continued onward, but her harsh features relaxed a bit as she passed him. "No harm done, lad."

"Excuse me, ma'am." He hurried after her. "But I'm lookin' for a family named Farringdon. Do you know them?"

"They live just over there." She pointed to the house he'd been watching, and kept walking. "But they're not lookin' for staff."

"Are you sure, ma'am?" he asked. "I heard they've just lost two footmen, and I've references."

"They haven't lost any footmen," she said, slowing her footsteps and turning to look at him. "And I ought to know. I'm well acquainted with their housekeeper."

Wiggins desperately tried to think of a way to keep this woman talking, but as she wasn't a young girl he could flirt with or a young lad he could lure to a teahouse with the promise of a sweet bun, he wasn't certain what to do. "I guess my friend was wrong, then," he finally said. "I'm sorry to have troubled you, ma'am."

"Don't worry, lad. It was no trouble," she replied as she continued walking. "You might try at the Addison house. They live just around the corner at number seven Connaught Square. No, don't bother goin' there—they get their staff from a domestic agency. Are you with an agency?"

"No, ma'am."

"But you have references?" She suddenly stumbled and pitched forward. She threw out her arms in a futile attempt to catch her balance and would have fallen flat on her face if not for Wiggins. He managed to grab her shoulders and pull her back onto her feet.

"Gracious! Thank you, lad." She was panting hard, frightened by losing her footing. "You saved me from taking a nasty fall. That was kind of you"

"Are you all right, ma'am?" He kept his hand on her elbow as he steadied her. "There's a nasty crack in the pavement there. Someone could really hurt themselves. The council ought to do something about that."

She was still panting and had gone quite pale. "Yes, I suppose they should. But I suspect they won't bother until someone breaks a limb and threatens a lawsuit."

Wiggins whipped off his cap. "Excuse me for bein' so bold, ma'am, but you've gone quite white. I think you need a cup of tea to calm your nerves. There's a Lyons teahouse just up the road . . ."

"There's a café around the corner." She pointed back the way she'd come. "Which is a lot cheaper than a Lyons. I'd be pleased to buy you a cup, young man. You're unemployed and you've just saved me from hurting myself. Let's introduce ourselves properly. I'm Matilda Jones. What's your name?"

Wiggins couldn't believe his luck. Ten minutes later, he was sitting across from Mrs. Jones at a window table with a cup of hot tea in front of him. Her shopping basket was on the chair beside her.

"I'm sorry there are no positions available at the Farringdon house," she said. "They treat their servants quite well."

"That's why I wanted a position there," he replied. "I 'eard they're real decent. Mind you, I also 'eard some other strange bits, but I didn't pay any attention, as it was just gossip."

Wiggins was making it up as he went along, hoping she'd supply him with some information. He'd noticed that if you acted as though you knew something, people often felt a need to tell you what they knew or had heard about the same subject.

"If you're referring to that silly rumor about Maria Farringdon poisoning the Whitfield man, it's nonsense." She sniffed disapprovingly. "Mrs. Farringdon wouldn't do such a thing."

"I'm sure you're right, ma'am." He took a quick sip and tried to think of the best way to keep her talking.

"There are far too many people in this world who have nothing better to do than sit around making up outlandish stories and gossiping."

"You're right, ma'am. I shouldn't 'ave even mentioned I'd 'eard rumors about the household," he said quickly.

"The very idea that someone of her class and background would do such a thing is absurd." She paused and took a deep breath. "Of course she's not from the same background as her husband, but according to Mrs. Mulch—she's their housekeeper and my friend—Mrs. Farringdon works very hard to be a credit to Mr. Farringdon. She takes great pains to ensure she observes all the proper social etiquette."

"I'm sure she does."

"Mrs. Farringdon does occasionally take her diligence a bit too far—at least that's what Mrs. Mulch thinks, and I quite agree with her." Mrs. Jones leaned across the table and dropped her voice. "When she goes to a really posh party, she brings home the wine bottles."

"Wine bottles," he repeated.

Mrs. Jones nodded. "She has her footman go around to the kitchen and fetch them for her. Mrs. Mulch says the footmen hate doing it."

"Maybe it's just as well there aren't any positions available with the Farringdons," he said thoughtfully. "I don't think I'd much enjoy doing something like that, either. What does she do with all of 'em?"

Smythe stayed far enough behind Betsy that she wouldn't spot him, but not so far as to lose her completely. There wasn't enough privacy for them at Upper Edmonton Gardens, and he needed to speak to her. They couldn't go on this way. He had to talk to her. He was going to be making the rounds of the pubs in the Whitfield neighborhood again today, and as they weren't open yet, he thought it would be a good time for the two of them to clear the air.

He watched her pull open a door and step into a grocer's

shop. Smythe hurried over and stood just outside the window. He peeked inside. The shop was empty of customers, save for Betsy. The clerk was up on a ladder behind the counter, putting tins on the top shelf.

Smythe stepped back. If he could see Betsy, she could see him, too. A few seconds later, he took another look. The clerk had climbed down off the ladder and was talking to Betsy. He was a young man, probably no more than twenty, tall and handsome in a foppish, silly sort of way.

The clerk dusted his hands on the front of his apron and said something to Betsy that made her laugh. She cocked her head coquettishly and made some comment in reply. Ye gods, Smythe couldn't believe his eyes. How dare she smile at a strange man like that? She was engaged to be married.

The clerk said something else, but Smythe couldn't hear the words. But whatever it was made her laugh again. Then she turned her head in Smythe's direction. He ducked back just in time.

When he looked again, she was smiling at the clerk and chatting as if they were old friends. Didn't the woman have any sense at all? That clerk was leering at her.

Smythe glared at her through the shop window. Now she was laughing again at something else the stupid git said. This was unbelievable. There was no mistaking her manner: she was out-and-out flirting. Blast a Spaniard, she was practically a married woman! Here they were engaged, and she was in there carrying on as though she'd set her cap for the man.

Just then she turned, and this time he wasn't quick enough. She saw him. Her eyes widened and her jaw dropped. Then she said something to the clerk, turned, and marched toward the door.

When she stepped outside, she did not look pleased to see Smythe. "Are you following me?"

"I just wanted to talk to you away from the house," he began. "So, yes, I suppose you could say I was following you."

"You were spying on me?" She put her hands on her hips and glared at him.

"No, I was waitin' for you. That's all. But I couldn't 'elp noticing you were battin' your eyes at that clerk like you'd set your heart on 'im."

Betsy's mouth gaped. "Set my heart on him? Don't be ridiculous. I was trying to find out something useful."

"I'll bet you found out plenty," he shot back. He was hurt, angry, and scared. Betsy was a beautiful girl, and any man would want her. What did he have to offer? Just money, and she wasn't interested in that.

"What do you mean? I was doing what I always do." Out of the corner of her eye, she saw the clerk start to move toward the door. A confrontation between an angry fiancé and a gallant young grocer's clerk was the last thing she needed. "Come on. If we're going to argue, let's get out of the street to do it. People are staring."

She turned on her heel and started up the road. When he just stood there, she whirled around. "Come on, then. Let's have this out once and for all."

"And where do you propose having this out?" he cried. He was starting to panic. It hadn't occurred to him that she'd force the issue this way. He could tell she wasn't talking only about this petty little incident. He wasn't sure he was ready for this.

"There's a park around the corner," she snapped. "We can talk there. I'm tired of all this. Let's get it out in the open, and we'll each have our say."

She stomped off toward the corner. Smythe hesitated. If

he turned and walked the other way, she wouldn't be able to end it for good. But that was the coward's way out, and by all the saints, he wasn't a coward. He hurried after her. Come what may, he'd face it. If she wanted it over, well, he could always go back to Australia.

"What did you think, sir?" Barnes asked as they came out onto Marylebone High Street. He waved at a hansom dropping off a fare farther up the road.

"I think Henry Becker is a bit eccentric, but not strange enough for us to discount his statement. Ah, good, you've got us a cab," Witherspoon said as it pulled up. He climbed in and slid to the far side, leaving room for the constable.

"Elm Park Gardens in Chelsea," Barnes called to the driver. He slipped in beside the inspector. "That was my impression as well, sir. Too bad his statement didn't really contain any information we didn't already know."

"True, but he did confirm Basil Farringdon's account of the evening," Witherspoon said.

"And he also gave us a bit of gossip." Barnes grinned. "That's always useful. Perhaps we'll have as much luck with Mrs. Graham."

"Let's hope the lady is at home." He frowned thoughtfully. "Becker did confirm the idea that any of them could have done it."

"The open bottle was sitting there for almost an hour," Barnes agreed. "It's too bad that so far none of our witnesses remembers exactly who went where at any specific time. But I guess people don't look at their pocket watches or a clock every time someone leaves a room."

"It would be most useful if people did," Witherspoon murmured. "After we finish taking statements, I want to go back to the Whitfield house and have another go at speaking to the servants. Perhaps one of them noticed if anyone spent any time alone in the drawing room. But then again, even if someone did go in there on his own, that would hardly prove he put the poison in the bottle."

"It might give us a place to start," Barnes said. "So far our best suspect is one of the Farringdons, and neither of them had any reason to want Whitfield dead."

Witherspoon smiled faintly. "Well, Whitfield did make light of Mrs. Farringdon's champagne cups last summer. She might still be a tad annoyed about that. But I hardly think the woman would commit murder over such a trifle."

Barnes laughed. "You never know, sir. Some women take their food and drink very seriously. What I really wonder is how they got the poison into the house. According to the postmortem report, a large amount of crushed leaves were found in the victim. That means the killer had to get them into the house and into the bottle of Bordeaux without any-one noticing. I don't think that would be particularly easy."

"Why not?" Witherspoon asked. "It seems to me that tucking an envelope filled with crushed leaves somewhere on your person would be simple. Then all the killer would need to do would be to wait till there was no one about, and tip the leaves into the bottle."

"An envelope," Barnes said thoughtfully. "I hadn't thought of that. In my mind's eye, I saw the leaves in one of those tiny glass vials or a little wood box. But you're right, of course. An envelope would be the simplest solution."

"And it would be easy to get rid of the remaining evi-dence," Witherspoon continued enthusiastically. "The killer could simply chuck the envelope into a fireplace or a stove. There would be nothing left for us to find."

"That's a dreary thought, sir," Barnes replied. "The last thing we need on this murder is a clever killer."

As the hansom made its way through the busy West End streets, they discussed what few facts they had so far. As the cab pulled up in front of the Graham house, a drizzle began to fall. Witherspoon turned up his collar and gazed at the four-story redbrick town house as he waited for Barnes to pay the driver. The dwelling was in excellent condition, the door freshly painted a bright blue, the black iron railing in the front free of rust, and the brass lamps brightly polished.

Barnes moved past Witherspoon and banged the heavy brass door knocker.

A few seconds later, a housemaid holding a feather duster opened the door and peered out at them, her expression curious. "Hello."

"We'd like to see Mrs. Graham," Barnes said. But the girl was already opening the door and gesturing for them to come inside.

"The mistress is expecting you," she said. She tucked her feather duster under one arm and motioned for them to follow. "If you'll come this way, please."

Witherspoon barely had time to whip off his bowler before the maid led them down a short hallway to a set of double oak doors.

"It's the police, Mrs. Graham," she announced as she stepped back and gestured for the two men to go inside the room.

Eliza Graham was sitting on a rose-colored sofa. She got to her feet as the policemen entered. "Good day, gentlemen. I've been expecting you." She smiled courteously.

Witherspoon tried not to stare. He'd seen her only last night at the Whitfield house, but he'd been distracted, and frankly the lighting hadn't been very good. She was past the first flush of youth, but she was still a remarkably lovely woman. He felt a surge of guilt as the image of Ruth

Cannonberry's sweet smile flashed through his mind. Witherspoon quickly brought his attention back to the matter at hand. "We'll try not to take up too much of your time, Mrs. Graham."

She sank back onto the sofa. "Please sit down. Would you care for some tea?"

"No, thank you, ma'am, though it's most kind of you to offer." Witherspoon sat down on the love seat next to the sofa.

Barnes sat down on a straight-backed upholstered chair and sighed in relief when it was actually comfortable. He glanced around, noting that the room was nicely decorated but lacked the grandiosity of the homes of the truly rich.

Instead of a crystal chandelier, there were wall sconces and hurricane lamps. The oak parquet floor was covered with simple but elegant rugs in rose and cream, and the furniture was good quality without being overblown. Pink muslin curtains hung at the windows, and the walls were painted a clean cream color. The mantel at the far end of the room was covered with knickknacks, and a huge gilt-framed mirror hung directly over the fireplace.

"I assume you've more questions for me," she said. "Though I'm not sure what I can tell you that will be of any use. I've no idea who might have wanted Stephen dead."

Barnes looked up sharply. "How did you know it was murder, ma'am?"

"You wouldn't be here if it wasn't," she replied with a weary smile. "And unlike the others last night, I knew the doctor wouldn't have sent for you if he wasn't fairly sure Stephen had been poisoned."

"Do you know if Mr. Whitfield had any enemies?" Witherspoon cringed inwardly as he did every time he had to ask the silly question.

"If he had enemies, he never discussed the matter with me," she replied.

"Had he been worried or upset about anything recently?" Barnes asked.

"No, I don't think so." She smiled sadly. "Though Stephen wasn't the sort of man to share his troubles. He was a very private person."

"How long have you known Mr. Whitfield?" Witherspoon asked.

"We met a year ago. As a matter of fact, we met at a funeral reception. Odd place to meet someone, I know, but nonetheless, that's where we were introduced. A mutual friend of ours passed away. We were introduced by Basil Farringdon."

"You brought Mr. Langdon to the dinner party." Witherspoon hesitated. He hated to be indelicate, but there was no way to ask this sort of question politely. "Yet I understand that Mr. Whitfield had intended to ask you to accompany him to Italy in the spring."

"That's correct," she replied without a trace of embarrassment.

"Was Mr. Whitfield upset when Mr. Langdon arrived with you?"

"I'd asked Stephen if I could bring a guest, and he'd told me it was quite alright." She looked down at the floor. "I feel very badly about this whole matter, Inspector. For some reason, Stephen seemed to think we had some kind of understanding between us."

"I take it that wasn't the case," Witherspoon said softly.

"No, it wasn't. He'd proposed to me, and he acted as if we were engaged. But the truth of the matter is that we weren't. I'd never agreed to marry him."

"Had you agreed to go to Italy with Mr. Whitfield in the spring?" Barnes interjected. "From what we understand, he'd already begun making plans and arranged for a letter of credit with his bank."

"Stephen could be very arrogant. He presumed too much." She shook her head. "He'd badgered me for an answer, but I'd not committed to that trip, nor had I agreed to marry him. We'd only discussed the matter."

"Yet Mr. Whitfield was confident enough of your response that he was preparing to make an announcement of your engagement at dinner that night. Isn't that correct?" Witherspoon pressed. He'd learned that when the questions took off in one specific direction, it was best to follow up.

"He was preparing to make some sort of announcement, Inspector." She smiled coolly. "But I've no idea what it might have been. He died before he could say anything."

"Mrs. Murray is quite certain he was preparing to announce your engagement," the inspector said. Rosalind Murray hadn't actually said any such thing, but she'd certainly implied it.

"She can say whatever she likes, but that doesn't mean it's true."

"Had you specifically told Mr. Whitfield you weren't going to accept his proposal?" Witherspoon asked.

She sighed, glanced down at the floor again, and then looked back up at the two men. "No, and for that I feel awful, especially now that poor Stephen is dead. I was trying to be kind, you see. It was Christmas, and I didn't want to ruin the holiday for him. He was making such a fuss about the season that I simply didn't have the heart to turn him down. I was going to wait until Boxing Day before I told him. That's why I invited Mr. Langdon to accompany me to Stephen's dinner party that night. I was hoping that Stephen would take the hint that it was over. But he didn't. He simply acted the fool and kept trying to make his announcement.

Oh, I might as well admit it. Rosalind Murray is correct. I do think he was going to announce our engagement, even though I'd not agreed to marry him." She laughed harshly. "Stephen was a great believer in taking matters into his own hands. He once told me that he'd managed to hang on to a great deal of money by taking direct action instead of waiting for life to reward him."

Witherspoon nodded in encouragement. "So his death . . ."

She interrupted. "Saved me a great deal of trouble and embarrassment, Inspector. But as I'd no idea he was going to do something quite so stupid, I could hardly have thought to bring along a supply of poison, could I?"

"We're not accusing you of anything," Witherspoon replied.

"You really ought to ask Rosalind Murray what she thought about Stephen's sudden declaration." Eliza smiled grimly. "She hated me, and what's more, I think she hated Stephen. He'd been playing her for a fool for years, and I think she finally got fed up with him."

"What do you mean?" Barnes looked up from his notebook.

"I mean that if anyone benefits from Stephen's death, it will probably be her. She'll inherit his house, and that's all she needs to live decently."

"You know this for a fact?" Witherspoon glanced at the constable and then back at Eliza Graham.

"Of course I do," she replied. "Why do you think I decided not to marry Stephen?"

"You weren't in love with him?"

She gave a short bark of a laugh. "Love? What's that got to do with marriage?" She waved her arm, gesturing at the room. "Have a good look around, Inspector. My late husband left me very little money. It looks comfortable enough here, but I don't own any of it. It all belongs to my dear departed husband's family, and they let me live here on sufferance. They don't quite have the nerve to face the gossip that would ensue if they actually chucked me out into the street. I have nothing more than a small allowance from his estate, so I've no choice: I must remarry."

"But Mr. Whitfield could have kept you quite decently," Barnes ventured.

"Only as long as he was alive," she said. "And I'm not going through that kind of misery again."

"I'm afraid I don't understand," Witherspoon admitted. "Why wouldn't you inherit Mr. Whitfield's estate if you and he married?"

"Because he doesn't own anything," she explained. "The house is going to Mrs. Murray, and all the income goes back into the annuity. It doesn't pass on to his heirs."

"Annuity? What annuity?" Witherspoon was terribly confused by this turn of events. "But who inherits the annuity? I mean, someone has to inherit it."

She shrugged. "I'm not certain of all the details about the wretched thing. You'll have to speak to Stephen's solicitor."

"Why would Mrs. Murray get the house?" Barnes blurted. He was a bit confused as well.

"Because the house belonged to his late wife's family," Eliza said. "Under the terms of his wife's will, he can live in the house for the remainder of his life, but upon his death, the property goes back to her family. The only one of them left is Rosalind Murray."

"Mrs. Murray inherits the house," the inspector repeated. He wondered why Rosalind Murray hadn't mentioned this fact during their interview.

"That's right." Eliza smiled cynically. "So it seems the

person who most directly benefits from Stephen's death is his dear sister-in-law. That's the only reason she agreed to move in and become his housekeeper, you know. She wanted to make sure the place was kept in good order. Everyone thought it was because she was in love with Stephen, but I don't believe that for a moment. She didn't care one whit about him, and she certainly didn't want to be tied down with another marriage."

"So Mr. Whitfield didn't own any property?" Barnes asked. "Is that correct?"

"As far as I know, he only had the house and the income from the annuity," she replied. "The Whitfield family estate was sold when the annuity was created, and that was years and years ago. The only other fact I know about the mess is that Stephen's heirs would receive nothing when he died, and as I've lived with that once before, it'll be a cold day in the pits of Hades before I do it again."

CHAPTER 6

Mrs. Jeffries tightened the ribbons under her chin as a blast of wind almost tugged her bonnet completely off her head. When she was satisfied that her hat was secure, she turned her attention to the Whitfield house, studied it for a moment, and then stepped back behind a lamppost. Even though there were no constables at the front door, she knew the police were lurking about the neighborhood.

She turned and surveyed the street, wondering if there were still constables doing a house-to-house. Then she realized that, due to the nature of the crime, it was unlikely the inspector had wasted police resources on talking to the neighbors. This murder was definitely a domestic crime, so to speak. The killer would hardly have lurked about outside, waiting for an opportunity to sneak in and chuck some foxglove leaves into an open bottle of wine.

The street seemed ordinary enough as people went about

their daily business. A few doors up, a housemaid swept the front steps; directly across from where she stood, a young lad was polishing the door lamps. A butcher's van pulled up at the house next door, and Mrs. Jeffries watched as a deliveryman leapt out, opened the back, and pulled out a large wicker basket, which he hefted onto his shoulders. As he started for the servants' entrance, their gazes met and he nodded respectfully. She inclined her head in acknowledgment and then began to walk down the street.

She couldn't linger here all day. She didn't want any of the neighbors peeking out their front windows and noticing an unfamiliar person loitering about the neighborhood. A murder in the area made people nervous. But she wasn't overly disappointed that she had to move on: she hadn't expected to actually talk to anyone from the Whitfield household. She wasn't as skilled as the others at getting information out of strangers, but nonetheless she'd wanted to see where the murder took place.

A blast of wind slammed into her so unexpectedly, she stumbled backward.

"Careful, Mrs. Jeffries. This wind is the very devil," a familiar female voice said.

Just then she felt a hand on her back, steadying her. Mrs. Jeffries whirled about. "Gracious, it's Mrs. Bowden. Goodness, this is a surprise. I haven't seen you in ages. How are you?"

Geraldine Bowden laughed. She was a tall, broadshouldered woman with blue eyes and graying brown hair. "I'm well, thank you. I've been trying to catch up with you. I saw you on the High Street, coming out of the draper's shop, and followed along, hoping to say hello."

"That was most kind of you." Mrs. Jeffries smiled broadly. She liked Geraldine Bowden. She was a widow who supplemented her late husband's pension by doing a bit of extra cleaning. She worked for the domestic agency that Mrs. Jeffries used when they needed extra help with the heavy spring cleaning. "Are you working in this neighborhood now?" Unless Mrs. Bowden's economic circumstances had changed greatly since they'd last met, she couldn't afford to live in a posh area such as this one.

"Indeed I am. But I'm no longer with the domestic agency," she explained. "I was offered a position as a live-in housekeeper and caretaker. The house is just around the corner. That's one of the reasons I followed you: I was hoping you'd have time for a cup of tea."

Mrs. Jeffries couldn't believe her good fortune. Perhaps this case wasn't going to be as difficult to solve as it first appeared. "That would be wonderful. I should love a cup of tea. It's so very cold out."

"Come along, then, and we'll have a nice long natter." She took Mrs. Jeffries' arm and led her up the road, talking as they walked. "It's quite a grand place," she said as they rounded the corner. "And I never thought I'd be living in such splendor."

Mrs. Jeffries stared at the six-story redbrick house and nodded in agreement. "It's certainly huge. How many staff does it take to keep it in good order?"

"Right now there's just me." Geraldine Bowden pulled a set of keys out of her pocket and charged up the steps to the front door. "Come on inside, and I'll tell you all about how I came to be here."

Ten minutes later, the two women were sitting in the kitchen, and Geraldine Bowden was handing her a cup of steaming tea.

"How long have you been here?" Mrs. Jeffries asked.

"And more importantly, how can you possibly run a place this size with no staff?"

"I've been here a little over a year." Mrs. Bowden took the chair opposite her. "And I can run it easily enough, as it stays empty most of the time. The man who owns it travels quite a bit. But he wanted someone to live in and keep an eye on the house. That's why I'm here all on my own. You know what London is like these days. You've got to be on the watch. Turn your back for a second and the silver's gone missing, if you know what I mean. Not like when we were girls. People kept to their own business back then."

"Times aren't as peaceful as they once were," Mrs. Jeffries replied. She didn't agree with that sentiment in the least. London had always been infested with burglars, thieves, and thugs. The only difference between now and when they'd been young was that back then there wasn't nearly as much access to daily newspapers. Nowadays crimes were reported in the press sometimes within hours and always within a day or two of their discovery.

"We had a murder just around the corner from here," Mrs. Bowden continued. "Can you believe it? If murder can happen in a neighborhood as nice as this one, it can happen anywhere." She paused briefly. "Oh, but you probably already know about the murder, don't you? I imagine that you hear about all of them, seein' as how you work for Inspector Witherspoon."

Mrs. Jeffries realized how very unskilled she was at this sort of thing. It was impossible to know whether to answer in the affirmative or whether it would be more effective to say little and give the other person a chance to show off what they knew. "Well . . . he did mention something . . ." she muttered.

"Of course he did," Geraldine continued cheerfully. "Every man likes to talk about his work. My Reggie, God rest his soul, used to go on and on about the factory. I expect your inspector is no different, especially as he hasn't a wife. The Whitfield murder has been the talk of the neighborhood, I can tell you that. He was poisoned at his own dinner party. One minute he was eating his soup, and the next, his face was in it. He died of foxglove poisoning."

"I believe the inspector did mention that as well." Mrs. Jeffries wasn't in the least surprised that details had already gotten out to the locals. In her experience, servants were very efficient when it came to finding out who, what, where, and why. "Are you here on your own right now?"

"Oh, yes, Mr. Owens is traveling." She grinned. "But not to worry. From what I hear, the killer isn't some maniac roaming the streets, looking for people to murder. It was someone Mr. Whitfield knew, someone who was at the dinner party, so I ought to be perfectly safe."

"That's reassuring," Mrs. Jeffries replied.

"Whoever killed Mr. Whitfield didn't just sneak into his house and poison the poor man; it was obviously planned. The poison was in a bottle of wine. Well, no one's given me any wine, and if I found anything to eat or drink on my doorstep, I'd chuck it away."

"Gracious, was the wine simply found on the man's doorstep?"

"Oh, goodness no, it was a gift from one of his dinner guests." Mrs. Bowden laughed. "Mind you, I don't think the Farringdons will be taking any more wine to the parties they attend, not now that poor old Stephen Whitfield keeled over from drinking the bottle they brought as a gift. Everyone says it was the wine that had the poison in it, but I expect you'd know more about that than me, seeing as how you work for the inspector in charge of the case." She eyed Mrs. Jeffries speculatively. "Has he said anything about the murder?"

Mrs. Jeffries believed that to get information, one had to give a bit back. "Of course he's very discreet," she began, "but he did mention that the wine had come from the Farringdons and that it had been a Christmas gift. He also mentioned the Farringdons were the only guests who brought a gift that night. He thought that very odd."

"But it wasn't, you see. The Farringdons had to bring a present," Geraldine protested. "Mr. Whitfield had started sending them one of his bottles of port for Christmas, so they had to show up with something. As to the other guests not bringing anything, well, I'm not surprised. Henry Becker is a bachelor and doesn't have a wife to remind him of his social responsibilities."

"He's never married, then?" she asked. As she wasn't hearing anything she didn't already know about the Farringdons, she was happy to move on to one of the other suspects.

"Oh, no, women of his own class wouldn't have him, and Becker is too much of a snob to consider marrying anyone but his social equal. Not like Basil Farringdon. Mr. Farringdon was quite happy to marry a woman of inferior social status."

"Why wouldn't a woman of his own background have him?" Mrs. Jeffries asked.

Geraldine took a sip of tea. "From the gossip I've heard, there's more than a touch of madness in the Becker family. And it's the bad kind, not the harmless, silly kind, if you get my meaning."

"I'm not sure that I do," Mrs. Jeffries replied.

"There's a bit of violence in the family tree." Geraldine bobbed her head for emphasis. "Years ago, Henry Becker's father stabbed his mother with a carving knife. Pulled it right out of the Christmas goose and stuck it in the poor lady's arm."

"Gracious, that's terrible."

"And all that blood put everyone right off their dinner," Geraldine added. "They had guests, you see. That's how the story got out and everyone heard about the incident. It kept poor Henry from ever having much of a chance to find a wife. His sister, Drusilla, had to go all the way to Canada to find herself a husband. But Henry didn't really like to travel, so he hadn't much hope of finding anyone from his own class that was willing to overlook the fact that they are a half-mad lot."

"But surely one incident years ago . . ."

"Oh it wasn't just one incident," Geraldine interrupted eagerly. "There was terrible gossip about Henry's grandfather as well. Supposedly he was so insane, he was locked in the attic for doing terrible things to the servant girls. People aren't as willing to overlook those sorts of things as they once were, and Henry Becker ended up an old bachelor."

"Perhaps he didn't wish to marry," Mrs. Jeffries murmured.

"Oh, but he did. He proposed to Isadora Hallowell, but even though he'd lots more money, she turned him down and married Stephen Whitfield instead. Rumor has it that she didn't want her children tainted by the madness of the Becker blood. But seein' as how poor Isadora and Stephen never had children anyway, I suppose it turned out not to matter much."

Mrs. Jeffries took another sip of her tea to give herself time to think. She hadn't remembered Geraldine Bowden being such a chatterbox, but then again she'd only ever known the woman in the capacity of employer to employee. "How sad for poor Mr. Becker."

Geraldine nodded in agreement. "It doesn't seem fair. Despite the lunacy that runs in the family, Henry Becker was never violent with anyone, at least not that I have heard."

"Perhaps he was just better at hiding his faults," she replied.

"Perhaps so," Geraldine said. "People can get very clever at hiding their true selves from others, can't they?"

"I suspect that's a characteristic we all have, to some degree or other."

"I certainly do." Geraldine grinned broadly. "Many a time, if I'd said or acted upon my true thoughts, I'd not have had a position. If Mr. Owens actually knew my real opinion of his character, he'd sack me on the spot. Thank goodness he's gone most of the time."

"I take it when he's here he's not very pleasant."

"He's a right old tartar." She laughed. "But like I said, he's gone most of the time, and all in all I can't complain. The work is easy, I live well, and I like the neighborhood."

"And you're very well informed about the locals," Mrs. Jeffries said admiringly. "You seem to know more about the Whitfield household than the police do."

"Only because I have tea every week with Flagg. He's the Whitfield butler. He's a bit sweet on me, but nothing will come of it. If I were to take another husband, I'd lose my Reggie's pension. I don't want to do that. Besides, having tea once is week is nice. Actually putting up with another husband would be something else altogether."

"This isn't a park—it's a cemetery," Smythe yelled at Betsy's back as she charged through the open iron gates of the West of London and Westminister Cemetery.

"The dead won't bother us." She looked over her shoulder at him. "And we'll have a bit of privacy here."

He cast a quick glance around as he tried to keep up with her. Mausoleums, statues, and crypts were scattered amongst the uneven rows of graves. Leafless trees and winter-dead bushes swayed eerily as the wind whipped around them, tossing bits of dried grass and brittle leaves into the air. The raw odor of newly turned earth reached his nostrils, and he saw that at the far end of the nearest row, two men were digging a grave. This wasn't the sort of place he'd have picked to try to talk some sense into Betsy. But then again, he'd not been given a choice.

He increased his pace and came abreast of her. She didn't look at him but instead kept moving straight ahead up the central drive. They walked in silence for a few minutes until Betsy pointed to a small path that veered off to the left. "There's a good spot. Come on, let's have this out."

She marched past a headstone of a tall, sword-wielding angel and a line of gravestones standing straight as soldiers in a field before finally stopping at a squat, stubby granite marker with ornate carving along the sides and a man's face carved in the center.

She turned and stared at him. "Now, what is it you want to say?"

Smythe froze. Now that they were here and alone, he was terrified. Why on earth had he pushed her into this confrontation? Why hadn't he let her work some of her anger off? Everyone had warned him to let her get a bit of her own back, but here he was, home less than three days, and he was pushing to get everything settled between them. At least when she was barely speaking to him, he didn't have to hear that she didn't love him, that she didn't ever want to be with him.

"Well?" she demanded. She folded her arms over her chest. "Has the cat got your tongue? You were in a big enough hurry to interrupt me when I was trying to find out information about our murder, so get on with it."

"We can't go on like this," he mumbled.

"I agree."

Blast a Spaniard, he was an idiot. Why hadn't he let well enough alone? "Uh, what do you want to do about it?"

"Do about what? Your spying on me and taking me to task for giving some poor grocer's clerk an innocent smile?"

"He was leerin' at you."

"Don't be daft. He was just a lad. And what's more, he was giving me some useful information about Rosalind Murray."

"Oh, well, I'm sorry, then. I didn't mean to interrupt you." Smythe looked down at the ground. "I just wanted to speak with you privately."

"About what?"

"About us," he replied. "About our situation."

"What do you want to do?" she asked. "You're the one who claims we can't go on like this."

"You agreed," he pointed out. He was getting very confused.

"Only because I didn't know what you wanted me to say," she replied. "Honestly, Smythe, you dog my heels like you don't trust me, when you're the one that ran off for six months, and now that we're alone, now that we've got a bit of time to ourselves, you're as tongue-tied as a green boy. What do you want to do? Just go ahead and tell me. But be quick about it. We've got a murder to solve, Christmas is coming, and you know how the Home Office gets."

"I want us to be together," he stammered. "I want you to still love me."

"Oh, for God's sake." She turned on her heel and stomped off back the way they'd just come. "Of course I still love you, you idiot. I wouldn't be here if I didn't."

He charged after her. "But—but—but . . ."

She whirled around to face him. For a woman who'd just professed her love, she didn't regard him with a particularly affectionate expression. "Smythe, listen to what I've got to say. I know you think you did the honorable thing when you left me at the altar . . ."

"I didn't leave you at the altar," he yelled.

"You left me only days before our wedding," she shouted. "You might have done the noble thing, and maybe it was even the right course of action, but you humiliated me in front of everyone I care about. Do you know what that's like for someone like me, someone who has always been at the bottom of the heap?"

"You're not at the bottom of anything," he cried. "You're the very best that there is . . ."

She paid no attention to him. "Then you didn't come back for six months . . ."

"I got back as quick as I could," he protested. "Australia's thousands of miles away. You don't get there and back in just a few days . . ."

"Nonetheless," she interrupted again. "You were gone a bloomin' long time." She turned her back to him and continued on.

"Betsy, listen to me," he said.

"I have listened to you," she replied as she stepped out onto the main drive. "And so far you haven't had much to say."

"You know why I had to go," he said.

"I do, and I gave you your time to do what you felt was right. You've got to give me mine." She dashed toward the main gate.

"What does that mean?" he cried as he scrambled after her.

"It means I've got work to do," she called over her shoulder. "We've got us a murder, in case you've forgotten."

He was almost running to keep up with her. For such a small woman, she could sure move fast when she wanted. "I've not forgotten a thing, and I've work to do as well. But this is important." He wasn't sure, but he thought he heard her give a snort of derision. "It *is* important," he persisted. "And you can take a few minutes out of your precious investigation to talk to me."

"I'll be happy to talk to you when you decide what it is you want to say," she retorted.

They reached the front gates just as a funeral procession entered. It was a big one, with six black horses pulling the hearse and half a dozen rows of black-clad mourners walking behind. A long line of carriages followed the mourners.

"But—but . . ." Blast a Spaniard, he did know what he wanted to say, but he could hardly shout it out here and now.

Betsy darted across the road to the other side. "I'll see you back at the house."

Smythe tried to cross after her, but the hearse was too close and he didn't want to spook the horses by dashing out in front of it. "Blast," he muttered. He yanked off his cap and stood respectfully until the cortege passed. By the time the last of the carriages had rumbled by, she was gone.

But he was in excellent spirits as he went out through the gates and onto the Fulham Road. She'd said the only words that really mattered to him. She still loved him, and that was all that counted.

Kerringtons and Stuart, Wine Merchants, was located on the ground floor of a small but very old building in Oxford Street. Witherspoon peeked through the leaded glass of the front window. "There don't seem to be many customers," he said to Barnes. "That ought to make the proprietors a bit more cooperative."

"Let's hope so, sir." Barnes opened the door, and the two men entered. The shop was paneled in dark wood, giving the room a gloomy, cavelike atmosphere. Shelves of wine, the bottles stored on their sides in racks, were lined up along the walls. A clerk in an old-fashioned black frock coat came out from behind the short counter on the far side of the room. Another clerk was at a small table with a well-dressed elderly woman. They were looking at a large open ledger book.

"May I be of assistance?" the clerk asked. He glanced over his shoulder at the closed door behind the counter.

"We'd like to see your manager, please," Witherspoon replied. "I'm Inspector Gerald Witherspoon and this is Constable Barnes."

The fellow gaped at them a moment, as though he'd never heard of such an outlandish request. "I'll see if Mr. Crick is available."

"If Mr. Crick isn't available, then perhaps we could talk with you," Barnes added.

By now the other clerk and the well-dressed matron had given up all pretence of minding their own business and were avidly watching everything.

"Me?" the clerk repeated. He looked quite alarmed by the prospect. "Goodness, no, that would never do. I'll go get Mr. Crick." He turned on his heel and scurried toward the counter.

"Sorry, sir," Barnes murmured. "But it's getting late and we need this information."

"I'm well aware of your 'methods,' Constable." Witherspoon grinned. Barnes was always reminding the inspector that his methods had become quite famous, and it was quite amusing to be able to turn the tables for once. "And I knew exactly what you were about. Most people would rather do anything than speak to the police. Everyone, that is, except Henry Becker."

"He was a strange one, sir," Barnes agreed. "Especially for someone of that class. But then again, perhaps we oughtn't to look a gift horse in the mouth."

The door through which the clerk had disappeared opened and he reappeared, followed by a short, balding man who did not look at all pleased. "I understand you wish to speak to me," he said, directing his attention to the inspector.

"That's correct," Witherspoon replied.

"Come along to my office, then. Let's not stand about out here." Crick waved them toward the open door behind the counter.

A few moments later the two policemen were standing in a tiny office opposite Mr. Crick, who had taken a seat behind a cluttered desk. Witherspoon started to introduce himself.

"My clerk told me who you are." Crick held up his hand. "What is it you want?"

Witherspoon paused for a moment. He couldn't for the life of him understand why so many people were hostile to answering a few simple inquiries. For goodness' sake, this was a murder investigation. Did honest merchants really want murderers running about the city killing people? You'd think that an old, respectable establishment such as this would be very much in favor of law and order. But the inspector could tell from the hostile expression on Crick's face that getting any reasonable information from the fellow was going to be difficult. Drat.

"We want to see your sales records for Mr. Basil Farringdon," Barnes said bluntly.

"Why should I show you my records?" Crick leaned back in his chair and folded his arms over his chest.

"We're investigating a murder, sir," Witherspoon said quickly. He was rather pleased that Barnes had taken a firm stand. "And your sales records might be very important evidence."

"I doubt that," Crick replied. "This is a very old and honorable establishment. My customers aren't the sort of people to be involved with the criminal element. Furthermore, I don't think they would appreciate having their privacy violated."

"Oh, for God's sake, man, you're a wine merchant, not a lawyer," Barnes snapped. "And unless you spend a great deal of time and effort getting to know your customers intimately, then you've no idea whether any of them are criminals or not. So don't waste our time blathering on about privacy. If you don't wish to cooperate, I'm sure we can ask Mr. Farringdon to come here with us and insist that you verify his story. However, I don't think you'll keep him or many of his friends as customers after that. People like Basil Farringdon don't appreciate being inconvenienced by uncooperative shopkeepers."

Crick's mouth opened in surprise, and he sat up straight. "Well, if you put it like that, I shouldn't like to inconvenience Mr. Farringdon. He is a good customer. Uh, what was it you wanted?"

"Can you verify that he and his wife purchased a half case of Locarno—it's a Bordeaux."

"I know what it is, Inspector." Crick turned around and pulled a ledger off the shelf behind him. He opened it up, leafed through the pages, and then nodded. "That is correct. A half case of Locarno, a case of Riesling, and three bottles of cordials were delivered to the Farringdons on the first of November."

"Did they buy Locarno often?" Barnes asked.

Crick shook his head. "This was the first time. Mrs. Farringdon came in and asked me if Locarno was a good Bordeaux. I confirmed that it is very good, and she ordered half a case. She was planning a large party and wanted to make sure she had plenty of good wine on hand."

"No, Samson, you have to stay inside." Mrs. Goodge gently hooked her foot under Samson's fat belly and pushed him away from the back door. "I'm goin' out to feed the birdies, lovey, and you'll frighten them."

Samson leapt off the offending foot, gave the cook a good glare, and then trotted off.

She pulled the door open and stepped outside. She held on to her cap against the strong wind as she crossed the small terrace. Leaves danced in the air, and the branches of the trees and bushes shook as powerful gusts whipped through the garden. She stepped onto the path and headed toward the clearance near the oak trees. As she came around a clump of evergreen trees, she saw a man sitting on the bench, smoking a cigar. He glanced up just then, saw her, and jumped to his feet.

"Sorry, ma'am," he said. He leaned to one side and jabbed the tip of his cigar against the metal armrest of the wooden bench. "I know we're not supposed to bother the residents or use the gardens, but I'm waiting for the foreman to come back and open up number eighteen. I'm one of the workers."

"Not to worry. You're not botherin' me and the birds," she replied. "Just don't let Mrs. Babcock from down the garden see you. What are they doing at number eighteen, knocking those two rooms together into one?"

"Yes, ma'am. It's to be a library, so we're also goin' to be building some shelves." He relaxed his lanky frame a fraction but didn't relight his cigar. "I appreciate you lettin' me stay here. Lots of people woulda run me out, and it's a lot more pleasant back here than it is hangin' about the front. Truth to tell, I've been wanting to have a gander at these gardens," he said.

"Are you interested in flowers and shrubs, then?" she asked, more to keep him talking than anything else. She was always on the lookout for someone who might have a morsel of gossip to pass along, so she was quite happy to keep on chatting with the fellow. He looked a bit rough—his clothes were stained with paint, and the long gray coat he wore had seen better days—but he was a laborer, and no doubt these weren't his Sunday best.

"I am, ma'am." He grinned broadly. Half of his teeth were missing, and the ones he had left were stained and rotten. "You could say I was once in the trade. I used to work as an undergardener."

"Where at?" She reached under her cloak and into her apron pocket. Pulling out the rolled newspaper containing the bread crumbs, she opened it up and tossed them into the air.

"I started out at a nursery in Chelsea and then got a position as an undergardener at the communal gardens just off the Redcliffe Road. Quite posh they were, too, but the residents' association was deadly cheap. They wouldn't pay enough to keep body and soul together. That's one of the reasons I'm now in the building trade and not gardening. A man's got to make a living."

Mrs. Goodge had gone still. Redcliffe Gardens was near

the murder house on Redcliffe Road. "How long ago did you work there?"

"It's been more than ten years ago." He smiled ruefully. "And I really loved the work. There's something very satisfying about muckin' about in the earth. But like I said, a man's got to make a living."

"Ten years ago, eh?" Mrs. Goodge silently debated whether he might have any useful information to impart. But then she decided she might as well risk it; she'd not had much luck today with any of her other sources. "That's a long time. Have you been in the building trade ever since you left the communal garden?"

"I have," he replied. "And it's been good to me. Even though I'm just a laborer and not a proper carpenter or joiner, my wages are still better than my cousin Ned's. I tried to get him to leave with me, but he wanted to stay on. Mind you, he's now the head gardener—well, leastways that's what he calls himself, but as he's the only gardener, I reckon it makes no difference."

"Your cousin stayed on working at the communal garden?"

The workman nodded and pulled his coat tighter against a gust of cold wind that rushed past them. "I wish the foreman would hurry up. It's right cold out here."

This was her chance. "Why don't you step into my kitchen," she said, pointing toward the inspector's house, "and I'll fix you a nice hot cup of tea?"

He hesitated. "I don't want to be any trouble."

"It's no trouble at all," she assured him. "I was going to make myself one anyway, and it is dreadfully cold out here."

"That's awfully kind of you, ma'am. Truth to tell, the rest of them have gone to eat, so it might be awhile before we start work again. My name is Lester Parks," he said.

"I'm Mrs. Goodge. Come along, then—it's just over here."
She was sure he was hungry as well as cold.

Twenty minutes later, her assumptions proved correct.
Lester Parks had eaten two slices of seed cake and three
slices of brown bread, and eagerly accepted a third cup of
tea. But she'd learned absolutely nothing useful from the
fellow. He knew nothing of their victim nor of any of their
suspects.

"So you've never heard of Stephen Whitfield?" she demanded. "You're absolutely sure?"

"Never 'eard of the fellow." Lester Parks looked down at
his empty plate. "That was a lovely feed, Mrs. Goodge. You're
a good baker."

"Or of Basil or Maria Farringdon?" she urged. She didn't
want to be the only one with nothing to report this afternoon, and her next source wasn't due here until after the
meeting.

"Like I said, I've never heard of them, either."

She glanced at the carriage clock on the pine sideboard.
"It's getting on, I'm sure your foreman is back by now."

"Thanks ever so much for the lovely food." He smiled
and got to his feet. "I was right hungry."

"What about Henry Becker?" she tried one last time.
"Are you certain you've never heard anything about him?"

"Sorry, I wish I knew something, but I don't." He started
toward the back door. "Most people don't bother talkin' to
the likes of me."

She got up and followed him down the hallway. She'd
brought up the murder but had learned nothing; he'd not
heard a word, and he certainly hadn't read any newspapers
lately. This had been a waste of time.

"Thanks again, Mrs. Goodge." He reached for the door
handle. "I'll be able to work this afternoon, and then maybe

the foreman will keep me on to help out tomorrow. Truth to tell, I've not eaten in two days, and I was so light-headed from hunger, I wasn't able to do very much this mornin'. Mr. Mayer—he's the foreman—told me that if I couldn't pull my weight, he'd not be needin' me."

That brought her up short. She stared at him as he stood there in the dim light. She realized then that he'd been out in the gardens resting so he'd have the strength to work. He was one of London's desperate poor. He probably spent his wages on gin, hadn't a proper home, and managed to keep body and soul together with only casual labor. Before she'd come to work here, she'd have thought he deserved his fate, that he'd brought his lot in life upon himself by his own actions. She didn't believe that anymore. "I'm glad I was able to help," she said softly. "Wait, let me give you something to take with you." She started back down the hall. The others would just have to do with a little less food for their afternoon tea.

"No, ma'am," he called. "Don't be troublin' yourself. You've been more than kind to me."

But she ignored him and went on into the kitchen. She grabbed the newspaper that was lying on a chair and hurried to the table. Spreading it open, she put in the remainder of the bread and cut two more slices of cake. Then she folded it into a neat parcel and took it back down the hall. He was still at the back door.

"Take this," she instructed as she handed it to him. "You'll be able to work tomorrow if you have food."

He stared at the package and then looked up at her. "Thank you. It's not often that people do me a kindness."

"Get on now. You don't want to lose your position because you're late," she warned, leaning past him and opening the door.

"I did remember something I heard about one of them names you mentioned," he said as he stepped out onto the terrace.

She didn't believe him. He was merely grateful for the food. "Did you now? That's interesting."

"Rosalind Murray," he continued. "That's the one I heard about. Mind you, it weren't much, but she and her husband used to live in a small flat at the top of one of them big houses that backed onto the gardens."

Mrs. Goodge had no idea whether this was true or not, but she'd give him a chance to salvage his pride for accepting the food. "Go on," she urged.

"He died, and the only thing he left her was some shares in a tea plantation out in the Far East. The poor lady had to move in with a relative just to keep a roof over her head."

Everyone was back at Upper Edmonton Gardens in time for their afternoon meeting. Mrs. Jeffries noticed that Betsy and Smythe seemed to be a bit more relaxed with each other. He'd arrived only moments before Betsy, and Mrs. Jeffries had seen the maid smile at him as he helped her off with her jacket. Good, she thought. It was important for these two to straighten out their differences. They loved each other too deeply to let foolish pride and hurt feelings keep them apart.

"Hurry up, everyone," Mrs. Goodge urged. "The rag-and-bone man is due here at five, and I'll want a few minutes with him before I have to start the inspector's dinner. Joseph always has the latest gossip. He does like to talk."

"It's already gone four," Wiggins protested. "What if our meetin' runs late? I've got a few bits to report on, important things that everyone should hear about."

"Joseph only gets to this area every month or so, and if I

miss him today, I'll have to wait till the middle of January," the cook replied. "Let's just get on with this."

"I'm sure we'll finish in good time for Mrs. Goodge to meet with her source," Mrs. Jeffries soothed. "Wiggins, as you appear to have heard something of importance, please go first."

"I don't know that it's so important after all, but I did find out that Mrs. Farringdon collects wine bottles." Wiggins was a bit embarrassed that he'd made a fuss. When said aloud, the information he'd heard from Mrs. Jones sounded silly.

"Does she collect any particular kind of wine bottles?" Hatchet asked politely.

"I'm not explaining this right. What I meant to say was that when she goes to a posh party, if she drinks a wine she likes, she makes her servants go around to the kitchen to collect the bottle. She does it because she's workin' 'ard to be a credit to her husband," he explained. He told them about his encounter with Matilda Jones, and her conviction that Maria Farringdon suffered greatly from feelings of inferiority to her husband's social class. "I know it doesn't seem like such a thing could have anything to do with the murder, but sometimes the oddest bits come together when Mrs. Jeffries is sortin' out who the killer might be."

"That's true," the cook agreed. "You never know what's going to come in useful."

"Shall I go next, then?" Betsy asked. When no one objected, she plunged right ahead. "I didn't have a lot of luck, but I did find out that Rosalind Murray is very well liked by the local merchants. Apparently she makes sure all the bills are paid promptly." She broke off and shot Smythe a quick grin. "Unfortunately I was interrupted before I could find out anything else, but tomorrow I'm going back to Whitfield's neighborhood to see what else I can learn. Mrs. Murray does sound a bit too good to be true, and it seems to me she was the one who had the most to lose if he married Mrs. Graham. But it's early days yet, so I'm trying not to come to any conclusions."

"That's very wise of you, Betsy," Mrs. Jeffries said. She couldn't wait to tell them what she heard from Mrs. Bowden.

"Can I go next?" Luty asked. "I'm bustin' to tell my bits."

"Of course." Mrs. Jeffries told herself to be patient.

Luty leaned forward eagerly. "I found out that Eliza Graham's husband died of a heart attack, and what's more, he died when he was alone in the house with just his wife."

"Where were the servants?" Mrs. Goodge asked.

"They were gone. He died while he and his wife were on holiday. They were staying in a rented cottage on the South Coast." Luty grinned. "Mr. Graham's death happened just after supper, after the two servants that did for them had left for the day."

"Was there an inquest?" Mrs. Jeffries asked.

Luty shook her head. "No. His doctor had sent him on holiday because of his health. He suffered from heart trouble. Even his family didn't think his death was suspicious. But in light of what we know about Whitfield's death, I think we ought to keep our eye on her."

"You mean, if she thinks she got away with murder once, she thinks she could do it again?" Smythe reached for another slice of bread.

"It's a possibility," Luty replied.

"But what would be her motive?" Betsy asked. "Why would she want Stephen Whitfield dead?"

"Maybe she stands to inherit from his estate," Wiggins suggested. "After all, we know he was sweet on her."

"He might have been sweet on her, but I don't think she was goin' to inherit anything from the fellow," Luty said. "I did find out a bit about Whitfield's estate, and it's strange."

"What do you mean?" Mrs. Goodge demanded. "How can an estate be strange?"

Luty was a tad embarrassed. Despite her best efforts, she'd found out nothing more than a general rumor about the late Stephen Whitfield's estate. As the others had charged her with finding out whether or not the house was entailed, she felt almost as if she'd failed. "According to my source, Whitfield doesn't have control of any of his property except his personal property."

"Personal property." Wiggins frowned. "Does that mean just his clothes and hairbrushes and that sort of thing?"

"That's pretty much what it means," Luty said. "Everything else is tied up in some sort of annuity fund. My source wasn't real sure, but he said he'd see if he could find out more about the estate, but it might take a day or two. Sorry I couldn't find out other details. I know you was all counting on me . . ."

"That's all right, Luty. You've done very well," Mrs. Jeffries interrupted. "Much better than anyone could expect in such a short period of time."

"I heard the same, madam," Hatchet added smoothly. "There is something odd about the estate, and none of my sources knew what it was, either." He was annoyed that he'd not been able to get in to see his friend, the Farringdons' butler, but the fellow was still ill. But he was supposedly on the mend.

"Let's hope I get lucky tomorrow and my source comes through with something useful," Luty finished.

Mrs. Jeffries looked at Hatchet. "Would you care to go next?"

"I'm afraid I've found out very little," he said. "Unfortunately one of my sources is still very much indisposed, but I'm hoping that is only a temporary condition." He'd die before he'd let Luty know how depressed he was about his contribution to the case thus far.

"I'm sure you'll do better tomorrow." Luty reached over and patted him on the arm. She'd recovered from her feelings of failure. He glared at her.

"In that case, perhaps I ought to tell everyone what I've learned," Mrs. Jeffries took a deep breath. "While I was out today, I happened to run into Mrs. Bowden . . ."

Mrs. Goodge broke in. "You mean the lady that gives us a hand with heavy spring cleanin'?"

"That's right," Mrs. Jeffries replied. She reached for her teacup, and as she did, she happened to glance toward the kitchen window. She could see the high wheels of a hansom pulling up in front of the house. "Oh dear, I think the inspector is home early." She leapt and dashed across the room.

"But it's not even half past four," Wiggins cried.

"What's he doin' home this early?" Mrs. Goodge complained. "That's goin' to ruin everything. I don't want to have to stop and get supper now. I want to speak to my rag-and-bone man."

"It's the inspector," Mrs. Jeffries hissed over her shoulder.

Luty and Hatchet were already on their feet and heading for the back door. "We'll be back tomorrow morning," Hatchet promised.

"Come for breakfast," Mrs. Goodge offered. "That way we'll have plenty of time for our meeting."

"Isn't that just like a man?" Betsy looked at Smythe. "Always popping up where you least expect them."

CHAPTER 7

The next morning, Luty and Hatchet joined the household for breakfast. While they ate their bacon and eggs, Mrs. Jeffries told them about her encounter with Geraldine Bowden. She also gave them the information she'd learned from Witherspoon the previous evening while he'd eaten his dinner. The house was now quiet and empty, with everyone out about their business.

Mrs. Jeffries glanced around the kitchen. Mrs. Goodge was at the counter, taking the mince tarts she'd baked early this morning off the cooling tray and putting them onto a serving platter. "Your sources are going to be lucky today. Those look delicious. They smell wonderful as well."

"Thank you. I'm hoping these will help loosen a few tongues. I didn't have much luck yesterday," she replied. The morning meeting had been so rushed that she'd not mentioned her garden conversation with Lester Parks.

"Some days are like that." Mrs. Jeffries smiled sympathetically. "No matter how hard we try, we simply don't hear a word about our suspects or our victim."

"I heard something, alright." The cook sighed. "I'm just not sure it's true."

"What was it?"

Mrs. Goodge laid the last tart onto the platter and then looked up. She might as well repeat what he'd told her. The poor fellow deserved at least that much. Besides, it wasn't the sort of tidbit that would do any harm to the case. "My source mentioned that the only thing Rosalind Murray's husband left her when he died was some shares in a tea plantation in the Far East." She shrugged. "But I don't think this source is particularly reliable, and what's more, even if the information was true, I don't see that it has any bearing on Whitfield's murder. But not to worry—I've an old friend coming around this morning, and I'm hoping she'll have something useful."

"I do hope so," Mrs. Jeffries said earnestly. "This case is becoming a bit of a puzzle."

"Aren't they all?"

"Of course they are," Mrs. Jeffries agreed. "But usually by now we have a few more facts to work with."

"What do you mean?" The cook picked up the clean tea towel she'd laid next to the serving platter and draped it over the tarts. "Seems to me we've got lots of information—we know plenty of things."

"But we don't," Mrs. Jeffries argued. "And the things we don't know are important. For instance, we've still no idea who will inherit Whitfield's estate or even if there is an estate to be inherited."

"Luty has got her sources working on that problem." Mrs. Goodge picked up the empty cooling tray and took it over to the sink. "She seemed confident that she'd have an answer for us by this afternoon's meeting."

"But that's not the only issue I'm concerned about. There's something else equally puzzling." Mrs. Jeffries paused and took a deep breath. She wasn't sure she should even voice this concern aloud. "No one seems to have any reason to want Whitfield dead."

That was what really bothered her: there didn't seem to be a reason for Whitfield's murder.

"What about Mrs. Graham?" Mrs. Goodge grabbed a cleaning rag from the rack above the sink and ran it lightly over the surface of the tray. "Seems to me she'd decided to jilt Whitfield and had set her sights on Hugh Langdon. Perhaps when she told Whitfield it was over, he'd threatened to make trouble for her with Langdon."

"But what could Whitfield have done?"

"Perhaps he said he'd tell Langdon that Mrs. Graham had been his mistress and that they were engaged," Mrs. Goodge replied. "Some men would think twice before stealing another man's fiancée."

"But they weren't engaged," Mrs. Jeffries pointed out. "Eliza Graham was very insistent on that point. She told the inspector she'd never agreed to marry Whitfield."

"True, but we've only her word to go on." The cook grinned. "She could be lying. After all, Whitfield is dead, and by her own admission, his death saved her a lot of trouble and embarrassment."

"That's true," Mrs. Jeffries murmured. "And from what the inspector told us, Mrs. Graham didn't try to hide the fact that she needed to remarry for financial reasons. I guess what I'm concerned about is why she would jilt a known quantity like Whitfield for a man who had a reputation as a bit of a cad."

"Perhaps Mrs. Graham saw Langdon in a different light." The cook slid the tray onto the bottom shelf of the work-table. "Maybe she fell in love. We both know that love makes people do foolish things. Just look at Betsy and Smythe."

"They seem to be a bit easier with one another, don't you think?"

"Yes, I noticed that as well," Mrs. Goodge replied. "And I'm glad of it. All that tension around the table was hard on my nerves. But back to our problem. The inspector said Mrs. Graham knew that the Whitfield estate wouldn't go to her even if she did marry Whitfield. So she'd be no better off married to him than she is now. Maybe she saw Langdon as a safer bet."

"So you're thinking she might have decided she could get Langdon to propose, and when she tried to break off the relationship with Whitfield, he threatened her in some way?"

"That's one possible motive." Mrs. Goodge shrugged. "Whitfield may not have taken kindly to being publicly jilted. Especially as he'd already made plans to go to Italy, called his solicitor to change his will, and told his mistress of many years that it was over."

"When you put it like that, I see what you mean," Mrs. Jeffries replied. "Perhaps Eliza Graham did have a motive. Gossip can sometimes have devastating consequences to women of her class. Who knows what Whitfield might have threatened when she told him the two of them were fin-ished?"

"And Mrs. Murray has a motive as well," the cook said quickly. "Remember the old saying: Hell hath no fury like a woman scorned." There was a loud knock on the back door. "That's probably my friend."

Mrs. Jeffries took the hint and quickly rose to her feet.

"I'll leave you to it, then. I've a busy day planned, so I'll see you this afternoon."

Mrs. Goodge waited till Mrs. Jeffries had disappeared up the back steps before she opened the door. She smiled at the small, sparrowlike woman standing on the stoop. "Hello, Emma. It's been a long time. Do come in."

"It has been a long time, hasn't it?" Emma Darnley agreed as she stepped inside. She had gray hair, deep-set brown eyes, and a sharp chin. "I was ever so surprised to get your note. But then I happened to run into Ida Leacock on Oxford Street the other day, and she said you'd been getting in touch with some of your old acquaintances."

"That's right." Mrs. Goodge ushered her guest down the hall toward the kitchen. "How have you been? It was Ida who told me that you'd moved to London."

"I came to London ages ago," Emma replied as they came into the kitchen. She stopped and surveyed the room. "This is very nice, not at all what I expected. Ida mentioned that you worked for a policeman."

"A police inspector," Mrs. Goodge replied.

"Even an inspector couldn't afford a house this size," Emma retorted. She took off her gloves and hat.

"He's private means as well," Mrs. Goodge said. Emma always had said exactly what she thought, and apparently the passage of the years hadn't changed her in the least. Good. "Give me your things and take a seat. I'll brew us a fresh pot of tea. I've some lovely mince tarts. As I recall, you were always fond of mince tarts."

Emma smiled in pleasure. "You remembered that—how very kind of you." She slipped off her coat and handed it to the cook along with her hat and gloves.

"I remember a lot from the old days. It's the present that I have a hard time keeping up with." Mrs. Goodge tucked the gloves inside the hat and laid them on the sideboard, then put the coat on the rack.

"I was surprised to hear you were still working." Emma continued her study of the kitchen as she sat down at the table. Her gaze lingered for a moment on the almost new, very expensive cooker, before moving on to the slab of marble sitting atop the worktable near the sink.

"I've really no choice about it," Mrs. Goodge said. It was a lie: she had saved practically all her salary over the years she'd worked for the inspector, and she now had a tidy sum tucked safely away in a post office account. He was a most generous employer. But she had found she could get far more information out of her old colleagues if they felt just a bit sorry for her. "I've no family to speak of and, well, here I am, still cooking and baking."

Emma dragged her gaze away from the pine sideboard and turned toward the cook. She smiled sympathetically. "I'm lucky. I've got my Neville, and he's his railway pension. I left service some years ago, you know. Right after we had our Lilly."

"That's what I heard," Mrs. Goodge replied. The kettle, which she'd left on to boil, began to whistle. She took it off and poured the water into the waiting teapot. "Was Lilly your only child?"

For the next ten minutes, they chatted about family, old friends, the weather, the season, and how crowded the shops were these days. Then the cook moved in for the kill. "Have you kept in contact with any of the others from the old days?"

"Not really, though I did get a card from Lorraine Brown last summer. Do you remember her? She worked with us at Lord Lattimer's London house."

"I remember her. She was a nice girl."

"She's moved to Dorset to live with her sister."

Mrs. Goodge didn't have a clue who Lorraine Brown might be, but this was the opening she wanted. "Dorset? Are you sure? I heard she ended up working as a housekeeper for that man who was murdered the other day."

"Lorraine Brown hasn't worked in London in years. What on earth are you talking about, Mrs. Goodge?" Emma stared at her curiously.

Mrs. Goodge put the teapot onto the table next to the plate of mince tarts. "Oh dear, I'm getting muddled. It was Helen Brown who worked at the Whitfield house. You don't know Helen. I worked with her years after you and I worked together."

"Murder," Emma muttered. She frowned. "You mean that man who was poisoned at his own dinner party?"

"Yes, that's him. Stephen Whitfield was his name." She put two mince tarts onto a plate and placed it on the table in front of Emma. "Poor man was murdered in his own home. My inspector has got the case." She'd decided there was no harm in mentioning this information. After all, they were two old women gossiping together, and it would be expected that she'd discuss her employer.

Emma nodded her thanks, picked up her fork, and sliced into the pastry.

Mrs. Goodge poured the tea. "Of course, there were half a dozen people in the house when the fellow was killed, so even though my inspector is an excellent policeman, it'll take a bit of work on his part to get to the bottom of it all."

Emma shoved a bite of the tart into her mouth.

"Mind you, my inspector has solved every case he's ever had," she continued chattily. "So I've no doubt he'll solve this one as well."

"I wonder who was at the dinner party," Emma mumbled

as she swallowed her food. "The papers didn't mention any names."

Mrs. Goodge handed her guest a cup of tea. "The respectable papers never give out names in this sort of case. They don't like to embarrass the upper class."

"Really?" Emma asked curiously.

"Oh, yes," Mrs. Goodge assured her. "Whitfield's guests were all like himself—upper-class and wealthy." She rattled off the names of Whitfield's dinner guests and knew she'd struck gold when Emma's narrow face lighted up when Mrs. Goodge mentioned Hugh Langdon's name. That was precisely the reason she'd invited Emma today. She knew of Emma's connection to the Langdon household. She'd learned of it from Ida Leacock and sworn her to secrecy about the whole matter.

"Hugh Langdon," Emma exclaimed. "My niece works as a housemaid for him. But he's not a murderer. He's a decent employer. He treats Mary and the other servants very well— very well indeed."

"Really?" Mrs. Goodge looked doubtful. "I've heard he's something of a cad. You know, with the ladies. Are you sure your niece is safe with a man like that?"

She knew she was risking making Emma angry, but she wanted to get the woman talking, and sometimes people needed a bit of a nudge. A bit of temper often led to a loosening of the tongue.

"Mary's worked there for years. He's never laid a hand on her or on any of the other girls. Honestly, Mrs. Goodge, you shouldn't believe everything you hear." Emma took another bite of her tart.

"You're right, of course. I'm sure he's a decent fellow. It's strange he's never married, though, isn't it?" She sipped her tea.

"He was engaged, but his fiancée died," Emma replied.

"I've never heard that."

"It was years ago," Emma said. "Right after Mary started working for him. He was going to marry a lady named Ellen Bannister. It was a very sad occurrence. She died on a trip to Paris to buy her trousseau."

"That's awful. How did she die?"

"She contracted some kind of fever and was dead before he could bring her back here for medical treatment. You know what they say about French hospitals, don't you? They're dreadful places." Emma nodded knowingly. "But if you ask me, the fact that he was willing to marry someone like her in the first place speaks well of the man."

"What was wrong with her?"

"There was some ugly gossip about her." Emma waved her hand dismissively. "Supposedly she was a tad free with her favors, if you get my meaning. But Mr. Langdon didn't let the opinions of others influence him. He was man enough to ignore the gossip and propose to her."

"That does speak well of him," Mrs. Goodge agreed. "I wonder how he ended up with his current reputation."

Emma shrugged. "I expect it's because he's not been much interested in getting married all these years. According to Mary, he likes women but is always very honest about his intentions. But then again, he's not old money, is he? So he's not as concerned about the social aspect of his situation. He made his fortune all on his own."

"So he's stayed single all these years?" Mrs. Goodge probed.

"Not for much longer, though," Emma replied. "When Mary came around for tea last week, she told me that she was sure he was finally going to do it—he was finally going to get married."

"To Eliza Graham?" Mrs. Goodge asked.

"Yes, that's her name. How did you know?"

"She was one of the people at the dinner party," the cook reminded Emma. "She'd brought Mr. Langdon."

Emma frowned slightly. "Mary said the staff wasn't particularly happy about her coming in as mistress of the household. Mr. Langdon's always been on the lenient side, but they're all worried they'll have to work a lot harder if he takes a wife."

Betsy hesitated for a brief moment. The girl she'd been trailing had stopped and was looking in a shop window at a display of ladies' gloves. She was a young woman who looked to be in her early twenties. Her brown hair was neatly tucked up under a gray and black hat that had seen better days, her black coat wasn't long enough to completely hide the last two inches of her gray broadcloth skirt, and her feet were encased in sturdy but rather ugly thick black shoes. Betsy had seen her come out of the Farringdon house and had guessed she was a housemaid.

She sidled up next to the young woman. "Those are lovely. I wish I could afford a pair like that." She pointed to a pair of black kid gloves.

For a moment, the girl didn't reply. She kept her gaze on the gloves; then she turned and looked Betsy directly in the eye. "You've been following me. Why?"

Betsy blinked in surprise. She thought about denying the charge and then realized she'd only be making a fool of herself if she did. The girl's tone had made it clear that she wasn't asking a question; she was stating a fact. Perhaps it was time to try another tactic. "You're right. I have been following you. But only because I'm desperate for a position, and I heard a rumor that your household might be hiring a scullery maid."

"I'm just a housemaid. I don't do the hiring," she replied. But her expression had softened.

"No, but you could tell me if there were any positions available and . . and . . . ." Betsy looked down at the pavement.

"And what?' the girl asked softly.

"And put in a good word for me." Betsy sniffed. "I'm sorry. I know it was wrong, but I'm desperate for work."

"Oh, don't start sniveling on me," the girl said harshly. "Look, come along and let me buy you a cup of tea."

"You don't 'ave to do that." Betsy slipped easily into the dialect of her old neighborhood.

"Don't be daft, lass. It's only a cup of tea I'm offering. I've been out of work myself, and I know what it feels like."

Betsy swiped at her cheeks and lifted her chin. She'd actually made her eyes water. "Thanks ever so much. I'd love a cup of tea. I'm stayin' at a lodgin' house, and I've not had breakfast because it costs extra."

"There's a café just around the corner." The girl started off. "Come along, then. My name is Rachel Webster. What's yours?"

"I'm Polly Johnson," Betsy replied as she trailed after the girl. "And I'm ever so grateful." She always used a false name when she was on the hunt. There was a chance that Inspector Witherspoon might end up interviewing the girl, and you never knew what might or might not be said.

They went into a small workingman's café on the Edgware Road. This late in the morning, there were only two other customers inside and they were sitting at a table by the counter, chatting with the counterwoman. Rachel ordered their tea and motioned for Betsy to take the table by the window.

Betsy sat down in the rickety chair and hoped it wouldn't

collapse on her. She glanced toward the counter just as
Rachel opened her tiny black change purse. A wave of guilt
washed over her as she watched Rachel counting out coins.
Even a cup of tea was an expense when you made as little
money as maids usually earned. She promised herself she'd
find a way to get the money back to the girl.

Rachel picked up their cups and started across the small
space. "This ought to warm you up a bit." She put the tea in
front of Betsy.

"Thanks ever so much," Betsy replied. She waited until
Rachel had sat down before speaking again. "I'm ever so
grateful."

"You've already said that," Rachel retorted, but she was
smiling.

"I know, but it's so cold out and you're bein' so nice to
me. Uh, I hate to ask, but are there any positions available
where you work?" she asked. She looked down at the tabletop as she spoke, trying her best to act as if she really was
looking for work. She'd already decided that Rachel was no
fool, and she'd see through this trick in a heartbeat if Betsy
wasn't careful.

Rachel shook her head. "No, and no one's thinkin' of
quittin', either. Why did you think there might be? Mrs.
Farringdon would never hire off the streets. She always uses
an agency."

"That's why I thought there might be a position." Betsy
had an answer at the ready. "I'm registered with the
Clements agency, but it's been two weeks now and they've
not even got me an interview. I was checking in with them
yesterday when I overheard the manager give out your
address—I mean, the address of the house I saw you come
out of this morning. So I went around and waited, hoping

that someone would come out and I could find out if there was any positions goin'." She sighed heavily. "But it looks like I wasted my time."

"You really must be desperate," Rachel said.

"I am." Betsy took a sip of her tea. "What's it like there? Are they decent?"

Rachel shrugged. "They're nice enough, I suppose. But the work is hard, and it's been really difficult lately as the ruddy butler's been sick and taken to his bed. That means the housekeeper is takin' on his duties and we're doin' most of her work. But the missus is alright. She's a bit of a stickler for the social niceties, but usually she's alright."

"She sounds very upper-class," Betsy murmured.

"Not really. Her father made a lot of money in trade," Rachel said. "It's Mr. Farringdon that's upper-class. She married up."

"So she had the money and he had the breeding," she murmured. "One of them marriages of convenience, I suppose."

"Then you'd suppose wrong," Rachel said tartly. "They love each other a lot. He's devoted to her, and Mrs. Farringdon works hard to do everything just right. She wants to be a credit to him. Leastways that's what the housekeeper says when she's had a few too many sips from the brandy bottle."

"That's nice—I mean, that they're so devoted like that. Not many couples seem to care that overly much for one another. The master and mistress in my last household hated each other," Betsy said. "That's one of the reasons I'm lookin' for work. Mr. Summers decided that Mrs. Summers didn't need as much help in the house, so he sacked me and the scullery maid." She wasn't sure she ought to be saying so much. It was important to keep the conversation on the Farringdons. "Are they newlyweds?"

"No, they're old. He's in his late sixties and she's not much younger. They've been married for years." Rachel leaned closer. "He saved her life once."

"Really?" Betsy repeated eagerly. She was relieved that Rachel hadn't wanted any additional details about the made-up Summers household. "That sounds ever so romantic. What happened? That is, if you don't mind my asking. I don't mean to be bold, but this sounds like a lovely story."

"You're not bein' bold," Rachel said. "And it is a good story, all the more interestin' because it's true. It happened a few summers back, a year or two before I started workin' for 'em. They'd gone sailing with some friends, and some part of the sail come flying around and knocked Mrs. Farringdon clean overboard."

"My goodness, that's awful," Betsy exclaimed. She wasn't really acting now. "Could Mrs. Farringdon swim?"

Rachel shook her head. "Not a bit. But Mr. Farringdon leapt right in and grabbed hold of her. He held her up until they could pull them both back into the boat. He's not a very strong swimmer, and the sea was rough, but he held her above the water, even though she was scared and strugglin' something fierce. She was thrashin' about so much he ended up with bruises all over his face. But if he'd not done it, if he'd not gone in after her, she'd have drowned."

"That's so wonderful." Betsy sighed prettily. "He must really care for her."

"He does." Rachel smiled.

Betsy wanted to get Rachel talking about the murder. "It must be the most exciting thing that ever happened to them. I mean, almost drowning isn't very nice, but it is an adventure."

"I'm not sure they'd see it that way," Rachel laughed. "Mind you, they were at a dinner party just a few days ago where the host was murdered. So that's a bit of excitement as well."

"Gracious, what happened?" Betsy remembered she was supposed to be cold and hungry, so she took a quick gulp of tea.

"Their host was poisoned right there at the dinner table." Rachel leaned closer again. "The police think the poison was in the wine the Farringdons brought with them to the man's house."

Betsy's eyes widened. "The police think your master and mistress are murderers?"

"Not really." Rachel shook her head. "I overheard Mr. Farringdon tellin' Mrs. Farringdon that the police think anyone could have put the poison in the bottle. But I know they're both upset over all the bother. They didn't much like havin' the police come 'round. Mrs. Farringdon had hysterics when he told her they'd been to the house. She was terribly concerned that the neighbors might have seen."

"I suppose that could be right upsettin' for a lady," Betsy ventured.

Rachel snorted. "Seems to me she ought to be worried about one of them gettin' arrested, not what the neighbors might think because they see a copper goin' up your walk-way to the front door."

Betsy gaped at her. Again, she wasn't acting. "Do you think they might have done it?"

"I don't like to think so." Rachel shrugged. "But you never know about people, do you? And I know that Mrs. Farringdon didn't like the man. She didn't want to accept his dinner invitation when it come, but she'd no choice. Still, it's not nice when your host gets murdered with the wine you've brought to the party. Mind you, the wretched stuff Mr. Whitfield used to send to them tasted like it had poison in it; leastways that's what Mrs. Farringdon claimed. She was really annoyed when another bottle of the stuff arrived this Christmas. I thought she was going to have a fit when he brought it by."

"Mr. Whitfield?"

"He's the man who was poisoned," Rachel explained. "He came around to see the Farringdons just a few days before he was murdered. He brought them a bottle of his special port—leastways that's what he called it when he handed her the bottle. He came himself with just a young housemaid helpin' him. He'd brought the port as a Christmas present."

"And Mrs. Farringdon didn't like getting a present?"

"She didn't like him and she didn't like his wine. Last year she called it pigs' swill and poured it down the sink. But when he showed up at the front door, Mrs. Farringdon was polite enough. She said all the right words and acted like she was ever so pleased, but as soon as he'd gone, she grabbed the bottle and took it up to her dayroom."

Hatchet stopped on the top stair of the servants' entrance to the Farringdon house. He took one long last look at Connaught Street to make sure there were no signs of the police. The Farringdon butler was an old friend of his, but even so, he didn't want to be in a position of having to explain his presence here to Inspector Witherspoon. That could get very awkward. But he didn't see any constables patrolling the street on foot, and the road was free of hansom cabs.

He went down the short flight of steps and knocked on the door. Within moments, a young scullery maid stuck her head out. "You're not the butcher's lad," she said.

As he was wearing a full top hat and elegant black greatcoat, he could understand her surprise. "Indeed I am not."

He smiled at the surprised girl. "Is Mr. Emery Richards able to receive visitors? I'm an old friend of his."

"I'm not sure. But he seems a bit better today." She pulled the door wider. "Come on in, and I'll see if he feels up to seein' ya."

Hatchet stepped into the hallway. "Thank you."

"You wait here," the girl ordered.

An older woman wearing a white apron and a cook's cap peeked around the corner. "Tell the butcher's lad he's late. I've been waiting for that joint . . ." Her voice trailed off as she spotted Hatchet.

"It's not the butcher's boy," the scullery maid called over her shoulder as she disappeared into a doorway at the far end of the passage. "It's someone to see Richards."

"How do you do, ma'am?" Hatchet swept off his hat and bowed toward the cook.

"Humph." She nodded and went back into the kitchen.

Five minutes passed before the maid stepped back into the hallway. Hatchet spent the time trying to learn as much as possible about the household. He'd been here before, of course, but then he'd been seeking information about people other than the occupants. But without standing at the kitchen door and shouting questions at the staff, he couldn't find out much of anything except that the hallway was freshly painted and the floor cleaned and polished.

"Come on back," the maid called. "He'd like to see ya."

As Hatchet passed the door to the kitchen, half a dozen pairs of eyes watched him curiously. He nodded to them politely, slowed his steps, and tried to observe as many details as possible. But the only things he actually saw were a row of copper molds and a whole shelf full of copper pans. They had very expensive kitchen equipment, but as he already knew the Farringdons were rich, that fact wasn't going to do him any good.

"It's just there." The maid pointed to an open door at the end of the hallway. "He's sitting up. But don't you stay too long, or you'll tire him out."

"Thank you, miss," he replied.

Inside the small butler's pantry, Emery Richards, attired in a long plaid wool bathrobe and slippers, was sitting at a table. A cup of tea was in front of him. He was a small fellow with a headful of gray hair, blue eyes, and a very pale complexion.

He smiled wanly and tried to get up as Hatchet came into the room. "It's so very good of you to come see me, old friend."

"Don't get up, Emery." Hatchet waved him back to his chair. "We've known each other far too long to stand on ceremony. How are you feeling?"

Emery Richards was a friend from the old days, the days when they'd both been wild and young and ready for any adventure. They'd had more courage than sense, and some would even say they'd been incredibly foolish.

Hatchet watched Emery carefully as he crossed the short space. There were only a few people from his past who had known him when he'd been in the grip of the demon rum. Emery Richards was one of them. But his old friend was hardly in a position to judge him or anyone else. Back in those days, Emery had had a few problems of his own.

"I'm getting better. But a few days ago, if you'd asked me that question, I'd have told you I was dying. It certainly felt that way." Emery grinned and pointed at the chair opposite him. "Sit yourself down, man. I've told Daisy to bring tea."

"And I've done just that, Mr. Richards." Daisy, the maid who'd let Hatchet into the house, elbowed the door open and stepped into the pantry. She was carrying a tray. She put it down and unloaded a small china pot, another cup, a cream pitcher, and a sugar bowl. "But you mustn't stay up too long, Mr. Richards. Remember what Doctor said: bronchitis can come back very quickly."

"Thank you, Daisy," Emery said. "I'll not overdo it."

"Should I pour?" she asked.

"That's all right, miss. I'll manage," Hatchet said quickly. He could see that his old friend wasn't as much on the mend as he'd pretended, and Hatchet didn't want to be responsible for a relapse.

"Right, then, I'll just close the door on my way out," Daisy said.

Hatchet poured his tea and then looked at Emery's half-empty cup. "Should I top you off?"

"Nah, I've had so much of the stuff, my bladder feels like it's going to burst," Emery replied. "Are you still working for that crazy American woman?"

"I am indeed."

"You still snooping around in that inspector's murder cases?" Emery shook his head. "I know that's why you've come to see me. Though, in all fairness, you've done your part over the years to keep in touch."

Hatchet laughed. He wasn't in the least concerned that Emery knew the real reason he was here. He'd used Emery as a source on two of the inspector's previous cases and knew the man could keep his own counsel. "You never were one to beat about the bush. I wonder what the Farringdons would think if they knew you as well as I do."

"The old man would have a stroke, and the good wife wouldn't give a toss as long as I did my job properly." He grinned broadly. "They're good people, even if he is a bit of a stick. Now, I don't know how much longer I can sit upright, so why don't you get on with it?"

"Emery, I'm not just here to get information. I want you to know that," Hatchet said softly. "I was concerned when I heard you were ill."

"I know. You've been a good friend over the years."

"As have you." Hatchet picked up his teacup. "What can you tell me about the Farringdons? More specifically, what can you tell me about their relationship to the late Stephen Whitfield?"

"Whitfield and Basil Farringdon went to school together, but they go back even further." He broke off and coughed lightly, covering his mouth with his hand. "Sorry, where was I?"

"Whitfield and Farringdon go back further than their school days?" Hatchet thought that odd. "Are they related?"

"No, but they are in the same tontine, and that was started the year they were born. So I guess you could say they've known each other from birth."

"Tontine?" Hatchet repeated. "Good Lord, I haven't heard of one of those for years. Aren't they illegal?"

"They were outlawed a good while back. I can't remember the exact year. The tontine was started by the parents the year they were all born. There were originally ten of them in it, and as was the custom, they were all close to each other in age," Emery explained. "That was sometime around 1825, well before the government outlawed tontines."

Hatchet thought for a moment. "Why wasn't the tontine disbanded or stopped when they were made illegal?"

"Because none of the principals wanted it to stop." Emery grinned. "They were making too much money off of it. I once heard Mr. Farringdon tell Mrs. Farringdon that when the law banning them was passed, they had their solicitors do something like rename it as a trust or an annuity, but basically the terms didn't change. It's still a tontine. It was a big one as well. Each family chucked in over ten thousand pounds."

"Was the money invested?" Hatchet asked. He wasn't completely sure he understood how a tontine functioned.

"It was, and this investment brought in substantial incomes to the participants, which is, of course, the reason they had it renamed instead of disbanded." He chuckled, which then turned into a cough. "You can see why the government outlawed the practice. Let's face it: That kind of money would tempt a saint, let alone a bunch of impoverished aristocrats living off the yearly dividend."

"Are you alright?" Hatchet put down his cup and started to get up.

Emery waved him back to his seat. "I'm fine. It's just a cough. Don't mind what Daisy says—I'm not on death's door yet. Speaking of which, if you're thinking that Mr. Farringdon murdered Whitfield to get his hands on all of it, think again. He doesn't need the money."

"But I thought you just referred to him as an 'impoverished aristocrat'?" Hatchet pointed out.

"He would be if he hadn't married Mrs. Farringdon. She's the one with the money. She's rich."

"Tell me more about the tontine." He was amazed they'd not learned about this as yet. Then again, most of the people involved probably had no reason to tell the police about it and, thus, show that they had a motive for wanting Whitfield dead.

"What else is there to say?" Emery asked. "The original charter had ten members. From what I've overheard Mr. Farringdon tell Mrs. Farringdon, two or three of them didn't survive childhood, so that got the number of participants down to seven. The money was invested wisely and, as I said, the fund—or annuity, as it's now called—has paid out a handsome dividend over the years. But the real prize will go to the survivor. He'll get everything." He started coughing again. He put his hand over his mouth, his head bobbed with every choking gasp, and it sounded as if his poor lungs were about to explode. Finally, just when Hatchet had made up his mind to call Daisy, the attack subsided.

Emery slumped back against his chair.

Hatchet got up. "You're too ill to continue this. You must get back to bed."

"Don't be stupid," Emery choked out. "This has done me a world of good. I'm so sick of lying in that bed that even your homely face is welcome. Sit your arse back down and tell me what you've been doing."

Hatchet hesitated. As much as he wanted information, he wouldn't get it at the price of his friend's health.

"For God's sake, sit down," Emery ordered. "I'm not dying. It's just a bad cough."

"Are you sure you wouldn't like me to fetch someone?" Hatchet asked. "You sound terrible."

Emery grinned again. "The only reason I'd want you to fetch a doctor is so I could have more of that lovely cough syrup he dispenses so sparingly. But considering my earlier problem with that very substance, I don't think the doctor will oblige me unless I'm literally at death's door, which I'm not. So, as I said, sit your arse down and talk to me."

Hatchet chuckled and did as commanded. He was pleased that Emery had told his doctor about his problem with opium. Years ago Emery, like so many others, had become addicted to the substance. As it was now used in many medicines, Emery had been wise to tell the physician about his earlier predicament. Apparently his doctor had felt there was a chance of his becoming addicted again, and had been very stingy with the cough syrup. But it was awful to see Emery suffering so much. "The madam and I have been quite busy lately," Hatchet said. "Madam especially enjoys playing detective. Being of service has given her a whole new perspective on life. She's the happiest I've ever seen her."

"You're very devoted to her, aren't you?" Emery asked.

"Of course. She saved me. As you know, I was once in the same position as you found yourself, but mine was because of drink, not opium. If it hadn't been for her, I'd have been dead years ago. She found me drunk and starving in an alley in Baltimore, took me home, cleaned me up, and put me to work. I think she liked my accent."

"I was saved by a thief, not a crazy American," Emery replied. "Who would have thought that getting all my money stolen and then finding myself left to rot in a Bangkok jail cell would end up saving me?"

"You never did tell me how you got out of that cell," Hatchet said. He'd have liked to ask more questions about the Farringdons, but he'd learned enough. Now it was time to just talk with an old friend.

"I didn't actually get out." Emery grinned. "The building caught on fire, so they unlocked all the cells and trooped us out into the street. But the guard got into an argument with a street vendor, and when his back was turned, I took off, as did most of the others. I managed to throw myself on the mercy of an Englishman I ran into, and he hid me in his hotel. He was a decent bloke, a former butler to a Scottish lord. He's the one that taught me the trade, you know. He forged a few references so I could get my first position. You know, Hatchet, sometimes in life, you just get lucky."

"I know."

"And today's your lucky day." Emery smiled wanly. "I'm going to tell you the rest of what I know about the tontine."

"You don't need to do that. I'm quite happy simply to sit here and visit with you. I should have come more often to see you."

"I could have gone to see you as well," Emery replied. "All of us get busy with our own lives. Now, what else do you need to know?"

For a moment, Hatchet's mind went blank. Then he thought of something useful. "I've heard a rumor that Stephen Whitfield and Mrs. Farringdon weren't overly fond of one another. Is that true?"

"Whitfield was a dreadful snob. He looked down on Mrs. Farringdon because her family made a fortune in trade." Emery snorted. "Mind you, his family may be old and aristocratic, but he wouldn't have had a pot to piss in without the dividend from the tontine."

Hatchet laughed. "How many people are left in the tontine?"

"There were three, but now that Whitfield is dead, there's only two left: Mr. Farringdon and Henry Becker."

CHAPTER 8

Hugh Langdon lived in a six-story brown brick town house in Bulstrode Street in Marylebone. Witherspoon and Barnes stood inside the entrance while the housekeeper went to fetch Langdon.

As was his habit, Barnes studied the reception hall. Experience had taught him that a man's home could often give you a hint or two about his character. The walls were painted a pale cream; the floor was made of simple, polished oak; and directly opposite him was a wide staircase. A brass umbrella stand and coat tree were the only furniture in the foyer.

Hugh Langdon stepped through a set of double doors farther down the long hallway and motioned them forward. "Good day, Inspector. I've been expecting you. Do come inside, please."

They went into the drawing room. Barnes noted that the

walls were painted the same shade as the foyer. A lovely peacock blue and brown carpet covered the wood floor, and blue and cream striped curtains hung at the three tall windows facing the street. Like those in the foyer, the furnishings were simple, attractive, and well crafted. The fittings and the furniture here hadn't been done to impress anyone, but rather to provide comfort for the occupants.

Langdon waved them to a pair of overstuffed chairs. "Please sit down, gentlemen."

"Thank you, Mr. Langdon," Witherspoon responded. "We'll try not to take up too much of your time. We do understand that you've a business to run."

"Would you or the constable care for a cup of tea?" Langdon asked. He sat down on the love seat opposite them.

"No, thank you," Witherspoon replied.

"Then I expect you'd like to get on with your questions." Langdon smiled sardonically. "I'm sure you're busy as well."

"I understand you were only recently introduced to Mr. Whitfield. You met him shortly before you went to dinner at his home," Witherspoon began.

"Actually, that's not quite true," Langdon interrupted smoothly. "I'd met Stephen Whitfield years earlier."

Witherspoon was taken aback. According to their information, the two men had met for the first time only days before the murder. That was one of the reasons they'd left Langdon to be questioned last. Witherspoon had assumed that because Langdon and Whitfield hadn't known each other or had any obvious connections besides their relationships with Eliza Graham, Langdon would be the least likely of all the dinner guests to have wanted Whitfield dead. "I'm afraid I don't understand. Mrs. Graham specifically told us she'd introduced the two of you only a few days before the murder."

"And she was telling the truth. Eliza had no idea that I'd met Whitfield previously, and it seems he'd forgotten our meeting as well," Langdon replied. "I apologize, Inspector. I ought to have mentioned this before, but the truth of the matter is that I met Stephen Whitfield thirty years ago."

"How did you meet?" Barnes reached in his pocket and pulled out his notebook

"We ran into Stephen last week when we were on our way into the Adelphi Theatre."

"No, I meant, how did you meet thirty years ago?" the constable clarified.

"Oh, sorry," Langdon said. "I wanted to become a member of the Bonfire Club. I was very young and trying my best to make my way in this hard old world, and I thought being a member of that particular organization would help me in business."

"And you met Whitfield at the club?" Witherspoon asked.

"Not quite. Whitfield was the chairman of the membership committee. I went to him and asked for a recommendation." Langdon grinned broadly. "Apparently that was the worst possible course of action. Whitfield took great offense that I'd dare approach him—and not only that, he blackballed me from membership in the club."

"That must have made going to his house for dinner a bit awkward," Witherspoon commented.

"Not really. As I said, he hadn't remembered me when we met that night at the theater." Langdon shrugged. "There was no reason why he should—the incident obviously hadn't been particularly important to him."

"Did you join another gentlemen's club?" The inspector watched Langdon's face as he asked the question. He was trying to determine how important membership to this club might have been for Langdon. Being blackballed from a society he was keen to join could be a motive for murder. In Witherspoon's experience, people were capable of holding grudges for a very long time. Old sins cast long shadows.

"No. I knew that if I couldn't get into the Bonfire, none of the other clubs would have me. Word gets about when you've been blackballed. But it was a long time ago, Inspector," Langdon said. "As the saying goes, it's all water under the bridge now."

"On the night you went to dinner at his home, did you inform Mr. Whitfield that you'd met before?" Barnes asked. "Or that he'd blackballed you?"

"Indeed I did." Langdon leaned back and crossed his arms over his chest. "I hadn't planned on mentioning the matter, as I didn't wish to cause Mrs. Graham any embarrassment. After all, I was her escort. Whitfield took us into the morning room to see the Christmas tree he'd had put up, and afterwards, when I'd gone back to the drawing room, he followed me. He said he wanted to have a word with me. But as I found his conversation somewhat objectionable, I'm afraid my good intentions about being polite went right out the window, and I took the opportunity to remind him that we'd met many years earlier." Langdon paused. "He didn't seem pleased by the news."

"Why did you go back to the drawing room?" Barnes asked quickly.

"I wanted to get some fresh air. The smell in the morning room was overpowering. The candles on that tree were blazing away, there was incense burning, and the ladies had doused themselves quite liberally with perfume. When my eyes began to water, I knew it was time to make a graceful exit into another part of the house."

"What did you mean when you said that Whitfield

didn't seem pleased to know you'd met previously? Did he tell you that specifically?" Witherspoon asked.

"He didn't say a word, Inspector. He just stood there, staring at me. But I could tell the news bothered him."

Barnes looked up from his notebook. "How could you tell, sir?"

"It was dead easy," Langdon replied. "You're a policeman, and I'll bet you know what I'm talking about. I'm sure you do it all the time when you're questioning suspects or taking a statement. You're doing it now as we speak. You appear to be making notes, but I can see that you and the inspector are observing me very closely. You see how my expression changes whenever you ask a question, or you watch the way I hold myself when I give you my answers. Very few people are skilled at truly hiding their feelings, and Whitfield was no exception. His face was as easy to read as the front page of the *Times*."

"I imagine it was," Barnes agreed.

"What did you find so objectionable about Whitfield's conversation when he followed you into the drawing room?" Witherspoon asked.

"Everything." Langdon uncrossed his arms and leaned forward. His expression hardened. "He tried to speak to me about Mrs. Graham. But I cut him off. My personal relationships are no one's business but mine."

"Do you know why he'd wish to discuss such a matter with someone he considered a stranger?" Witherspoon asked. Past experience had shown him that matters of the heart were always sensitive subjects.

"He wanted to warn me off her, Inspector. But I wasn't prepared to discuss her with Stephen Whitfield under any circumstances. I may not have been born to an upper-class family, but I am a gentleman when it comes to the women in my life. I certainly wasn't going to stand there and let him denigrate her character because she'd chosen me over him."

"So you knew that Mrs. Graham and Mr. Whitfield had been seeing each other?" Barnes asked.

"Mrs. Graham told me about her relationship with him from the very beginning," he replied. "Furthermore, she also told me he'd presumed that simply because they'd seen one another socially, she was willing to marry him. She wasn't."

"But he had proposed to her," Witherspoon stated.

"True." Langdon smiled sadly. "But Eliza had been candid with him. She'd told him she needed time to think about the matter. Yet even though she'd been honest and hadn't made any promises, she was sure he assumed she was going to consent to marry him."

Barnes said, "How long had you been seeing Mrs. Graham?"

"We met this past summer at a charity ball. We've been seeing one another ever since."

"And you didn't mind that she was still seeing Stephen Whitfield?" Witherspoon stared at him doubtfully. Men who'd made as much money as Hugh Langdon hadn't done so by sharing what they possessed. "You didn't object to that, sir?"

Langdon flushed angrily. "Of course I didn't like it, Inspector. But Mrs. Graham had her reasons for continuing to see him, and frankly, at the time she told me about him, I'd no idea how our relationship might progress. She needs to marry, and as I wasn't willing to commit to such a course of action until very recently, I could hardly object to her continuing a relationship with Whitfield. He had made it perfectly clear that he did want to marry her."

"And apparently you decided you did as well," Barnes

murmured. He suddenly felt sorry for Stephen Whitfield. He might have been an arrogant, upper-class twit, but he'd been playing second fiddle for months and hadn't even known it.

"Yes, I did," Langdon declared. "Mrs. Graham and I are very well suited to one another. I proposed to her. That's the reason I wanted to accompany her to the dinner party that night. I wanted her to break it off with Stephen, and I wanted to be there when she did it."

"Yet you refused to discuss her with him when he brought the subject up," Witherspoon reminded him.

"That's right, Inspector." Langdon said. "I did. I wanted Eliza to do the telling. I only wanted to be there in case he got angry or abusive."

"Was there any reason to think he might react badly?" Witherspoon asked.

Langdon's eyes narrowed. "Of course there was. He had quite a bad temper."

"Did Mrs. Graham tell you that?" Barnes looked up from his notebook.

"She did not. I knew about Whitfield's temper from my own experiences with the man."

"But you hadn't seen him in years," the constable argued.

"So what, Constable? A leopard doesn't change his spots just because he's grown a few gray hairs around his snout," Langdon snapped. "Thirty years ago, when I asked him for help in getting into that stupid club, he became so enraged by my temerity, by my even daring to approach him with such a request, that he tried to strike me."

Witherspoon's eyebrows rose. "That is hardly the act of a gentleman."

Langdon sank back against the love seat. "It didn't really matter, Inspector. He was middle-aged, and I was young and fit. I easily avoided his fists and even got in a blow or two of my own."

That's the real reason he blackballed you, Barnes thought. You didn't let him cuff you about and pretend that his kind still rule the world.

"But you can understand why I wanted to be here when she told him it was over between them. I didn't want him taking his anger out on Eliza," Langdon continued. "But as it turned out, I needn't have worried. Before she could speak to him alone, he died."

Smythe whistled as he stepped through the door of the Dirty Duck Pub. Since he and Betsy had their little chat yesterday, life seemed just that bit brighter. They weren't back to normal yet, but they were getting there. He'd not lost her. She still loved him.

He pushed his way through the crowd to Blimpey's table. "Good day, old friend," Smythe said as he slipped onto the stool.

Blimpey grunted a greeting and then waved at the barmaid, caught her attention, and pointed to Smythe.

"What's wrong, Blimpey?" Smythe asked. "You look right miserable."

"I am miserable. Business is terrible." Blimpey snorted. "Half of London is gone to Scotland or Wales or some such other heathen place for Christmas. My sources at three of the busiest police stations are all down with the flu, and my man at the Old Bailey just told me he wants a raise. Can you believe it? Every time you turn around, someone's got their hand in your pocket or they're malingering in bed instead of doing their work properly." He broke off as the barmaid slipped a pint of beer on the table. She gave Smythe a quick grin and then scurried back to the bar.

"People can't 'elp it if they take ill." Smythe picked up his pint. "And you don't 'ave to give your Old Bailey source a raise. You can always say no."

"He's too good a source to risk." Blimpey frowned. "I've got to give him a raise. Blast it all. No tellin' what he'll be wantin' next year."

"And there is a nasty flu goin' around." Smythe took a quick sip of beer. "So you can't blame your other sources for takin' to their beds."

"Hah! Young people these days will find any reason not to do their jobs," Blimpey cried. "Not like when I was growing up. You didn't take to your bed at the first sign of a sniffle or a bit of a cough."

Smythe put down his glass and stared at his companion. Blimpey kept his head lowered, staring at the tabletop as if it were a treasure map. "What's really wrong? This isn't like you. You've never complained about your sources taking a bit of time to themselves. As a matter of fact, everyone knows you always treat your people decently. That's one of the reasons people work for you—you're good to 'em."

Blimpey said nothing for a moment, then he lifted his chin and looked Smythe in the eye. "Oh, blast it. I'm bein' silly, and I know it. Makin' excuses because I don't want you to think ill of me."

Smythe didn't like the sound of that, but he said nothing.

"The truth of the matter is, I'm a bit embarrassed. I've not got much information for you at all, and from the way my sources are droppin' off, I have grave doubts that I'm going to find out anything useful in the near future."

Blast a Spaniard, Smythe thought. That wasn't what he wanted to hear. "You have nothing for me?"

"I've got a little. But it's not much, and I don't think the

information has anything at all to do with your case."
Blimpey shrugged apologetically.

In an effort to hide his disappointment, Smythe forced a
smile. "Let's 'ear it, then." He'd been counting on learning a
few facts from Blimpey, especially as his own snooping had
turned up nothing. "Don't concern yourself on whether or
not your information is useful. You never know what little
fact 'elps solve the case. Who is it about?"

"Rosalind Murray."

Smythe relaxed a bit. "She's one of our stronger suspects.
What did you find out about her?"

"I got a tidbit out of one of her servants . . ."

"They always know what's what." Smythe smiled encouragingly.

"Actually, it was someone who used to work for her, a
housemaid."

"You mean the maid doesn't work in the household
now?" His smile faded.

Blimpey glanced at the fireplace and then back at his
pint. "The truth is, the girl left in September . . ."

"September," Smythe interrupted. "But that was months
ago. Cor blimey, Whitfield was just killed a few days ago.
How could this girl possibly know anything?"

"You said yourself that you don't know until the very end
what might or might not be of value, so just drink your pint
and have a listen," Blimpey retorted. "I've paid good money
for this, so you can at least do me the courtesy of pretendin'
you're interested."

Smythe took a deep breath. "Sorry. Go on."

"Rosalind Murray keeps a diary. She's done so for years.
My source read this diary."

"And what did it say?" Smythe didn't see how a diary

entry from three months before the murder could help, but he'd agreed to listen.

Blimpey eyed him appraisingly. "Your lot is lookin' at everyone who was at dinner the night Whitfield was killed, and wonderin' what their motives might be, right?"

"That's generally what we do. Why?"

"Because I'm thinkin' that, seein' as how the word I got was that Rosalind Murray was supposedly Whitfield's mistress for the past ten years, you're all thinkin' her motive for murderin' him is because he was goin' to jilt her for another woman, right?"

"Are we playin' guessin' games here, or are you goin' to tell me what you found out?" Smythe cried impatiently. He had the horrible feeling they were going to lose another one of their few motives for this murder.

"Alright, alright, hold yer horses. I'm gettin' to it. What I'm tryin' to tell ya is, if that's what you've been thinkin' about Mrs. Murray, you'd be dead wrong. Rosalind Murray wasn't jealous of Stephen Whitfield carryin' on with another woman." Blimpey grinned. "As a matter of fact, according to her own words, she was glad he'd taken up with someone else so she could get on with her own life. She had plans."

Smythe thought for a moment; then he shook his head. "Are you sure your source wasn't lying? This can't be right. We've a witness who claims Mrs. Murray and Whitfield 'ad a terrible row, and it was about him gettin' serious with Mrs. Graham."

"My source has no reason to lie," Blimpey declared.

"Did you pay her?"

"What's that got to do with the price of turnips? I pay all my sources. That's why I'm able to do what I do," Blimpey said indignantly.

Smythe studied his companion for a long moment. A dull red flush had crept up Blimpey's cheeks, and once again he was studying the tabletop as though it could tell him where King Midas' gold was buried. "She came to you after you'd put the word out that you were lookin' for any information about the Whitfield household, didn't she?"

Blimpey nodded. "But she's a good source, Smythe. I made sure of that. I asked about, and she's not a greedy lass who'd make something up for a bit of coin, nor is she one of them kind that lies just to get people to notice her."

"You know your business, Blimpey," Smythe said. "I'm not questionin' that. It's just—this doesn't make sense . . . or does it?"

"You mean you're wonderin' if maybe the dustup between the Murray woman and Whitfield didn't 'ave sod-all to do with him takin' up with the Graham woman? Maybe you just assumed that's what she was goin' on about, because that's what made sense to you."

"That is what I'm startin' to think," Smythe admitted. In which case, he wondered how many of their other assumptions might be wrong.

Blimpey shrugged. "I wouldn't know whether or not there was some misunderstandin' on what the two of 'em were squabblin' about, but I do know what my source reported."

Smythe nodded, his expression thoughtful. "The girl claimed that Mrs. Murray had plans. Did she know what those plans might be?"

"Nah, she only got to read a few pages of the diary before she had to chuck it back when she heard Mrs. Murray comin' up the stairs." He laughed.

"Rosalind Murray was in the house when the girl was readin' her diary?" Smythe asked incredulously. "That was brave of her."

"Not really." Blimpey laughed again. "She'd already given her notice, and claimed that she didn't much care if she got caught. I don't think she liked the Whitfield house very much. But she's not lying—I'm sure of it. She's a good girl."

"Good girl, my foot," Smythe snorted. "She's a slyboots, she is. She read Mrs. Murray's diary. What does that say about her character?"

Blimpey's eyebrows rose. "It says she was curious. Not everyone who started out in service was lucky enough or clever enough to go off to Australia and make a fortune."

"Even when I was just a coachman, I'd never 'ave read someone's private papers," he replied.

"Climb down off your high horse, Smythe." Blimpey plopped his elbows on the rickety table and leaned forward. "Have you forgotten what bein' in service is like for most young girls? They're worked harder than cart horses, abused by their employers, and constantly dodgin' the lecherous advances of the master or his sons. You can't blame them for wantin' to get a little of their own back."

"But Rosalind Murray had a reputation for treatin' staff decently," Smythe said.

"Maybe so, but even the decent employers work most of their servants harder than slaves, begrudge every bite of food they put in their mouths, and treat 'em lower than dirt."

"Not every household is like that," Smythe said defensively. But he was a bit ashamed. Blimpey had a point. "Besides, you was just complainin' about your people takin' to their beds and wantin' more money."

"Yes, but I was just makin' excuses to cover up bein' embarrassed because I'd found out so little," he said smugly. "You said it yourself—I treat my people real well, and I do it because I know what it's like to work my fingers to the bone for not much more than a crust of bread. Most of the prosperous ones in this town don't have any idea what life is really like for workin' people. Euphemia Witherspoon was a decent sort, and your inspector's a good man as well. But neither of them was from the upper class, were they? Neither of them was trained from birth to see the rest of the human race as slaves put here to do their bidding or make their lives easy. You've had it better than most, Smythe, but not everyone is as lucky as you. Not everyone has a chance to get out."

Smythe stared at him for a long moment. "I 'ave 'ad it better than most."

Blimpey blushed. "Sorry, I didn't mean to go on and on. Cor blimey, you probably think I'm soundin' like one of them ruddy Socialists. But sometimes they have a point."

"Yeah, there is some injustice in this old world." Smythe took another sip of his beer. "And most servants do get treated badly."

"My mother was in service," Blimpey said softly. "Her master tossed her out when she got bronchitis and couldn't work anymore. She never even made it 'ome the night she died. She collapsed in the street."

"How old were you?"

"Ten."

"That's 'ard," Smythe said. No wonder Blimpey sounded so bitter.

Blimpey shrugged. "It was. I loved my mum, Smythe. She was a wonderful woman. Despite how little we had, she made sure I got a bit of education. She never knew I did any thievin'. She'd have hated that. But I think she'd have liked how I've turned out."

"You've become a very prosperous businessman," Smythe said quickly. "Your mum would have been very proud."

"Indeed she would have," Blimpey agreed. "I've money

in the bank, I've a nice house, and I own quite a bit of property, if I do say so myself."

"You've done very well."

"I've married a good woman and made a decent home for us," he continued. "But you know what she'd have been most proud of?"

"What?"

Blimpey smiled. "Most of all, she'd have been happy I managed to bankrupt the bastard that tossed her into the streets that night."

Barnes pulled open the heavy front door of New Scotland Yard and held it for the inspector. "What time are you seeing Chief Inspector Barrows?" he asked as Witherspoon stepped past him into the reception area. Barnes followed him inside.

"He said that anytime after three o'clock would do." Witherspoon stopped, pulled out his pocket watch, and noted the time. "So we can go right on up. He ought to be in his office." He nodded at the two policemen on duty behind the counter, and headed for the stairs.

"Is the chief expecting a full report, sir?" Barnes asked as they started up.

"Oh, I daresay he's hoping we've got the case solved"— Witherspoon sighed—"and that I'll walk into his office and tell him we're making an arrest today. You know how the powers that be hate having an unsolved murder over Christmas."

They reached the first-floor landing and turned down the long hallway to Barrows' office, which was at the far end. They were halfway down the corridor when the door just ahead of them opened and Inspector Nigel Nivens stepped out. He stopped when he saw them.

Nivens was a man of medium height who was running to fat. He had dark blond hair going gray at the temples; bulging, watery blue eyes; and a thick mustache. He was dressed in a gray-blue checked overcoat open far enough to reveal a dark blue suit and gray sateen waistcoat. A deer-stalker hat in the same fabric as the overcoat dangled from his fingers.

"Well, well, if it isn't the fair-haired lads of the Metropolitan Police Department." He sneered. "Here to give the chief an update on your latest case?"

"We're here to make a report," Witherspoon said politely as he swept past. He didn't like being rude, but he was aware that Nigel Nivens didn't like him and probably did in fact hate him. Their encounters this past year had convinced him that Nivens would like nothing better than to see him utterly destroyed.

Nivens slammed the deerstalker onto his head. He hurried after them, his boots pounding heavily against the wooden floor. "You'd better be close to an arrest, Witherspoon," he said in a loud voice. "If you can't get this case solved soon, they're going to give it to someone who will."

Barnes looked behind him and gave Nivens a good glare. Witherspoon ignored the man and kept on walking.

"That means me, Witherspoon," Nivens cried.

Barnes glanced at Witherspoon, but the inspector resolutely kept his gaze straight ahead.

"Did you hear what I said?" Nivens yelled. He was furious at being ignored—especially as some of the doors down the long hallway had opened and a number of policemen were now watching.

Witherspoon reached Barrows' office. He continued ignoring Nivens, lifted his hand, and rapped softly on the door.

Unable to stop himself, Barnes turned. Nivens had halted

a few feet away. "Don't worry, sir," the constable said. "You're not going to be overly burdened with additional work. Inspector Witherspoon has this case well in hand. An arrest is imminent."

"Good, glad to hear that." The voice came from behind him and belonged to the chief inspector.

Barnes turned slowly and saw Witherspoon staring at him with an expression of undisguised horror on his face. Chief Inspector Barrows was beaming. Barnes heard a snort from Nivens, who then turned and stomped off. As he moved down the hall, the constables who'd been watching quickly closed their doors and went back to their business.

"Actually," Witherspoon said quickly, "we're making progress, but I'm not sure we're ready to . . ."

"Don't be so modest, Witherspoon. As the good constable said, you've got the case well in hand." Barrows clapped him on the back. "You're always hiding your light under a basket. Come inside and give me a proper report. You, too, Constable." He ushered the two of them into his office and pointed at two chairs in front of his desk. "Take a seat."

"Thank you, sir," Witherspoon began.

"Don't mind anything Inspector Nivens might have said. His nose is more out of joint than usual. He lost a case in court this morning. Two burglars he nabbed were acquitted." Barrows frowned and shook his head in disgust. "Stupid fool should learn to make sure he's got the evidence before he makes an arrest."

Barnes exhaled the breath he was holding and sat down. He knew he should have held his tongue, but he hadn't expected Chief Inspector Barrows to pop out of his ruddy office. "Actually, sir, I spoke a bit too soon."

Barrows looked amused. "Of course you did, Constable. Your words were for Nivens' benefit. I know that. The man

gets on my nerves as well, especially when he makes the police look like incompetent fools in front of a judge and
jury, but he does have good political connections. But that
aside"—he looked at Witherspoon—"even if you're not close
to an arrest, I take it you are making progress."

"Yes, sir, we are. We're working very hard," Witherspoon
replied. "But there are some difficulties."

"Difficulties." Barrows frowned as if the word itself was
offensive. "What sort of difficulties?"

Witherspoon hesitated. "Unfortunately we've no idea why
Mr. Whitfield was murdered. There simply doesn't seem to
be any compelling reason for anyone at the dinner party or
any member of his household to have wanted him dead."

"The why is the least of it." Barrows waved his hand impatiently. "Are you absolutely certain the killer was one of
the dinner guests or someone in the household?"

"Yes, sir." Witherspoon nodded. "The wine he'd been
drinking was poisoned."

"I know that. I've read the postmortem report," Barrows
replied. "And you've determined that no one from outside
the household could have had access to the open bottle?"

"The butler was on duty near the front door, and if an unknown person had come in through the back, they would
have had to walk right by the kitchen, which had staff going in and out all evening long," Witherspoon replied. "It's
highly unlikely that an outsider could have gotten in, poisoned the wine, and left the premises without being seen."

"And I suppose it's impossible to determine which of the
guests might have been alone long enough to have had
access to the bottle," Barrows said.

"They were all milling about, sir," Witherspoon replied.
"Mr. Whitfield had one of those decorated Christmas trees

in the morning room, and all the guests were dashing about everywhere. No one seems able to recall who might have been where at any given moment in time."

"It would only take a second to put the crushed leaves in the wine, sir," Barnes added.

Barrows leaned back, closed his eyes, and rubbed his forehead. "You'd have thought the man would have noticed leaves floating in his bloody glass, wouldn't you?" He opened his eyes and straightened up.

"They were crushed very fine," Witherspoon explained. "And it was nighttime, sir. There were only gas lamps and candles burning. I expect that the leaves were hardly noticeable under those circumstances."

Barnes, trying to make up for his earlier mistake, said, "The witnesses all stated that Whitfield was drinking the wine as fast as he could get it down his throat, sir."

"In other words, he was slogging it back so quickly he'd not have noticed a ruddy rat floating in it." Barrows sighed again. "This is no good. Christmas is less than a week away. Do you have any other leads? Did you get any useful tips from the neighbors or the house-to-house?"

"We didn't do an extensive house-to-house, sir," Witherspoon told him. "It was obvious right from the start that it was an inside job, so to speak. But we did interview the neighbors on each side of the Whitfield house. They neither saw nor heard anything unusual that night. There was no one suspicious lurking about the area, and none of them knew of anyone who might have wished Mr. Whitfield harm."

"Have you questioned the servants in the adjoining houses?" Barrows rubbed his hand over his chin.

"We have, sir. But none of them saw or heard anything unusual, either." Witherspoon glanced at Barnes. The constable gave a barely perceptible shrug. All of this information was in their preliminary report, which was currently open on the desk right in front of the chief.

"Question the Whitfield servants again." Barrows yawned. "They might know more than they were willing to tell the first time around. And have another go at the dinner guests. We've got to get this one solved, and we're running out of time."

"Yes, sir. We intended to speak again to everyone who was there that night," Witherspoon assured him.

"I don't mind telling you, we're getting pressure from the Home Office on this one." Barrows smiled cynically. "They don't like it when a member of the upper class gets murdered. It scares them. Of course, if it had been some poor sod from Stepney that had gotten it in the neck, they'd not be so concerned." He clamped his mouth shut. "Sorry, I didn't mean to go off on a tirade. It just annoys me that the HO seems to think the life of a rich man is worth more than anyone else's."

"I understand how you feel, sir," Witherspoon replied. "I promise you, we'll do our very best."

Barrows nodded and got to his feet. "Keep digging, Inspector, and please, let's try to have an arrest before Christmas if at all possible."

"We'll keep you informed of our progress, sir," Witherspoon said as he and Barnes got to their feet.

Neither policeman said anything until they were out of Barrows' office and almost to the staircase.

"Sorry, sir," Barnes began. "I shouldn't have spoken up when we ran into Inspector Nivens."

"That's quite alright, Constable." Witherspoon smiled faintly. "The chief inspector made it very clear he knew what you were doing."

"Yes, but he still wants an arrest before Christmas," Barnes muttered.

"Only because he's getting pressure from the HO. Poor man. He looks very tired."

"Do you think he's right, sir?" Barnes started down the stairs. "I mean, about the why of a murder being the least important part."

"No." Witherspoon pulled his gloves out of his coat pocket. "With all due respect to him, I think he's dead wrong about that. In my view, once you discover the why, you find the killer. Now, I think if we hurry, we can have a quick interview with Whitfield's solicitor. He's supposed to be back in his office today."

"This has been an inconvenient time for the man to come down with the flu," Barnes said as they reached the bottom of the stairs. He glanced at the clock over the counter behind the duty constables and saw that it was just past four. They'd never make it to the solicitor's offices on Addison Road and then get back to West Brompton in time to speak to the servants before nightfall. "But what about the servants at the Whitfield house, sir? Should we leave them until tomorrow?"

"I think so." Witherspoon pulled open the door and stepped out.

They were lucky enough to find a hansom right away, so despite the heavy traffic over the bridge, the found themselves at the law offices of Runyon & Gable within twenty minutes.

John Runyon had been expecting them. He ushered them both into his office and instructed the young clerk in the outer office to see that they weren't disturbed. "I'm sorry I've been unavailable," he apologized. "My clerk said you'd been here twice before, but I've been ill."

"That's quite alright, sir," Witherspoon replied politely. "I do hope you're feeling better."

"Thank you. I'm on the mend, as they say. Please sit down." Runyon motioned toward two chairs in front of the desk. He was a slender man with bushy eyebrows. Though elderly, he had very clear blue eyes. He was holding a white handkerchief to his nose and blew gently into it as he walked around the desk and took his seat.

"We won't keep you long, sir, but we do have a few questions about your late client Stephen Whitfield," Witherspoon said. He took off his bowler and sat down. The constable took the chair next to him.

"I know why you're here, Inspector." Runyon picked up a pair of spectacles that were lying on top of an open file on his desktop, and put them on. "My client was murdered, and you're trying to determine who might have had reason to want him dead." It was a statement of fact, not a question.

"That is correct, sir. As his solicitor, you're in a position to tell us who benefited the most from his death," Witherspoon said. "We understand that he had made a will."

"Of course he did," Runyon replied. "In the interest of saving time, I've made a list of his bequests. I take it that's what you're most interested in hearing about?"

Witherspoon nodded eagerly. "Indeed."

Runyon looked down at his desk and began to read. "Let's start with the servants first. He left fifty pounds to the cook, Hannah Walker, and a hundred pounds to the butler, Jeremiah Flagg."

"Nothing to the other servants?" Barnes asked.

"No, they'd not been with him long enough to warrant an inheritance." Runyon glanced up at the constable. "The butler and the cook were family servants. They'd been there for years." He picked up the paper and continued reading. "His other bequests are simple enough. He left his gold watch, two sets of sterling silver cuff links, an onyx ring, and his rosewood jewel case to Rosalind Murray, his sister-in-law. All of his clothing is to be sold and the proceeds used to pay for a memorial plaque at St. Stephen's Church in Holcomb Street." Runyon put down the paper, took off his spectacles, and looked at the two policemen. "Is there anything else I can help you with?"

Witherspoon stared at him incredulously. "Is that it? I don't understand. Wasn't he a rich man?"

"As long as he was alive, he was quite well-off," Runyon replied. "But the house belongs to his late wife's family and will now go to Mrs. Murray; he didn't own any other property; and the only company he ever owned stock in went bankrupt twenty years ago."

"What do you mean, as long as he was alive?" Witherspoon asked.

"As long as Mr. Whitfield was alive, he collected an annual dividend from an annuity that was established many years ago."

"What happens to his share of the annuity, then?" Barnes asked. "Who inherits that?"

"No one." Runyon smiled ruefully. "His share of the dividend becomes part of the annuity capital."

"How long ago was this annuity established?" Witherspoon was beginning to understand.

"When Mr. Whitfield was born," Runyon admitted. "In those days, it was referred to as a tontine. There were ten infants on the original charter. Their families each put in ten thousand pounds, and the money was invested—very wisely I might add. Each child, as he grew, was entitled to one-tenth of the total dividend share. Over the years the investment has grown substantially, and the dividends have increased accordingly."

"So as the shareholders died off, the dividends got bigger and bigger," Barnes muttered.

"That is correct," Runyon said.

"But tontines are illegal," Witherspoon sputtered.

"As well they should be." Runyon nodded in agreement. "There hasn't been a tontine established in over fifty years. But this one was established well before that time."

"We heard that Mr. Whitfield recently sent for you," Barnes added. "He was going to change his will. But why would he bother if all he had to leave was a few bits of jewelry?"

"He wanted the jewelry to go to—" Runyon broke off, looked down at the file, and pushed aside the top page. He picked up the one underneath it. "A woman named Eliza Graham. He said they were engaged."

CHAPTER 9

"Good afternoon, madam. We're so pleased you could join us." With a broad smile, Hatchet greeted the last one to appear at their afternoon meeting. He'd been the first to arrive.

Luty stopped just inside the doorway and stared at him. Her eyes narrowed as she took in his bright expression and barely controlled exuberance. He was fairly bouncing in his seat. "You're grinnin' like the cat that got the cream. You found out somethin' important, didn't ya?" She continued across the room, her skirts rustling as she headed for her usual place at the table.

"Everything we learn is important, madam. This is a group effort, so all of our contributions are essential to solving the case. However, I will admit that I've had some modest success today," he replied. He got to his feet and pulled out her chair.

"Humph," Luty snorted as she flopped into her seat. "Then you have to go last. That's only fair, seein' as how my contributions to catchin' this killer ain't amounted to so much as a hill of beans."

"You mustn't think that, Luty," Mrs. Jeffries said quickly. "You always do your share. You've given us lots of facts we couldn't have gotten without you. You know as well as I do that we never learn until the very end what bit of knowledge led us to solve the case."

Luty smiled wanly. "That's nice of ya to say, but some days it's discouragin'. Tryin' to get people to talk today was like pullin' hens' teeth."

Hatchet stared at her sympathetically. She really did look downhearted. "I take it you weren't able to uncover any details about the distribution of Whitfield's estate?"

"Nope, and I didn't find out much of anything else, either. All in all, it was a right waste of my time. I talked to every lawyer I know and even tried bribin' a couple of clerks, but no one knew anything—or if they did, they weren't tellin'."

"Don't be sad." Wiggins reached over and patted her on the arm. "I 'ad a miserable day, too, and I didn't find out anything, either."

"Some days are simply like that," Mrs. Goodge added. She put a plate of scones onto the table, next to the teapot. "If no one objects, I'd like to go first." She paused briefly and then continued. "Yesterday I heard some gossip about Rosalind Murray. Namely, that the only thing she inherited from her husband when he died were some shares in a tea plantation out in the Far East."

"How come you didn't tell us this at our meeting?" Betsy helped herself to a scone.

"If you'll recall, the inspector came home earlier than

expected." The cook grinned. "And at breakfast this morning, there wasn't time. Besides, as I've already told Mrs. Jeffries, I'm not all that convinced my source was very dependable, so I wasn't sure I should even mention it at all. But today I did talk to someone quite reliable, and I found out some very interesting facts about Hugh Langdon." She repeated what Emma Darnley had told her, taking care to ensure that she didn't forget any of it.

"So he wasn't the sort the man to be concerned about gossip," Mrs. Jeffries said thoughtfully.

"And it appears that he was going to marry Mrs. Graham," the cook added. "So that means she certainly didn't have a reason to want Whitfield dead. He wasn't a danger to her."

"There's another suspect gone," Betsy muttered.

Mrs. Jeffries looked at her sharply. She'd thought she was the only one to realize the case was going badly.

Hatchet leaned forward, his expression puzzled. "Pardon me, but I don't quite see how you reached that conclusion." He looked from the cook to the housekeeper and then to the maid.

It was Mrs. Jeffries who answered. "Our assumption has been that Eliza Graham's motive might have been that she was afraid Whitfield could somehow stop her marriage to Langdon."

"I don't see 'ow," Wiggins said. He looked as confused as Hatchet.

"Don't be daft, lad," Mrs. Goodge said. "Among many women of her class, even a breath of scandal would be enough to stop a man from proposing. But from what we've now learned about Langdon, he wasn't the sort of man to pay any attention to scandalmongering or rumors."

"But we don't know whether Eliza Graham knew that," Betsy said hopefully. "We don't know that she had any idea he'd ever been engaged. Mrs. Goodge found out because, well, that's the sort of thing we do. But that doesn't mean Langdon told her about his previous fiancée." She glanced at Smythe. "Some men are very secretive about their pasts."

"I wasn't tryin' to hide anything from you," Smythe said defensively. "You never asked me any questions about my past. I'd 'ave told ya anything you wanted to know."

"Of course you would have. But I didn't ask." Betsy turned her attention back to the others. "That's what I'm talking about. Maybe she didn't ask Langdon any questions, either, and perhaps he didn't think his past was any of her business. Or if he did tell her, he might not have said a word about his first fiancée being the object of vicious gossip."

Mrs. Goodge crossed her arms over her chest and stared at the maid. "Come now, Betsy, you don't really believe that, do you? How could she not know about his past? It's true that we make a point of finding out what we can about our suspects, but do you honestly think that Eliza Graham, a woman we know had to marry for money and position, wouldn't find out everything she possibly could about Langdon before she let their relationship get to the point where he'd propose marriage?"

"The inspector said she was quite candid about her circumstances," Mrs. Jeffries added. "And she obviously found out enough about Stephen Whitfield's financial situation to decide he wasn't a particularly good prospect. She knew the house didn't belong to him."

"But she didn't stop seeing him," Wiggins said.

"Why should she?" Mrs. Goodge answered. "Mrs. Graham wasn't getting any younger. I've no doubt she considered Whitfield her fallback position in case Langdon didn't come through with a proposal."

"But she knew that Whitfield didn't even own his

house," Smythe said. "Why not just break it off with him altogether?"

"She isn't a fool," Luty said. "Even if she wasn't goin' to marry Whitfield, if it didn't work out with Langdon, Whitfield was her entry into high society."

"Do women really think like that?" Wiggins looked very disturbed. "That sounds right cold'earted."

"She had no other choice," Betsy replied. "It's not as if someone of her class could go out and find work. I suppose that you're all right, though: Mrs. Graham must have known something about his past, and that means she probably knew about his previous engagement." She broke off and grinned at Smythe. "Maybe you and I should have a nice long natter about your past."

Relieved that she could make light of the matter, he laughed. "As soon as this case is solved, you can ask me anything you want."

"Whatever you can say about Mrs. Graham, she didn't try to 'ide what she wanted with her gentlemen," Wiggins said. "She told the inspector she 'ad to marry for money."

"That's true," Betsy murmured. "And if we could find out so easily about Hugh Langdon's past, so could she. It wasn't a secret."

"I expect Eliza Graham knows everything there is to know about the feller," Luty added. "Includin' how much he's worth and whether or not he's got any relatives."

"Were you able to find out anything else?" Mrs. Jeffries asked the cook. She wanted to move the meeting onward, away from any potentially disastrous discussions of what Smythe might or might not have told Betsy about his past. The girl had smiled at her fiancé, but Mrs. Jeffries had seen a flash of pain in her eyes when she said the two of them should have a "nice long natter" about his past.

Mrs. Goodge shook her head. "Not really. Emma spent the rest of our time together talking about her grandchildren. She has six of them, and to hear her tell it, they're all perfect little angels."

"Who would like to go next?" Mrs. Jeffries looked around the table.

"I'll have a go," Betsy offered. "I didn't find out all that much, but I was able to have a cup of tea with a maid from the Farringdon house." She told them about her meeting with Rachel Webster. She paused occasionally in her recitation, casting her mind back to the café and to Rachel's face as she spoke. It was a trick Betsy used to help herself recall information. When she was finished, she was thirsty, so she picked up her cup and took a long sip of tea.

"So Basil Farringdon and his wife are quite devoted to one another," Mrs. Jeffries muttered.

"They must be," Luty said. "Most people are scared of rough water, especially if you ain't a strong swimmer."

"But the important thing you found out is that Maria Farringdon really did hate Whitfield," Mrs. Goodge said. "We ought to have a closer look at her. She's a strange one, she is. Pourin' good port down the sink when she could have sent it into the kitchen to use for cooking, collecting wine bottles . . ."

"She wanted the labels," Betsy said quickly. "Rachel told me that as well. I almost forgot. She mentioned it as we were leaving. She said that one of her responsibilities at the house was steaming the labels off the empty bottles."

"What did she want the labels for?" Wiggins asked.

"Mrs. Farringdon put them in a big book and then made notes at the bottom of the page on what sort of food was served with that particular wine. Rachel said it was hard to get the labels to come off, so they used a teakettle to steam them. But she said that most of the time they ripped in half or fell to bits."

"Why would anyone want wine labels?" Smythe asked. "I could understand wantin' the bottles. You could use them for brewin' peach brandy or summer wine."

"She got the bottles from social events that she'd attended with her husband. Everyone said she worked hard to be a credit to him, and if you'll recall, Mrs. Farringdon didn't grow up knowing anything about wine. I think it was very clever of her to use the labels to figure out the right food to serve with the right wine when she had her own dinner parties," Betsy explained.

"I still think she's a strange one," Mrs. Goodge said. "Mind you, she's not as odd as Henry Becker. He's another one we need to keep our eye on."

"That's all I heard today," Betsy finished.

"I'll go next," Smythe volunteered. "It seems we might be wrong about Rosalind Murray bein' a woman scorned. Accordin' to my source, she was relieved that Whitfield turned his attentions to Mrs. Graham. She had plans of her own and was glad to get him off her 'ands, so to speak."

"But she had a row with him over his engagement," Mrs. Jeffries said. "And when she was telling the inspector about his plans to go to Italy with her, the inspector was sure she seemed a very bitter person."

"But was the argument really over his engagement, or was it over somethin' else? All we know for sure is that the two of them 'ad a right old dustup, but we don't really know what it was about. As for her bein' bitter, lots of people get soured on life. Besides, my source was repeatin' Rosalind Murray's own thoughts and words. She keeps a diary."

"And your source read this diary?" Mrs. Jeffries asked.

"She did. The girl was a real little slyboots, and she

wanted to get a bit of her own back." Smythe told them what details he could without revealing how he'd obtained the information.

"That means that as far back as September, she was makin' plans of her own," Luty said speculatively. " 'Course, it could be that one of them plans was killin' Whitfield—that's one way of gettin' rid of him."

"But why wait until now?" Betsy asked reasonably. "She's known for ten years that the house was hers when he died. Why wait until now to kill him? The inspector told Mrs. Jeffries that Mrs. Murray seemed sure Whitfield was going to marry Mrs. Graham. That means she *was* finally getting rid of him."

"Maybe she was scared he was going to toss her into the street," Wiggins suggested helpfully. "It was his 'ouse as long as he lived, right?"

"He couldn't toss her out," the cook replied. "Whitfield's situation is very common. I worked in two places where the same thing happened. A man ends up living in the wife's family home. Usually he's given a lifetime right of residency, but that's all. He has no control over whether other family members can live in the house as well. Believe me, his wife's family will have made sure of that."

"I've no idea what any of this might mean," Mrs. Jeffries murmured. She had a horrid feeling that she was deluding herself. Though she hadn't had time to think about all of this as thoroughly as she'd like, so far it seemed they were losing motives left and right. "But it's getting late, and we've yet to hear from Hatchet." She looked at the coachman. "Were you finished?"

"I was. Let Hatchet 'ave his turn now." Smythe grinned wickedly. "He's been very patient, even though it's obvious he's bustin' to talk."

"I am indeed quite eager to say my piece." Hatchet took a deep breath and paused dramatically, making sure that he had everyone's undivided attention. "I found out the details about Whitfield's estate." Without mentioning names, he told them everything he'd learned from his old friend Emery Richards.

He took his time in the telling, explaining the complicated nature of the tontine as best he could. When he finished, he leaned back in his seat and waited for the inevitable questions and comments.

"A tontine." Mrs. Jeffries shook her head. "No wonder we had so much trouble finding out about the estate."

"You can bet yer bottom dollar that none of his fancy lawyers talked much about it," Luty added indignantly. "They'd not like those details bein' bandied about, now, would they?"

"But this one was started before the government outlawed 'em,' Wiggins said. "So why was it so 'ard for us to find out? Annuities are legal, and that's what it is now."

"The legal issues aside," Hatchet began, "I expect it was kept quiet because none of them wished to be associated with an institution that essentially gives those involved a reason to be delighted at the death of one of their peers. There's something quite disgusting about the entire idea."

"Their income went up every time one of them died?" Wiggins wanted to make sure he understood the facts. "So tontines were outlawed. But did people really kill each other so they'd be the sole survivor?"

Mrs. Goodge stared at the footman in disbelief. "Knowing what we do about murder, how can you even ask that? Of course people really murdered one another, and for all we know, that may end up being the motive in this case."

"That's right," Hatchet replied. "As I said, there were

originally ten members. Three didn't survive childhood, which left seven. Over the years, the others have died off, and now with Whitfield gone, there's only two left."

"Henry Becker and Basil Farringdon," Mrs. Jeffries said.

"And neither of them need the money enough to kill for it," Smythe muttered. "Becker's wealthy, and Farringdon's wife has plenty enough for both of them.'

"Maybe Basil Farringdon was tired of depending on his wife," Betsy speculated. "Maybe he wanted a bit of his own."

Mrs. Jeffries shook her head. "I don't think so, Betsy. He jumped into a rough sea to save her life. If he wanted money of his own, he could have just let her drown."

Inspector Witherspoon was late getting home that evening. Mrs. Jeffries met him at the front door. "Gracious, sir, we were beginning to worry," she said as she reached for his bowler hat.

"I stayed to finish up some reports," he said. He slipped off his overcoat and handed that to her as well. "And there was a dreadful traffic jam just this side of the park."

She hung up his things and looked at him. He appeared very depressed. His face was paler than usual, there were dark circles forming under his eyes, and tufts of his hair were standing straight up. "Are you alright, sir?"

"I'm just tired," he admitted. "I do hope Mrs. Goodge hasn't gone to too much trouble over my dinner. I'm not really hungry."

"It's a simple grill, sir. Pork chops and potatoes. Stewed apples, too." She watched him carefully as she spoke, hoping that he wasn't coming down with that awful flu that was going around. "Shall I bring it up to the dining room?"

"Not yet. I think I'd like a sherry first. Do come along

and join me." He led the way down the hall and into the drawing room. Mrs. Jeffries hurried past him and went to the cabinet. He sat down while she poured both of them a glass of sherry.

"Now, sir, tell me what's wrong," she ordered as she handed him his glass.

"It's this case, Mrs. Jeffries." He sighed heavily, sank back into the chair, and took a sip of sherry. "I've no idea what to do next."

"Is that all that's bothering you, sir?" she asked, striving to sound as unconcerned as possible. "I was worried you were coming down with something. There's a terrible flu going around."

"Mrs. Jeffries, I am deadly serious. I think this is going to be the case that I will not be able to resolve. I've no idea who killed Stephen Whitfield, and the more that I learn, the more muddled I get."

As she felt exactly the same way, it was rather difficult for her to dredge up the right words to bolster his confidence. "But that's the way you always feel just before you find the solution, sir," she replied. She hoped the words didn't sound as false to his ears as they did to hers. "It's always the darkest just before the dawn," she continued, "and I've no doubt whatsoever that your inner eye has already seen that one perfect clue that will lead you to the killer."

"Inner eye," he repeated. "I thought you always told me I had an inner voice."

"It's the same thing, sir," she said cheerfully. "It's that part of your mind that takes in the facts, observes the suspects, and then points you in the right direction. I believe some people call the phenomenon 'intuition.' It is a process that hasn't failed you yet, sir, and you must have faith that it won't let you down this time."

"I do hope you're right," he replied earnestly. But he didn't look convinced.

"Did you find out anything useful today, sir?" She sat down on the settee and took a sip from her own glass. In truth, she was also dispirited. Time was marching onward, and she had no idea who had killed Whitfield.

Witherspoon told her about his day. She heard every detail of the meeting with Hugh Langdon, with the chief inspector, and with Whitfield's solicitor. She listened carefully, asked questions at appropriate intervals, and made occasional comments. When he told her about the tontine, she contrived to look surprised. She even managed to hold her tongue when he described his meeting with Inspector Nivens.

The conversation continued when he went into the dining room for his dinner. By the time he'd finished his stewed apples, he was in a much better frame of mind. "I do feel better." He put his serviette on the table and pushed his empty saucer to one side. "A thorough discussion of the facts of the matter always seems to help so very much."

"Perhaps all you needed was a good meal, sir," she murmured. Her own frame of mind hadn't improved one whit.

"Mind you, if I don't make some headway within the next few days, I may ask the chief inspector to turn this case over to someone else," he commented. A yawn escaped him, and he clamped his hand over his mouth. "Good gracious, where did that come from? I must be more tired than I thought." He pushed back the chair and got to his feet.

Alarmed, Mrs. Jeffries leapt up as well. "You're not serious, sir, are you? Who could possibly take over the case? You're the best detective in the Metropolitan Police Force."

"That's very kind of you, Mrs. Jeffries." He smiled wanly. "But despite my past successes, if I can't solve this one, I may not have any choice."

"Surely the chief isn't going to listen to anything Inspector Nivens has to say," she replied.

"Nivens has many friends in the Home Office," Witherspoon said. "But even so, I don't think Chief Inspector Barrows would take me off the case just because of Nivens' machinations. But he can resist only so much pressure to get the wretched thing solved, and if I can't do it, he'll have no choice but to bring in someone else. I'm not going to let it get that far—if I don't make any real progress in the next few days, I'm going to ask that it be assigned to someone else."

"But, sir, that's simply not right. You must give yourself enough time . . ."

"I've had time," he interrupted. "And frankly, I'm no closer to a solution now than I ever was. But I'm dreadfully tired, Mrs. Jeffries. I really must retire. Can you ask Wiggins to take Fred for his walk?"

She knew when to stop. "Certainly, sir. Sleep well."

Later that night, when everyone in the household had gone to their beds, Mrs. Jeffries crept down to the kitchen. She put her lamp on the kitchen table and got a tin of silver polish and two cleaning rags from the bin under the sink. She put her supplies on the table, spread out yesterday's *Times*, and put the polish on top of the pages. Going to the pine sideboard, she knelt down and pulled open the bottom drawer.

Inside were three flat silver trays, each of them wrapped in soft gray flannel drawstring jackets. She grabbed the trays and heaved them out, groaning a little as she felt the strain on her knees. Putting the stack on the table next to the open newspaper, she slipped the first tray out of its jacket and positioned it next to the tin of polish. Then she sat down and picked up a rag.

Mrs. Jeffries knew she'd not be able to sleep, so she hadn't even bothered to try. She'd decided to clean the trays for two very good reasons. Firstly, she hoped a dull, repetitious task would help her mind come up with some idea of how to solve this case; and secondly, Christmas would be here in a few days, and they needed the trays cleaned.

As she went about her task, she tried not to dwell on any details of the case. She wanted her thoughts to wander freely, moving haphazardly from one fact or bit of information to the next. But try as she might, she couldn't stop herself from thinking.

She smeared a gob of polish over the top of the tray and reached for the other cloth. Rosalind Murray had been the strongest suspect, and now it looked as if she'd no motive at all. But there was still the matter of the house. With Whitfield dead, Mrs. Murray could finally get control of it. A house in that neighborhood and of that size was worth a huge amount of money. Perhaps Mrs. Murray's plans had included selling the place and going off on her own. Yes, that made sense, especially if she was afraid that a new, relatively young wife might spur Whitfield on to a long and vigorous life.

Mrs. Jeffries rubbed the cloth along the top of the tray in long, even strokes. But would getting her hands on the family home be enough of a motive for Rosalind Murray? she wondered. That was the question.

"What on earth are you doing?" Mrs. Goodge asked softly.

Startled, Mrs. Jeffries dropped the cloth. "Gracious, Mrs. Goodge, you gave me a fright. I couldn't sleep, so I thought I'd get started on the silver. We do like using it for Christmas."

Mrs. Goodge came into the kitchen. Samson trailed at

her heels. She wore a long gray wool robe and a pair of red carpet slippers. "You can't sleep, can you? The case is keeping you awake."

"No, I can't. I don't mind telling you that this one has got me baffled. What's more, I think the inspector is ready to hand it off to someone else," Mrs. Jeffries said. It felt good to confide in someone.

"We'll not let that happen." The cook slid into the seat next to Mrs. Jeffries, pushed her chair back, and then patted her lap. Samson jumped up, glared at Mrs. Jeffries, then curled into a ball and began to purr.

Mrs. Jeffries picked up the polishing cloth and continued her task. "I'm not sure we can stop it. Every time we have a meeting, I learn something that convinces me that no one had a motive for actually wanting the man dead."

"Nonsense." Mrs. Goodge stroked Samson's broad back. "You're only saying that because it's late at night and you're tired. You'll feel differently in the morning."

"No, I won't. We're running out of motives, Mrs. Goodge. After what we heard about Hugh Langdon, you must see that Eliza Graham didn't have a motive. He wouldn't have given a toss about gossip about her, and he wasn't even willing to listen to Whirfield when he tried to discuss her."

"Perhaps she wasn't as sure of him as we think," Mrs. Goodge said. "Perhaps Eliza Graham wasn't . . . Oh, you're right. She's been seeing the man socially for months now, so she must have some idea of his character. Alright, I'll admit that it appears as if she no longer has a motive, but we've plenty of others. I still think that Rosalind Murray might have done it. Despite what plans she may or may not have had, she might have hated him enough to kill him."

"And risk being hung instead of getting on with her

life?" Mrs. Jeffries put the rag to one side. "I don't think that's likely."

"What about Henry Becker? There's madness in his family. He might have done it. Perhaps he was tired of always losing at whist. That might be a sufficient motive for an insane person."

"But we don't know that he is insane. True, there's a bit of lunacy in his family, but I expect if you looked hard enough at many families, you'd find evidence of strange or violent behavior. Becker had no motive. We've no evidence that he hated Whitfield, and he certainly doesn't need the money from the tontine."

"Basil Farringdon doesn't seem to need the money, either," Mrs. Goodge murmured, "and they are the only two left in the tontine."

"Which means we can rule that out as a motive." Mrs. Jeffries picked up the flannel jacket and slipped the tray inside.

The cook reached across and pulled the drawstring tight. "You've still got Maria Farringdon as a suspect. She did hate Whitfield."

"But did she hate him enough to kill him?" Mrs. Jeffries shook her head. "I don't think so. Nor do I think that Hugh Langdon had a motive for murdering him, nor did any of Whitfield's servants, either. The killer went to a great deal of trouble to commit this murder."

"But all they had to do was chuck a few leaves into an open bottle of wine," Mrs. Goodge retorted. "That doesn't seem like much effort."

"That part wasn't. But the actual planning of the murder must have been thought out well in advance. This is the middle of winter, so they would have had to plan it months ago, when foxglove was abundant."

"It's not the sort of plant that people bother to grow in greenhouses," Mrs. Goodge agreed.

"Whoever did it must have picked the leaves, dried them, and stored them somewhere for months before they decided to act." She put the lid back on the tin of polish and slapped it into place. There was no point in trying to do the other trays. She'd not be able to concentrate, and she had a feeling that as long as she was in the kitchen, the cook would feel compelled to keep her company. Mrs. Goodge needed her rest. "I just don't see any of our suspects having a motive strong enough to go to all that trouble."

"Someone did," the cook reminded her softly.

"I've thought and thought and thought about everything we've learned," Mrs. Jeffries said. She looked at the cook. "Frankly, I don't see how any living person could have committed this murder."

The next morning, Mrs. Jeffries' spirits hadn't brightened any, but she went to great pains to keep her thoughts from the others. They were all so eager to be out and about—on the hunt, so to speak.

"I thought I'd 'ave a go at talkin' to a servant," Wiggins said as he tucked into a fried egg.

"If you're goin' to the Whitfield house, be careful," Mrs. Goodge warned. "I overheard the inspector mentionin' to Constable Barnes that they were goin' to go there this mornin'."

"Maybe I'll try the Farringdon house or Henry Becker's servants," Wiggins muttered.

"Where are you going, Betsy?" Smythe asked.

Betsy swallowed the bite of toast she'd popped into her mouth. "I haven't been to Becker's neighborhood, either. I thought I might talk to those local shopkeepers."

"What are you goin' to be doin' today, Mrs. Jeffries?" Wiggins asked.

"I thought I'd give the drawing room a good clean," she replied. She caught the cook's eye and nodded almost imperceptibly, letting her know that though she was ready to give up, she wasn't going to say anything to discourage the others. "I find that doing boring, repetitive tasks helps me to think things through, and we're at the point in this investigation where a good think is in order."

But despite everyone's best efforts when they met for their meeting that afternoon, none of them had anything new to report. It was the same the next day and the day after. Wiggins talked to half a dozen housemaids, footmen, and tweenies. He learned nothing. Betsy had chatted up every grocer's clerk, fishmonger, and baker in three different neighborhoods, with equally dismal results, and Smythe had spent so much time in pubs that he declared the smell of beer actually made him half-sick.

Nor had Inspector Witherspoon done any better. He'd questioned the dinner party guests and the Whitfield servants a second time, but none of them had anything to add to their original statements.

But at the brief morning meeting on the fourth day, there was a glimmer of hope. "I know we seem to be hittin' a dry spell, but my friend Hilda Ryker is back in town," Luty announced. "She loves to gossip and always knows what's what in London. I know I'll have something for ya by this afternoon; I just know it."

"I certainly hope so, madam," Hatchet replied. "We've none of us found out anything these past few days, and Christmas is almost upon us."

"That's not true," Mrs. Goodge corrected. "We did find out that Mrs. Murray's late husband did leave her something valuable. That tea plantation he left her shares in has done very well the last few years."

Inspector Witherspoon had found out that bit of information when he'd interviewed Rosalind Murray for the second time. She'd been quite candid about her plans. She was selling everything, including the house, and moving to Canada to start a new life.

"Let's hope you're very successful today," Mrs. Jeffries said to Luty. "And I know the rest of you will find out lots of useful things as well."

Mrs. Goodge waited till everyone had left, and then she turned to the housekeeper. "Are you going to tell them about the inspector, about what he wants to do?"

"I think I should, don't you?"

"Yes. They'll be disappointed, but they'll get over it." She sighed heavily. "Mind you, I do hate the idea of him giving up on a case. Are you sure he was serious?"

"He was deadly serious," Mrs. Jeffries replied. "When I was serving him his breakfast this morning, he made it quite clear that unless he finds another avenue to investigate, he's going to ask Chief Inspector Barrows to give the case to someone else."

"Did he say when he planned on doing this?" the cook asked. She didn't like the idea of quitting, either. But unless they had a miracle, she didn't see that there was much hope.

"The day after tomorrow."

"That's Christmas Eve."

Mrs. Jeffries nodded. "Let's hope that someone comes up with something useful. Otherwise we'll have failed."

"Of course I'm acquainted with Maria Farringdon." Hilda Ryker said to Luty. "She's a very nice woman, much smarter than her husband, but that's only to be expected. Her family actually worked for what they've acquired. Basil Farringdon's family, on the other hand, has managed to fritter away just about everything they ever had, and believe me, they had plenty. The Farringdons once owned a good share of Norfolk. His mother was a cousin to the duke."

"You sure know a lot about 'em," Luty commented. She was sitting in the drawing room of Hilda Ryker's elegant town house on Ridley Square. Hilda and her husband, Neville Ryker, were old friends of Luty's.

When the Rykers weren't traveling, Hilda spent her whole life immersed in the London social whirl. If there was anything worth knowing about any of the guests who'd been at Whitfield's dinner party on the night of the murder, she'd be the person to ask. Luty was determined to have something for their afternoon meeting. Mrs. Jeffries was doing her best to keep everyone's spirits up, but they were all getting discouraged.

"Of course I do." Hilda's long face creased in a grin. "Gossip is one of my favorite activities. I know we're never supposed to admit such a thing, but it's true nonetheless. If you're not interested in other people, you might as well be dead; that's what I always say." She cocked her head to one side and stared at Luty speculatively. "Why are you so interested in the Farringdons? They can't possibly be friends of yours. He's a bore, and she's far too conventional to appreciate you."

Luty wasn't sure whether she was being complimented or insulted, but she found the comment funny nonetheless. She laughed. "I'm not. I just happened to overhear that they were at the dinner party where that Whitfield fellow got murdered. I was just curious; that's all."

"You're always curious about murder." Hilda poured

another cup of tea from the silver pot on the trolley next to her chair.

Luty held her breath. She hadn't expected Hilda to remember that Luty had come around once before, asking questions about the murder of Harrison Nye, one of their previous cases. She started to mutter something inane, but before she could get the words out, Hilda continued talking.

"I expect it's because you're friends with that police inspector. I find murder fascinating as well, certainly far more exciting than conventional gossip." Hilda reached for the sugar tongs and delicately placed a lump into her tea. "Would you care for another cup?"

"No, thanks. I'm not finished with this one yet."

"But as to Maria Farringdon, I do hope she's not the murderer." Hilda said. "Despite her being a stickler for convention, I quite like her. She's very social, so I see her quite frequently. We always have a nice chat when we run into one another. But, come to think of it, I haven't seen her since Lady Emmerson's party last September. Of course Neville and I have been gone quite a bit since then. Neville does so love to travel, but frankly, I always miss London when we're gone. Foreigners, especially the French, can be so difficult."

"You said she's smart." Luty didn't want Hilda bringing up her husband. Neville Ryker was Hilda's favorite subject, and once his name was uttered, getting her to talk about anything else was almost impossible.

"She is," Hilda replied. "Before she married Basil Farringdon, she helped run her family's business."

Luty wasn't sure how much to press, but on the other hand she didn't want the woman shutting up, either. Right now she needed all the information she could get. She started to ask another question, but Hilda hadn't finished.

"And she's observant as well . . ." Hilda's voice trailed off and her eyes widened. "Oh my goodness, I've just realized something. It was Stephen Whitfield that Maria was talking about when she told me about the cheese incident. Do you think I ought to mention it to your inspector friend? Oh dear, I do hope not. Neville wouldn't like me actually talking to a policeman, even one as respectable as your Inspector Witherspoon."

"Why don't you tell me about this here . . . er . . . uh . . . cheese incident? If it's something that ought to be passed on, I'll mention it to him," Luty suggested. She couldn't believe her good fortune. Maybe their luck was changing. "That way, you won't go gettin' Neville upset, but you'll have done your part in seein' that justice is served."

Hilda looked doubtful. "It probably means nothing. I'd have never thought of it if we'd not started talking about Maria Farringdon."

"Well, what was it?" Luty urged. "Go ahead—you can tell me."

"I've only just realized it was Stephen Whitfield that Maria was staring at as she was telling me about it. I knew who he was, of course. Despite his age, and his being a widower, he was considered quite an eligible catch."

"Go on," Luty pressed. "Tell me what happened." She glanced at the ornate baroque clock on the mantelpiece and saw that it was twenty till four. If she could ever get this woman talking sense, she just might make it back to Upper Edmonton Gardens before the meeting ended. "I'm a good listener."

"I feel so silly. It was such a minor incident, and I think I've made too much of it." Hilda smiled weakly.

"Tell me anyway," Luty ordered. She was tired of pussy-footing around.

"All right, if you insist. As I said, it was in September. Neville and I were getting ready to leave. It had been quite a tedious party, really. Not at all amusing. Neville sent for our footman and then went off to get my wrap. Suddenly Maria Farringdon came up and stood next to me. I'd not seen her that evening, so we started to chat—as I said, she's an interesting woman. We both saw Stephen Whitfield across the room. He was speaking to our hostess, and his expression was, well, very earnest if you know what I mean."

Luty wasn't certain she understood, but she didn't want to interrupt.

"He must have been quite rude to Mrs. Farringdon that day," Hilda continued thoughtfully. "She was glaring at him, and then she said, 'He's trying to recover from having made a fool of himself.' "

"You actually heard her say those words?" Luty confirmed.

"Indeed I did." Hilda nodded. "I asked her what she meant, and she turned, looked at me, and laughed. Then she said, 'He might find it amusing to make fun of my champagne cups, but the man obviously can't taste a thing. I just overheard him commending Lady Emmerson on the lovely Stilton she'd had served. Stupid fool. Lady Emmerson won't forgive that faux pas for a good long while.' I don't like cheese, so I had no idea what she was going on about, and I asked her what she meant. She laughed again and said that it hadn't been a Stilton that was served but a Wensleydale. Apparently our hostess had sent all the way to Somerset for the Wensleydale and was annoyed that it wasn't fully appreciated."

Luty struggled to keep from showing her disappointment. This gossip didn't help one whit! They already knew

that Maria Farringdon disliked Whitfield. Blast—this had
been Luty's last hope. She had nothing to take back to the
others.

She was beginning to think they were never going to
solve this case.

CHAPTER 10

"Despite all my big talk this mornin', I ain't found out one thing that's goin' to help us much," Luty admitted. She watched the faces of the others around the table as she described her meeting with Hilda Ryker. Every one of them looked as disappointed as Luty felt. When she'd finished, she sat back, folded her hands in her lap, and shrugged. "Sorry I wasn't able to learn anything we didn't already know about Maria Farringdon."

"You did your best, and you mustn't feel badly. Perhaps Wiggins has found out something useful." Mrs. Jeffries looked at him hopefully.

But he shook his head. "I don't think so. Matter of fact, what I did 'ear makes me 'ope the lady isn't the killer. Mrs. Farringdon is a bit of a soft'earted one. She hired a scullery maid back who'd gone off and 'ad a baby. The baby died, and as the girl 'ad no husband, Mrs. Farringdon took pity on her and let her come back to work."

"That would never have happened in my day," Mrs. Goodge murmured. "Back then, if a girl got in trouble, she was let go and it was her hard luck. Thank goodness times have changed for the better." Not only had times changed, but since she'd become a member of this household, the cook's attitudes had changed as well.

Mrs. Jeffries agreed with the sentiment but realized they had now lost their last suspect. She'd been clinging to the belief that perhaps Maria Farringdon's hatred of Whitfield was so fierce that it was the motive for the murder. "Mrs. Farringdon obviously isn't a cruel, callous woman, or she'd have never hired the girl back."

"Which means she probably isn't mean enough to kill Whitfield over a few insults about her food or her background," Smythe said.

"I agree. But that puts us very much at a loss here," Mrs. Jeffries said morosely.

"Because we're now completely out of any genuine suspects," Hatchet said glumly.

"What about Henry Becker?" Wiggins wasn't ready to give up yet. "With Whitfield dead, he'll get a bigger dividend now."

"He's rich as sin already," Luty reminded him. "He can't spend what he's got now, and he might be strange, but we've never heard of him actin' nasty or violent to anyone."

Mrs. Jeffries started to speak and then thought better of it. She looked down at the tabletop. Perhaps she should wait? Perhaps today the inspector would find the clue that pointed them in the right direction. She glanced up and caught Mrs. Goodge looking at her.

The cook's features hardened a fraction. "I think Mrs. Jeffries has something to tell us," she prompted.

Mrs. Jeffries was aware they were all staring at her, waiting for her to say something. She cleared her throat. "I do have something I need to say. You've all realized this case isn't progressing very well at all."

"You don't have any idea who did it?" Wiggins asked plaintively.

"No, I'm afraid I don't."

"Are you sure?" He couldn't quite believe it.

"I'm positive," she replied. "Inspector Witherspoon is at as much of an impasse in the case as we are. A few days ago he told me that if he didn't make progress soon, he was going to ask Chief Inspector Barrows to assign another officer to it."

They all started talking at once.

"That's ridiculous," Hatchet snapped. "Surely the chief inspector will give him more time."

"Cor blimey, there's plenty of time left to get it right," Wiggins complained.

"He's lost his confidence," Mrs. Goodge muttered darkly.

"Oh, no, that's awful. We can't let him give up," Betsy exclaimed.

Mrs. Jeffries held up her hand for silence. "I appreciate and agree with all your sentiments. But unfortunately I don't think he's going to be dissuaded from this course of action. Unless we can come up with more evidence by tomorrow, he's going to see the chief."

They discussed the matter at great length but could come up with no way of stopping the inspector from asking to be taken off the case. Nor did any of them have a clue as to who might have killed Whitfield. Finally they lapsed into silence, which was broken by the clock striking the hour.

"It's five o'clock, madam," Hatchet said to Luty. "We must get home so you'll have time for a short rest before dinner. Lionel Burston and Lady Fenleigh are coming at eight."

"Oh, nells bells, I'd forgotten all about that stupid dinner," Luty muttered as she got to her feet. She looked at Mrs. Jeffries, her eyes hopeful. "Should we be here at our usual time tomorrow?"

Mrs. Jeffries wasn't sure there was anything left for any of them to do. Yet just as she decided to tell them it was no use, she felt a tug at the back of her mind. It was only a wisp of an idea, and it was gone before she could grab it long enough to make sense of anything; but nonetheless it was real, it was there, she felt it. For the first time in this case, her own "inner eye" was opening. Or perhaps she was simply grasping at straws. "Yes, please. We're not going to give up just yet. We've all day tomorrow to continue the hunt."

"Good." Luty beamed approvingly, and even Hatchet seemed satisfied as he helped her with her coat.

As soon as the two of them had gone, Mrs. Goodge went to her room to put on a clean apron, Wiggins took Fred for a short walk, and Mrs. Jeffries went upstairs to finish polishing the furniture in the inspector's study.

Betsy was still at the table, staring straight ahead, her eyes unfocused and her shoulders relaxed. Smythe wasn't sure this was the best time to broach the subject, but as it was the first time he'd been alone with her in days, he wasn't going to waste the opportunity. "Can I talk to you?"

Betsy looked at him. "Someone's bound to come back in a minute or two, so you'd better be quick about it."

"Are we still engaged?" he blurted. That was what he

needed to know; that was what had been haunting him since he'd returned. "You said you still loved me, but do you still want to marry me?"

She said nothing for a moment, just stared at him with an expression he couldn't read. Finally she said, "Do you still want to marry me?"

"Of course I do," he cried. "I want to marry you more than anything. You've got to tell me. Not knowin' is tearin' me apart. Are we still goin' to be married?"

As Betsy had predicted, they heard footsteps coming toward the kitchen. "Yes, we're still engaged," she hissed as she got up and began to clear the table. "And if it's all the same to you, we'll keep this to ourselves until after this case is solved."

"It might never be solved." He got up and reached for the nearest dirty plates.

"Then we'll talk about it after Christmas," she replied. She picked up the sugar bowl and the jam pot and walked to the counter.

"Boxing Day, then. We'll make our plans on the Feast of St. Stephen." He followed after her.

"Feast of St. Stephen," Mrs. Goodge repeated as she came into the room. "I've not heard Boxing Day called that in years."

"It was on the notice board outside the church." Smythe ignored Betsy's warning look, put the plates down, grabbed her by the shoulders, and enveloped her in a hug. "We'll sort everything out then."

Mrs. Goodge beamed at them.

Upstairs, Mrs. Jeffries poured a dab of Adam's Furniture Polish onto her rag and rubbed it on the top of the inspector's desk. She moved her hand in a long circular motion, applying the polish evenly over the wood surface as her thoughts began to float free. What was it that had pushed at her earlier? It was an idea or a thought that had bubbled into awareness while they were discussing the case. She cast her mind back to the moment she'd felt the tiny nudge, it had been when . . . when . . . She shook her head. She couldn't recall what was being said when it had happened. Drat.

She finished all the furniture in the study and had moved on to the drawing room when she heard the inspector coming up the front steps. Putting the rag down, she hurried out into the hall, arriving just as Witherspoon stepped inside.

He didn't look good. His face was paler than usual, his glasses had slid completely down his nose, and his bowler was askew. "Good evening, Mrs. Jeffries," he said politely. He took off his hat and hung it on the coat tree, then began pulling off his gloves.

"Good evening, sir," she replied. "Have you made any progress today?"

He tucked his gloves in his overcoat pocket, shrugged it off, and handed it to her. "Not really. I spent the day going over all the statements and seeing if there is something I might have missed. But honestly, I didn't see anything."

"Don't give up, sir. I'm sure you'll find the solution soon," she said. She hung up his coat. "Are you still going to ask the chief to assign it to someone else?"

"I must. Perhaps a fresh approach is what's needed," he said. "But I did have one bright moment this afternoon. I ran into Lady Cannonberry on Holland Park Road. She's invited me to come early on Christmas day—you know, before the others arrive."

The inspector was having Christmas dinner with Ruth Cannonberry and some of her relations. She was their neighbor and his special friend.

"That's very nice, sir. I'm sure you'll have a lovely time," Mrs. Jeffries replied. "Would you like a sherry before your dinner?"

"Not tonight, Mrs. Jeffries. I'll have my meal and then I think I'll retire for the evening. I don't like to complain, but reading all those statements and going over the postmortem report has given me a dreadful headache."

In the darkness of her room, Mrs. Jeffries lay in bed and stared at the ceiling. She couldn't sleep. Fragments of conversation and bits of gossip from their many meetings played about in her head, jostling for position and trying to get her attention. She didn't want to delude herself, but she was sure her own inner voice was trying to tell her something, trying to show her something that was right under her nose.

Mrs. Jeffries recalled a maid's words that Wiggins had repeated. *"He'd got one of them wine corkers from Germany. But he did make a terrible mess."* Now why had that sprung into her mind?

She rolled onto her side and let her mind drift where it would. Rosalind Murray had already made plans to sell the house. She wondered what the argument between Mrs. Murray and Whitfield had really been about. If she had truly wanted to be rid of him, then it couldn't have been about his relationship with Mrs. Graham.

She closed her eyes and took a deep breath. Whitfield was planning on taking Eliza Graham to Italy in the spring. But she'd already decided not to marry him. Had he suspected she was going to decline his proposal?

"Now it looks as if I'm going to another funeral come January." Those words popped into her mind. Her eyes flew open and she frowned, trying to remember who'd made this statement.

It was Inspector Witherspoon, and he'd been repeating Henry Becker's words. She'd lavished so much praise on the inspector about his ability to recall conversations and statements, and he now took great pride in repeating things word for word.

She flopped onto her back again and looked up at the ceiling. She heard the *clip-clop* of horses' hooves outside and the rattle of wheels as a hansom trundled past the house. Finally she drifted off into sleep.

"Last year I gave it to my next-door neighbor. But he's dead now, so I was rather stuck with the stuff." Mrs. Jeffries jerked away as those words rang in her ears. She squinted into the night, trying to think where she'd heard them. Then she remembered. Henry Becker. Once again the inspector had repeated Henry Becker's own words to her.

She sat there for a moment, letting the idea that was forming in her mind strengthen and take shape. Ye gods, it was right under her nose.

She tossed the covers to one side and leapt out of bed. Ten minutes later, she was downstairs putting the kettle on to boil as she came up with a plan. By the time she heard Mrs. Goodge's bedroom door open, she knew what had to be done.

"I thought I heard someone moving about in here. What are you doing up so early?" Mrs. Goodge stood at the doorway. She was still in her nightclothes. Samson was at her feet.

"I couldn't sleep. I've been up for ages. I think I know what happened, but I'm not saying a word until I have a few things confirmed."

"Let me put Samson out." The cook continued down the hall.

Mrs. Jeffries went to the doorway and stuck her head out. "Do you know what a foxglove plant looks like?" she asked.

"Of course I know what it looks like. They grow all over the place." Mrs. Goodge unlocked the top bolt on the back door and opened it, letting in a blast of frigid air. Samson gave a plaintive meow, but the cook used her foot to nudge him gently outside. "Go on now. Go out and do your business."

"Would you know what a winter-dead one looked like?"

"I imagine it just looks like a stalk of weed," Mrs. Goodge called over her shoulder as she closed the door.

"That's what I thought as well." Mrs. Jeffries moved to the stairs.

"Where are you going?"

"Up to get Wiggins and Smythe. They'll need to move quickly today."

Mrs. Goodge started back to the kitchen and was midway down the hall when she heard soft thuds against the back door. "Oh, he couldn't have done his business that quickly," she muttered, but she retraced her steps and opened the door. Samson, a sheen of wet on his fur, shot through the back door and raced toward the kitchen.

By the time Mrs. Jeffries returned to the kitchen, the cook was nowhere to be seen, but the kettle was on the boil. She made the tea while she waited for the others. She put the sugar, milk, and jam on the table, then went into the wet larder for a pot of butter. She'd come back and was starting to slice a loaf of bread when Mrs. Goodge appeared. This time she was fully dressed.

"What's all this about, then?" she demanded as she crossed the room to the worktable. "Here, I'll do that." She took the knife from the housekeeper and commandeered the spot in front of the breadboard. "I heard the others coming down the stairs. Young Wiggins makes enough noise to wake the dead. Let's hope he doesn't wake the inspector this early and have him down asking what we're all doing. You finish making the tea."

Wiggins, his hair on end and his shirttail flapping, came in first, followed by a yawning Smythe. Betsy trailed behind the two men.

"Sorry to get everyone up so early, but you must get out and on the hunt." Mrs. Jeffries put the teapot on the table. "Everyone sit down and listen to what I have to say. Please don't ask me any questions, because I could be dead wrong about my theory. But if I'm right, we've lots to do today."

Mrs. Goodge put the plate of sliced bread next to the butter pot and sat down. "Should we send Wiggins for Luty and Hatchet? They're not due here for another hour at the earliest."

"That won't be necessary." Mrs. Jeffries poured the tea into the cluster of mugs she'd put on the table earlier. "In any case, they can't do their part until later today. But I need these three out and about early." She finished pouring and waved her hand, indicating they were to help themselves.

No one asked any questions. They all knew the housekeeper wouldn't tell them what she suspected until she was certain she was right. For the next few moments, the room was silent as they fixed their tea to their liking, buttered bread, and came fully awake.

"All right, Mrs. J, what is it ya need me to do?" Smythe asked.

She thought for a moment, trying to sort through the best means to confirm her suspicions. There were several ways one could go about this task. She wanted to be as efficient as possible. "Luckily, the inspector isn't due to see the chief until tomorrow, so we're not going to be too badly rushed. But I think I'd like you to go to the communal gardens at the Whitfield house. Find out if there's foxglove growing anywhere in the garden. This time of year it might look like a weed, so perhaps it would be best if you found the gardener or the groundsman and asked him."

"Is that it?" He didn't want to point it out, but he needn't have been awakened at the crack of dawn for such an errand, especially as they weren't pressed for time.

"For the moment." She turned to Wiggins. "Can you find that housemaid you spoke with before, the one that told you about going with Whitfield to deliver his bottles of port to his friends?"

"That'd be dead easy. She should still be at the Whitfield 'ouse."

"Excellent. I want you to find out how many bottles of port were delivered and, more importantly, where."

Wiggins glanced at the clock. "You want me to go now? Isn't it a bit early?"

"That's the best time to try to see the girl without the butler or housekeeper catching you," Mrs. Goodge answered. "It's the young girls that must get up early to light the fires and make the tea. The cook won't come down until eight, so if you hurry, it ought to be just the younger girls up and about the kitchen."

"What about Fred's walkies? Usually the inspector likes me to take 'im out."

"Don't worry, lad—just be off with you," the cook ordered. "We'll take care of Fred's walkies. The exercise will do me good."

"Alright, alright, I'm goin'." Wiggins took a quick sip of his tea, grabbed a slice of bread, smeared some butter on it, and rose to his feet. Smythe had got up as well, and the two of them went over to the coat tree.

"What about me?" Betsy asked.

"Your task is going to be quite difficult." Mrs. Jeffries

took a deep breath. She wasn't sure she should even send her on what might turn out to be a fool's errand. "I'm not certain you'll be able to track down this information, but I think it's important that you try. Last year one of Henry Becker's neighbors died. I'll need you to find out the person's name and the circumstances of the death."

Smythe was putting on his coat, but he stopped and started to say something. Betsy gave him a hard stare, and he clamped his mouth shut and started doing up his buttons. He grabbed his scarf and wound it around his neck. "Just be careful," he said to her as he and Wiggins made for the back door.

"Get back as soon as you can," Mrs. Jeffries called after them. She looked at the maid. "I'll understand if you don't wish to . . ."

"Don't be silly." Betsy laughed and pushed away from the table. "I'll find out something, Mrs. Jeffries. Don't you worry. But I've no idea how long it might take."

"Don't spend too much time on it," Mrs. Jeffries said. "I might need you for another task. Try and be back before too late this afternoon."

"I will." Betsy grabbed her long cloak and bonnet, checked the pocket for her gloves, and then hurried toward the back door.

"The house seems awfully quiet this morning," Witherspoon said. He looked up from his plate of bacon and eggs. "Is everything all right?"

"Everything is fine, sir." Mrs. Jeffries smiled brightly. "And you're correct, as usual. The house is quiet. I've sent Wiggins out on errands, Smythe has gone to Howard's to see to the horses in case you should need the carriage over the holidays, and Betsy's gone to Mrs. Crookshank's to borrow a recipe book for Mrs. Goodge." She laughed. "What an excellent detective you are, sir. Most people wouldn't have noticed the change in the atmosphere."

She was deliberately building up his confidence. She'd been dropping hints about her idea since he'd come downstairs, but so far she had no indication that she'd made any progress.

He beamed in delight. "You're giving me far too much credit, Mrs. Jeffries. Though, I will admit, a good night's sleep has restored my spirits a bit." The door knocker sounded. He broke off and gazed toward the front of the house. "I do believe that's Constable Barnes' knock. It's most distinctive."

As Barnes was expected, this was hardly brilliant detective work, but Mrs. Jeffries nodded in appreciation as she went out to the hall. She flung open the door, but before Barnes could open his mouth, she grabbed his arm and pulled him into the foyer. "Constable, I don't mean to be rude, but you must listen to me. You've got to get the inspector to question Maria Farringdon again. It's vitally important. Ask her to show you the bottle of ruby port that she received from Whitfield."

As the constable was well aware of Mrs. Jeffries' activities and had only the highest regard for her intelligence and abilities, he didn't waste time with needless questions. "What if she claims she tossed it into the dustbin?"

"It was a Christmas gift. She won't have done that." Mrs. Jeffries cast an anxious glance down the hall. "If she sticks to her guns over the matter, ask to speak to her servants. She'll know good and well that if she had really chucked out the wine, one of them would have fished it from the trash and kept it."

"Is that Constable Barnes?" Witherspoon called.

Barnes nodded that he understood. "It is indeed, sir, and I've come with some unsettling news," he announced as he stepped into the dining room.

Mrs. Jeffries followed him, but she stopped just inside the doorway.

"Unsettling news?" Witherspoon repeated. He half rose from his chair. "Egads, what is it now? What's wrong?"

"The chief inspector wants to see you this afternoon," Barnes said.

"But our appointment was for tomorrow morning." The inspector sank back to his seat.

"He changed it to today, sir. I stopped in at Ladbroke-Grove station on my way here. Griffiths had just come back from headquarters with a message from the chief. You're to go in at half past four today, sir." Barnes pursed his lips. "Griffiths thought Inspector Nivens might have something to do with this. The constable saw him coming out of the chief's office, lookin' right pleased with himself."

Witherspoon sighed and then shrugged. "I suppose it's just as well. There's no point in postponing the inevitable. But I will admit that after thinking about the matter, I had come up with some other ideas about the case."

"But you're not seeing the chief until late this afternoon," Mrs. Jeffries said. "You've still time to go to the Farringdon house."

He stared at her blankly, and she realized that even though she'd been dropping hints ever since he'd come downstairs, she'd not mentioned Maria Farringdon. "Oh, come now, sir. You know I'm on to your methods," she said hastily. "We've spent the last half hour talking about Whitfield's Christmas port. Of course you're going to want to speak to her again."

"Yes, I suppose I should." He still looked confused.

"I'm glad we're going back, sir," Barnes added. "I've wondered what she did with her bottle as well."

Smythe got back before either Betsy or Wiggins. Luty and Hatchet had been there but were already gone after having been given their assignments. When Smythe came into the kitchen, Mrs. Goodge was rolling out puff pastry and Mrs. Jeffries was pacing back and forth. She stopped in front of the sideboard.

"There's not a bit of foxglove anywhere in the communal garden," he reported. He expected her to be disappointed, but she merely nodded as though this was what she'd anticipated hearing. "You don't seem surprised."

"I was hoping you'd find it there. I didn't want to have to send you all the way to Dover."

"Dover?" he repeated.

"Specifically, I want you to go to the Thompson Hotel and see if there's any growing in their gardens." She looked over her shoulder at the carriage clock on the sideboard shelf. "It's already nine. Can you get to Dover and back here by half past three?"

He thought for a moment. "I should be able to manage. Why? I thought we weren't pressed for time on this one."

"We weren't, but we are now," Mrs. Jeffries answered. "The inspector's been ordered to report to the chief inspector at half past four today. If we don't have something useful on this murder by then, he's going to be pulled off it."

"And the case will probably be given to Inspector Nivens," Mrs. Goodge added. "We can't have that. Nivens is so desperate to make a name for himself and make our inspector look bad that he'll arrest the first person he lays eyes on."

Mrs. Jeffries nodded in agreement. "I couldn't have put it better myself."

"Blast a Spaniard," Smythe muttered. "I'd better get moving, then. I'll be back by half past. Don't worry—I'll not let you down."

"Why are you here again, Inspector?" Basil Farringdon narrowed his eyes, glaring at the two policemen standing in his drawing room. "This is the third time you've disturbed my household. It's becoming tiresome, and I'll not have it. If you don't leave immediately, I'll be filing a formal complaint with your superiors."

Witherspoon squared his shoulders and met Farringdon's gaze. "You may do as you see fit, sir. But a murder has been committed, and if I might remind you, you and your wife were the ones who brought the means of the murder into Mr. Whitfield's home."

Farringdon's jaw dropped. "How dare you . . . ?"

"I'm doing my job, sir," the inspector interrupted. "Now if you'll ask your wife to join us, we'll ask our questions and get out of your home."

"I'm right here, Inspector." Maria Farringdon appeared in the doorway. She stared at Witherspoon with undisguised hostility, crossed the room, and stood next to her husband.

"Good day, ma'am," the inspector began.

"Let's dispense with the social niceties, shall we?" she said coldly. "Just ask your questions and be on your way."

"You don't have to answer them," Basil said to her. "I'm going to make a complaint."

"We'd like to see the bottle of ruby port that Mr. Whitfield brought you," Barnes blurted.

She didn't answer. She simply stood there, staring at them. But Witherspoon noticed that her face had gone paler, and the hand at her side had suddenly balled into a fist.

"I've no idea where it is," she finally said.

"Oh for goodness' sake, Maria, show them the wretched thing so they'll leave. I'm sure Richards put it in the wine rack in the butler's pantry." Basil Farringdon glanced at his wife and then moved toward the bellpull beside the door. "I'll just call him."

"Richards was ill the day Stephen came," she said quickly. "So I didn't give it to him to take to the cellar."

Farringdon stopped. "What did you do with it?"

"I chucked it in the dustbin," she said. "I'm sorry, Basil. I know he was a close friend of yours, but I couldn't abide that dreadful stuff. So I threw it away." She looked at the two policemen and smiled confidently. "I'm sorry, Inspector, but I can't show you the bottle. It's gone."

"May we speak to your servants, then?" Barnes asked quickly.

Panic flashed across her face, but she caught herself. "No, you may not. I'd like you to leave."

"We'll leave if you insist, Mrs. Farringdon," Witherspoon replied somberly. "But we will take every one one of your servants with us."

"This is an outrage," Basil blustered. "What on earth are you talking about? You've no right to barge in here, bully us about, and then threaten to take my household God knows where . . ."

"We'd simply be asking them to accompany us to the station to help with our inquiries," Barnes added smoothly.

"It's alright, dear." Maria moved to her husband and took his hand. "Calm yourself. You know what the doctor said about getting overly excited."

He stared at her in confusion for a moment before the realization dawned that she knew more than she'd told him. "For God's sake, Maria," he whispered. "What is going on?"

"I didn't kill him." She looked directly into her husband's eyes as she spoke. "I promise you that."

"Of course you didn't. I know you're not capable of such an act." He seemed to have forgotten that he and his wife weren't alone. "But what's happening? You must tell me."

"Just listen, dear." She took a deep breath and turned to Witherspoon. "How did you discover what I'd done?"

As he still wasn't certain, he tried to be as noncommittal as possible. "It wasn't difficult to figure out, ma'am. But it would be helpful if you'd explain why you did it."

"I wanted to prove a point, Inspector. It's as simple as that."

"I still don't quite see . . ." He let his voice trail off, hoping she'd say a bit more.

"Stephen Whitfield was a dreadful man," she said harshly. "He made it obvious that he thought my husband had married beneath him."

"Maria." Basil put his arm around her shoulders and pulled her close. "Don't say such a thing."

"But it's true, dear—that's what he thought," she continued. "He was always insulting me in nasty little ways. At the summer fete, he pretended that my champagne cups were off, and at a dinner party last Christmas he complained that the wine I served didn't go with the fish course, when I know it did. So I wanted to show the whole world that his opinion was worthless, that he couldn't tell the difference between a ruby port and a Bordeaux." She paused. "When he gave me the port, I took it up to my room and pasted the label from the Locarno on top of his handwritten label. I save labels, you know. That's how I know the wine I served with the turbot was perfect. Lady Emmerson had served the same combination at one of her dinners."

"Maria, why didn't you tell me?" Basil looked at her. "If I'd known how he made you feel, I'd have made sure we avoided him. I'd never have accepted his dinner invitations."

"Don't be silly, darling." She smiled wanly. "You'd known him all your life. We were part of the same social circles, so it would have been impossible to avoid him. That's why I did it, you see. I wanted to teach him a lesson once and for all. I wanted to let him know that I could fight back. When he drank his own port that night, thinking he was drinking an expensive French wine, I was delighted. Once I saw him pouring it down his throat like a drunken sailor, I decided to tell everyone over dessert what I'd done. I was going to pretend it was a jest, something I'd done that was playful and festive. But he'd know the truth. He'd know I'd done it to show everyone that his opinions about food and wine were worthless." She gave a disappointed sigh. "But I never got the opportunity. He collapsed before we'd even finished the first course."

"Why didn't you tell us this?" Witherspoon asked.

"Are you serious, Inspector? I couldn't possibly confess to playing a nasty trick on a man who died at his own dinner party. How would that look? Then when I found out he'd been murdered, I was even less inclined to admit what I'd done."

Witherspoon wasn't certain what this development in the investigation meant, but he was beginning to have the glimmer of an idea. "So the bottle was never opened while in your possession here?"

"Of course not. That was the whole point of the exercise, to prove that he couldn't tell one wine from another. I simply put my label on top of his and gave it back to him. I had a bad moment when Basil handed over the bottle. Stephen stared at it for such a long time that I was sure he was on to me, but I needn't have worried. He was simply playing the exuberant host by pretending to be so touched by our gift."

"Maria, he was touched," Basil chided.

"Don't be silly. He was annoyed that we'd turned up with a better wine than that miserable port he gave to all his friends." She stepped away from her husband. "But even though the port was dreadful, Stephen had done a good job with the corking, so the bottle looked as if it came from a winery and not someone's cellar."

"I see," the inspector murmured. "What would you have done if he'd not drunk the wine in front of you?"

"My original plan was to ask him later how he enjoyed it," she replied. "If he said it was wonderful, which I hoped he would, I was going to tell him it wasn't a Bordeaux, but a port. The two don't taste at all alike, Inspector, and he'd have been terribly upset that I knew his little secret. Then I was going to spread the story all over town."

"What if he'd noticed the difference?" Witherspoon asked.

"But I knew he wouldn't, Inspector. That was the whole point. He had no sense of taste or smell, yet he acted as if he was a connoisseur."

"I see." Witherspoon didn't see at all. It seemed a silly and pointless trick.

"Frankly, I was amazed that none of your people discovered the truth. The police have had the bottle in their possession since the night it happened, Inspector. But then again, I did do a very good job of pasting the label in place," she said with a proud smile.

"The hard part was gettin' the names of all the tontine members out of that clerk." Luty chuckled and tossed her muff onto the table. "Once we had that, the rest was easy."

"It wasn't the least bit difficult once you started waving money about. I found it shocking that the clerk was so easily bribed." Hatchet pulled out her chair, seated her, and slipped into the seat next to her.

"You bribed a clerk?" Wiggins asked. He was grinning.

"It seemed the fastest way," Luty admitted. She glanced around the table. "Should I wait for Smythe before I start?"

"No, go ahead," Mrs. Jeffries replied. "We can't delay any longer. It's almost half past three."

"I'll tell it fast, then." Luty pulled a folded paper out of her muff and opened it. "There were seven charter members of the tontine who survived to adulthood. One of them died a long time ago of scarlet fever, two of them are still alive, and the other four died within the last four years." She began to read. "Whitfield just died. Last January, Jeremy McDevitt died of heart failure. Two years ago, also in January, Harold Stumps had a heart attack that killed him. And guess what—three years ago Martha Slade passed on of natural causes." She looked up at the rest of the group. "The clerk couldn't find out how she'd died, just that it was considered a natural death. The fourth one, Mr. Augustus Bromston-Brown, died four years ago, but he died in February."

"What killed him?" Mrs. Goodge asked.

"Same as most of the others—he had some sort of heart trouble." Luty put the paper on the table and looked at Mrs. Jeffries. "Does this help any?"

"Very much so, Luty," she replied. "And you have my sincerest thanks. You and Hatchet had a very difficult task, and you did it efficiently and quickly. I'm sorry you had to spend your money to bribe the clerk at Runyon's office . . ."

"Oh, I've done that kind of thing lots of times," Luty admitted. "So no thanks are needed. And I've got plenty of money. I don't mind spendin' some of it to catch a killer. I just hope that what we've learned helps."

"It does, but so far most of our evidence is circumstantial," Mrs. Jeffries said. She looked at Wiggins. "Were you successful?"

"Rosie was a bit surprised to see me, but I told 'er I was workin' for a private inquiry agency, and she was willin' to answer my questions." He smiled self-consciously. "She told me that when she helped Whitfield deliver the port, they only went to two houses—the Farringdons' and Henry Becker's. She said she didn't understand how he could have made such a mess in the cellar—he only corked up two bottles of the port."

"Very good. You've done well." She turned to Betsy. "I know your task wasn't easy, either."

Betsy laughed. "It wasn't hard, Mrs. Jeffries. I went into the local greengrocer's and asked if . . . Well, never mind how I found out. The fact is that Henry Becker has only had one neighbor who has died in the past year or so, and that was the poor man that lived next door. His name was Hiram Bates, he was fifty-eight, and he had a heart attack last January . . . Oh, my goodness, another one."

"There seems to be a rash of heart attack deaths in January," Hatchet said thoughtfully.

"It's Christmas that kills 'em," Mrs. Goodge declared. "All that rich food."

"I don't think it's rich food." Luty eyed Mrs. Jeffries speculatively.

"No, it isn't." Mrs. Jeffries cast an anxious glance at the clock. "But we don't have time to discuss this now. We've a decision to make." She took a deep breath. "We must stop Inspector Witherspoon from meeting with Chief Inspector Barrows. I'd hoped Smythe would be here by now—he may have the final piece of the puzzle, the final proof of my idea. But we can't wait any longer . . ." She trailed off as she heard the back door flung open, then the sound of steps pounding up the hallway.

Startled out of a nice nap, Fred leapt up and began barking. Samson, who'd been curled on Mrs. Goodge's lap, shot up, hissed, and ran for the safety of the cook's quarters.

"Easy, boy, it's just me," Smythe said to the dog as he charged into the room. He looked first to make sure Betsy was there and then focused his attention on Mrs. Jeffries. "There's foxglove in the hotel gardens, and what's more, I've got a witness that saw him collecting it last summer. One of the gardeners remembers him. They had words when the gardener asked him to stop pulling the leaves off the flowers."

"The gardener was sure it was him?" she pressed.

"Oh, yes." Smythe grinned broadly. "They knew him well. He's been going there every August for four years now."

"Who did they know?" Mrs. Goodge demanded. "Who are we talking about? I'm confused."

"Stephen Whitfield," Mrs. Jeffries said softly. "He's our murderer."

CHAPTER 11

"But he's the one that's dead," the cook cried. "How can he be the killer?"

"I'll explain later," Mrs. Jeffries replied. "Right now we must stop Inspector Witherspoon from meeting with Barrows." She turned to Smythe. "How long will it take you to get to New Scotland Yard?"

"This time of day, it'll be 'ard findin' an empty hansom," he began.

"The carriage is right outside," Luty interrupted. "We can take ya."

"And our coachman is an expert at finding alternate routes to avoid traffic," Hatchet added.

"Go and get him," Mrs. Jeffries instructed. "Tell him we've an emergency here at home, and he must come at once."

Smythe didn't move. "I'm not questionin' your decision, Mrs. Jeffries, but what's the rush here? Even if our inspector sees the chief and gets taken off the case, that'll not change the facts of the matter. Whitfield will still be the killer. We'll still be able to prove it."

"You don't understand. If Nivens gets it, he'll be the one in charge, and he'll never accept evidence he doesn't find for himself." She looked at the clock again. "And unless Whitfield took a terrible risk this time, which I'm not certain he did, we'll have no way of proving we're correct except with circumstantial evidence." There was one final item that might prove her theory correct, but she wasn't certain Whitfield had been desperate enough to actually poison both men.

"Nivens is out to make a name for himself," Mrs. Goodge pointed out impatiently. "He'll not be concerned with justice, and he's got enough political friends to make sure none of the evidence we find ever sees the light of day." She understood how the world worked.

"Let's go," Luty ordered. "We can just about make it in time if we hurry."

The three of them turned and rushed toward the hall. Smythe skidded to a halt at the kitchen doorway. "What kind of emergency is it to be?"

Mrs. Jeffries said the first thing that popped into her head. "Tell him that he must come home straightaway. Tell him that Mrs. Goodge has collapsed."

The hansom pulled up in front of the tall redbrick building that housed the headquarters of the Metropolitan Police. They climbed out, and Barnes stopped to pay the driver. A cold wind blew off the river, and Witherspoon grabbed his bowler to keep it from flying off as he rushed across the short cobblestone yard to the front door. The constable was right on his heels.

They went inside, nodded a greeting at the two policemen behind the counter, and started for the staircase. Barnes
slowed his steps and glanced over his shoulder, hoping to
see another hansom pull up and a member of the inspector's
household leaping out. He knew that once this case was
handed over to Nivens, any hope of justice would go right
out the window. But he saw nothing except a few pedestri-
ans, their heads bowed against the strong winds as they hurried toward the bridge.

"I think you ought to tell the chief we've made progress,
sir," Barnes suggested. "You found out about Mrs. Farringdon's little trick. It's only a matter of time before you solve
it, sir."

Witherspoon started up the steps. "I don't think that
matters now. Unless I can walk into Barrows' office and tell
him we're going to be making an arrest, he's going to take
me off the case. I don't think he's any choice in the matter."

"That's not fair, sir," Barnes protested. "No one can solve
a homicide in less than a fortnight."

"We've done it before, Constable," Witherspoon reminded him. "But it's a pity to lose it now. I'm beginning to
have an idea about what might . . . Oh well, it can't be
helped. Nivens wants this case, and he has powerful political friends."

They'd reached the first floor. The inspector started down
the long hallway, walking briskly with his shoulders back
and his spine straight. Barnes followed at a more sedate pace,
his mind working frantically to find a way out of the situation. Like the inspector, he, too, had an idea about the murder of Stephen Whitfield, and he didn't want to see the truth
buried under Nivens' incompetence or, even worse, watch an
innocent person be arrested.

But try as he might, he couldn't come up with one single

fact that might keep them from losing the case. Barnes sighed heavily as they neared the end of the corridor.

Barrows' office door was shut, but just then the one opposite it opened, and Inspector Nigel Nivens stepped into the hallway. He nodded curtly. "Witherspoon, Barnes. The chief is expecting us. He said he'd be free in a few minutes."

"Thank you, Inspector Nivens," Witherspoon said politely.

"You couldn't solve this one, could you?" Nivens gave them a smug smile. "It appears you're not quite as brilliant as you think."

"I've never claimed to be brilliant," the inspector said softly. "But I have had a decent record of homicide convictions."

"Humph." Nivens snorted and cast a quick glance at Barrows' door. "You've had help, and you've been damned lucky."

Witherspoon said nothing.

"We're very close to solving it, sir," Barnes said. "And that's what I'm going to tell the chief. All we need is a bit more time."

"Constable Barnes," Witherspoon warned.

"Time." Nivens sneered. "You've had over a week. You're not getting another minute on this case. I've seen to that."

Barnes was momentarily distracted by the sound of footsteps pounding up the staircase. He looked down the corridor.

The door to Barrows' office opened, and the chief inspector appeared. "I wasn't aware you were in charge of reassigning cases," Barrows said.

Barnes jerked his head around. Barrows stood just inside his office, frowning at Inspector Nivens.

"But of course I'm not, Chief Inspector." Nivens' smile

was strained. "That's your responsibility. I was merely jesting with the constable here. My little joke, as it were."

Barrows didn't smile back. He simply pulled his door open wider and gestured for them to come inside.

Three people suddenly appeared at the top of the staircase. Barnes sagged in relief as Smythe, Hatchet, and Mrs. Crookshank charged down the hallway, oblivious to the racket their pounding steps made against the wood floor.

"What on earth is that?" Barrows asked. He moved past Witherspoon and Nivens, both of whom had already stepped into his office, and stuck his head out.

"It's the inspector's coachman," Barnes replied.

"Who are those other people?" the chief demanded.

"Friends." The constable moved toward the rapidly approaching figures. "Is something wrong?" he called.

"The inspector's got to come home right away." Smythe tried to catch his breath. He smiled apologetically in the direction of the frowning chief. "Mrs. Goodge has collapsed and might be dying."

"Oh, my good gracious." Witherspoon pushed past Nivens and Barrows. "What happened?"

"Witherspoon, what is this?" Nivens had followed him out. "What kind of trick are you trying to pull now?"

"Sorry to interrupt, Inspector, Chief Inspector." Hatchet took off his top hat and bowed politely. "But Mrs. Goodge has taken seriously ill, and you must come at once. Luckily, the madam and I happened to be there when the unfortunate incident occurred, so we were able to bring Smythe along to fetch you."

"We'll take ya back in our coach," Luty added. "You come along now—there's no time to waste. She might not last much longer."

"Oh dear, this is horrid. Poor Mrs. Goodge." Witherspoon turned to the chief. "I'm dreadfully sorry, sir, but I must go home. My household is very dear to me."

"Of course you must go, Witherspoon." Barrows glanced at Nivens. "This can wait until tomorrow."

"Now, just a minute. It's a trick," Nivens yelled. "They're all in on it."

"We'd better hurry." Witherspoon clamped his bowler onto his head and started off. "I do hope it's not too late."

"You come along, too, Constable," Hatchet said as they turned to go. "We've plenty of room in the carriage, and you live out that way."

"Thank you," Barnes said as he fell into step behind them. "That would be very helpful."

"You're not going to let them get away with this, are you?" Nivens protested.

"Inspector Nivens." Barrows' voice was harsh. "Be careful what you say. Slandering a fellow officer is a serious offense and will not be tolerated."

"But it's a trick, I tell you, a trick. Tomorrow morning he's going to walk into your office and claim he's solved the murder."

Barnes sincerely hoped that would be the case.

"What do I do when the inspector gets here?" Mrs. Goodge asked worriedly. She wasn't one to complain, but she had no idea what they expected of her.

"Lie on the floor and pretend you're at death's door," Wiggins suggested.

"Lie on the floor?" she repeated. "Are you mad? It's too cold. I can look ill sittin' in my usual seat."

"But it would look better if you was lying there." He pointed to a spot in front of the worktable. "Make it more real-like."

"Mrs. Goodge can be resting in her chair," the housekeeper interjected, "and she isn't at death's door. She simply
fainted, and she feels much better now. But I do think a nice
warm blanket around her shoulders would be appropriate."

"I'll run fetch one," Betsy offered.

"There's a nice plaid traveling rug on the foot of my
bed," the cook said. "Get that one."

Mrs. Jeffries waited till Betsy had come back and draped
the brown and gold wrap over the cook's shoulder's before
she continued with her instructions. "When he arrives, try
to follow my lead. I'm not certain our plan will work, but as
it's the only one we have, we must do our best." She'd already told them about the hints she'd dropped into the inspector's ear this morning. "Let's hope that I was correct in
my assumption about Maria Farringdon, and that when he
interviewed her today, she admitted what she'd done." She
silently prayed that her own reasoning had been correct in
this matter, but after putting all the facts together, she'd
come to the conclusion that it was the only way Whitfield's
death made any sense.

They heard the sound of a carriage pulling up outside.
"Get ready, everyone," Mrs. Jeffries warned. "He's here."

Moments later, Witherspoon and the others raced into
the kitchen. "Is she all right?" He charged toward her.
"How bad is it? Has the doctor been here?"

"I'm fine, Inspector." Mrs. Goodge raised her gaze to
meet his. "I do feel such a fool, collapsing the way I did. I'm
so sorry you were disturbed."

"Please don't concern yourself with that, Mrs. Goodge.
You're more important than a meeting." He dropped to his
knees next to her chair.

Mrs. Jeffries saw that his face was pale and his mouth so

white it looked as if the blood had drained all the way to his toes. A pang of guilt shot through her as she realized her ruse had frightened him badly. She vowed she'd make this up to him somehow. But justice was a harsh mistress, and she couldn't risk an innocent person's being arrested.

"Thank you, sir." Mrs. Goodge's lips trembled. "You're very kind. But I'm truly feeling much better. It was just a faint."

"But you must see the doctor," he insisted.

"Oh, no, sir, that wouldn't do at all." Her voice caught, as though she were trying hard not to cry. "Doctors frighten me. I'm fine, truly fine. It was just a faint."

"But you might be very ill," he pressed.

"I'll see a doctor if it happens again," she said.

"I think that's a splendid compromise," Mrs. Jeffries said hastily. She was impressed by the cook's acting ability. She was doing a superb job. "I do think it was just a faint, sir. Mrs. Goodge got up very early this morning to finish her Christmas baking, and she didn't eat breakfast."

"That's right, sir—I didn't eat breakfast, and when you get to be my age, you shouldn't miss your meals." Mrs. Goodge gave him a weak smile. "I'll not make that mistake again, sir. Honestly, now that I've had something to eat and drink, I feel much better."

Witherspoon rose slowly to his feet. "Alright, then, I'll respect your wishes. But you must promise me you'll see a doctor if this happens again."

"Oh, I will, sir. I truly will."

"You should take it easy for the next few days," he instructed.

"Thank you, sir, and again, I'm sorry to have interrupted your work."

"Speaking of which, sir, did you see Mrs. Farringdon to-day?" Mrs. Jeffries asked. She was painfully aware of everyone watching her, waiting for her to take the lead.

"We did. She admitted that she'd pasted one of her wine labels onto the bottle of port that Whitfield gave them as a Christmas gift," he replied. He seemed unaware that he had a kitchen full of people staring at him. "It was most extraordinary, but it does reaffirm my idea."

"It's more than just an idea, sir," she said with a wide smile. "I'm sure the chief inspector was delighted when you told him you'd solved the case."

"Solved the case," Witherspoon repeated.

"Now, sir, don't be modest," she laughed.

"That's your problem, sir," Barnes added quickly. "You're far too modest. Not at all like that Inspector Nivens—he's always braggin' about his arrests. Now, sir, I know you probably don't want to speak too much about it until you've thought it through the way you always do. But seein' as how it's Christmas, maybe you can give us just a hint on how you came up with your idea."

"Oh, please, Inspector," Luty cried. "Do tell. We love hearing about your work." She grabbed Hatchet's arm and yanked him toward the table. He recovered in time to pull out her chair before taking his own seat.

"I think you're ever so clever, Inspector." Betsy stared at him in admiration. "Most people could never take just a few facts and put them together to catch the killer the way you can, sir."

"Well, er, uh, once I realized that none of the other dinner guests had any real motive for wanting Whitfield dead, I had to . . . uh, look at the crime from an entirely different perspective."

"Was that when you figured it out?" Mrs. Goodge asked.

She knew good and well that it had been Mrs. Jeffries' hints that had put that particular notion in the inspector's head. She was glad he remembered it.

"Well, certainly, that was a part of my reasoning," he replied.

"And today when Mrs. Farringdon admitted what she'd done, and that the Bordeaux was actually the bottle of port he'd given her, is that when you realized that with Basil Farringdon dead, there were only Becker and Whitfield left in the tontine?" Barnes said.

"Yes, er, that did occur to me," Witherspoon said eagerly. "That's precisely what I thought. Port is a man's drink, so I was certain it was meant for Mr. Farringdon, not his wife." The picture in his mind was becoming clearer by the minute. He suddenly understood what his inner voice had been trying to tell him since he'd come down to breakfast this morning. "Of course, proving all this is going to be very difficult."

"You'll find a way, sir," Smythe said.

"We could always press for an exhumation order on the other tontine members who have died in the past few years," Barnes suggested. He was fairly certain he now understood what had happened. "As you said, sir, it seemed that every January, Becker and Whitfield met at a funeral of an old friend. I'll warrant that most of those funerals were tontine members and that all of them had received one of Whitfield's Christmas bottles."

"Yes, I suppose we could do that." Witherspoon frowned in confusion as a dozen different courses of action whirled about in his brain. "But I'm not sure we'd get such an order. The courts are generally very opposed to digging someone up, especially on this kind of evidence. It's all circumstantial."

"Don't tease us, sir." Mrs. Jeffries laughed gaily. "That's not the only trick you have up your sleeve. Before you even ask for any sort of order, you're going to test the bottle of port that Whitfield sent to Becker. Am I right?"

"Yes, yes, you are," he cried. "And how did you know I was going to do that?"

"Because Whitfield was still planning on taking Mrs. Graham to Italy," she said. "And as he'd proposed and she'd not given him an affirmative answer, he took matters into his own hands."

"Go on." Witherspoon adopted the pose of a schoolmaster questioning a clever student.

"Have you ever seen the like?" Luty said in a voice just loud enough for the inspector to hear. "He's smarter than that Sherlock Holmes character." She hoped she wasn't overdoing it too much.

"Aha, I see you want me to show that I've been paying close attention to your methods," Mrs. Jeffries replied. "Well, sir, I shan't disappoint you. According to Mrs. Graham's own words, she needs to marry for financial reasons. As she'd not agreed to Whitfield's marriage proposal, he realized that she'd probably been able to ascertain his true financial situation and understood that marriage to him wouldn't give her what she wanted: lifelong security in the manner to which she was accustomed to living. Am I correct so far?"

He nodded.

"Therefore Whitfield concluded that the only way he could have her as his wife was to obtain money of his own, not simply an annuity that went back into the tontine pot upon his death." She paused. "As there were only three of them left, Whitfield decided that this year, he'd kill off Farringdon and Becker both."

"Which would mean that he got it all," Wiggins exclaimed. "Only he didn't count on Mrs. Farringdon sendin' 'is own poisoned wine back to 'im."

"That's correct, Wiggins." Witherspoon nodded in satisfaction. He was so proud of his household. He'd truly taught them to love justice. "And therefore, if my theory is correct, Becker's bottle should contain poison as well."

"That should be easy enough to check, sir," Barnes said. "All we have to do is have a good look and see if there's any leaves floatin' about in it."

"For a minute there, I thought we were doomed." Luty slumped down in her chair. "I was wonderin' if he was ever gonna catch on." She motioned for Hatchet to pass her the plate of apple tarts Mrs. Goodge had put out for their tea.

"I was fairly sure he'd understand," Mrs. Jeffries replied. "Inspector Witherspoon is no fool. He can add two and two and come up with four as easily as I can."

"But what if, when he gets to Becker's house this evening, the port doesn't have any poison in it?" Betsy asked. "What will we do then?"

"Oh, I shouldn't worry about that." Mrs. Jeffries smiled confidently. "Even if there isn't anything in Becker's port, we've still come up with enough evidence for the inspector to make a good case that the killer was Whitfield."

"What got you thinking that it might be him?" Hatchet helped himself to another tart.

"The realization that none of our other suspects had any genuine reasons for wanting him dead. I began to think I was looking at the whole matter the wrong way," she explained. "Once I learned about the tontine and that there were only three surviving members left, two of whom were already wealthy, I remember thinking that if it had been one of them who had died, then Whitfield would be the perfect suspect." That wasn't entirely true, but she could think of no other way to describe how it had all come together in that one bright moment of insight in the wee hours before dawn.

"And once you started down that path, then there was plenty of evidence that it had to be him." Mrs. Goodge bobbed her head for emphasis.

"We already knew that every January one of Whitfield's friends died," Mrs. Jeffries continued. "So I asked myself if these friends might have been other members of the tontine. Since we established that"—she gave Luty and Hatchet a quick, grateful smile—"then, even if Becker's port is free of foxglove, I imagine it will be easy to find out if these poor souls received a bottle of Whitfield's Christmas port."

"And every time one of them died, Whitfield's dividend went up," Smythe muttered.

"Once we found out that Maria Farringdon collected wine labels, then it made sense." Mrs. Jeffries raised her hand over her mouth to cover a yawn. "Oh dear, I am sorry."

Luty laughed and got up from the table. "Not to worry. We've got to be on our way. There's a Christmas ball at Henley House, and I've got to put in an appearance. But you let us know about Becker's port."

It was half past ten by the time Witherspoon came home that night. Mrs. Jeffries didn't even need to ask any questions—despite the late hour, he was grinning like a schoolboy. "The foxglove was there." He paused by the bottom stair. "You could see the crumbled leaves floating in the bottle. Whitfield was so confident he wouldn't be caught, he didn't even try to cover his tracks."

"Whitfield was arrogant, sir. He'd gotten away with it so

many other times, perhaps he thought he'd never be caught. Did Mr. Becker realize what you were doing?"

Witherspoon sighed. "He did. I felt sorry for the poor man. He considered Whitfield a friend. I don't think he has many friends." He started up the staircase. "Once I've handed in my report to the chief inspector tomorrow, we can put this matter to rest and enjoy our Christmas." He continued onward, but when he reached the first-floor landing, he stopped and looked back at her. "I do hope that Inspector Nivens doesn't raise too much of a fuss when he finds out the case has been solved."

But of course he did.

Christmas Eve was wet and cold. Witherspoon shook the rain off his bowler as he and Barnes walked down the hallway.

"He's here, sir," Barnes warned softly.

Nivens stood in the corridor outside Barrows' office. His eyes narrowed angrily as they approached. "I hope you're prepared to give up, Witherspoon," he warned. "I don't think the chief inspector is willing to put up with any more shenanigans out of you."

"Good morning, Inspector," Witherspoon responded politely. He moved past him to the office door, raised his hand, and gave a quiet knock. Barnes ignored Nivens completely.

"Come in," Barrows called.

Witherspoon twisted the knob and, as the door opened, Nivens shoved past him into the room. The other two followed.

Barrows looked up from the report he'd been reading and frowned. "Inspector Nivens, what is all this? You weren't invited to this meeting."

"I've a right to be here. You promised me this case."

Barrows stared at him a long moment. "The case has been solved. The inspector's report is right here." He tapped the pages on his desk. "So you've wasted time, which could have been properly used in keeping the peace, to come along and try to tell me how to do my job. I most certainly did not promise you this case. I said that if Inspector Witherspoon didn't solve it, I'd consider passing it along to you."

"My apologies, sir. I must have misunderstood you," Nivens replied coolly. "But as I'm here, may I ask who is being arrested for the Whitfield murder?"

Barrows pretended to think about it for a few seconds. He couldn't allow Nivens' insubordination to go unchallenged, but now that he'd reestablished his authority, he was inclined to be reasonable. Besides, he wasn't a fool. Nivens did have powerful friends. "No one is being arrested. Stephen Whitfield died by his own hand."

Nivens gaped at him in shock. "Are you saying the man committed suicide at his own dinner party? That's absurd."

Barrows looked at Witherspoon. "Would you care to explain?"

"Whitfield didn't deliberately take his own life. He was trying to murder Basil Farringdon. But Mrs. Farringdon played a rather odd trick on Whitfield—pasted a different label on the bottle and sent it back to him unopened. He drank it and died."

"How on earth did you reach that ridiculous conclusion?" Nivens snapped. He glared at Barrows. "This is just another one of his tricks. Now he even wants to take credit for the cases he couldn't solve. Are you going to let him get away with this?"

"Inspector Nivens, I've been more than patient with you." Barrows rose from his chair. "You are insubordinate, sir. If I say the case has been solved, then the bloody case has been solved. Now get out of here before I bring you up on formal charges."

Nivens' mouth opened and closed. Then he turned on his heel and stomped to the door. He banged his shoulder into Barnes as he shoved past, muttering to himself. He marched out the door, slamming it hard behind him.

"Gracious, sir, that was most unpleasant," Witherspoon said. "I am sorry that this case has caused you so much trouble. Inspector Nivens will be going straight to the Home Office."

"Let him do his worst." Barrows shrugged. "The man is an incompetent bully. Half of his arrests either result in acquittals or are tossed out of court. If he runs to his political pals and complains about what I've done, he'll be in for a nasty surprise. I've some weapons of my own I can use to defend myself and the department. Don't concern yourself on my account, Inspector." He tapped the report again. "You've done an excellent job here, and it was a very complex case."

"Thank you, sir." Witherspoon flushed in pleasure. "But of course it was a team effort. Constable Barnes and many other policemen worked very hard to help bring this matter to a close."

"I appreciate the fact that you got me the report so early this morning," Barrows continued. "I don't mind admitting, I had to read through it twice to make sure I understood how all the pieces came together. Whitfield was a fool and a murderer, but in the end he got what he deserved." He closed the report and looked Witherspoon directly in the eye. "It's a pity we can't go public with any of this. It looks as if your record is going to be a bit tarnished. Publicly, this must appear as if you couldn't solve this one."

"That's quite alright, sir," the inspector replied. "I understand."

Several years earlier there had been a series of unsolved murders in the East End, which had seriously undermined public trust in the Metropolitan Police Force. Jack the Ripper, as the press referred to the unknown killer, had never been caught. But as time passed, public confidence in the police had returned. If the true facts of this case were to come out, that faith could once again be shattered.

Witherspoon's report suggested quite strongly that Whitfield had murdered at least four people and he'd gotten away with it. The police hadn't had a clue that the crimes had even taken place.

"Have you had confirmation that it was foxglove leaves in the bottle you obtained from Henry Becker's residence?" Barrows asked. "We might as well get all the loose ends tied up nice and neat."

"Yes, sir. We stopped in at the station on the way here. There was poison in the bottle."

"I'm surprised we got confirmation so quickly." Barrows looked puzzled. "Surely a chemist or botanist couldn't have been found on such short notice."

"We fed it to some rats," Barnes answered. "When I walked into the station last night with Becker's bottle, they'd just caught some rodents. As rats will usually eat or drink anything, I suggested we see if the rats would drink the port. There were three of them, sir. So we poured out a bit of it in the top of a Cadbury cocoa tin and put it in the rat catcher's box. Two of them were dead this morning and the third was lying on his side, panting hard. He's probably dead by now, too. The cocoa lid was empty. As the rats looked healthy enough last night, we're pretty sure it was the poison that killed them."

"Ye gods, are you serious?" Barrows exclaimed. "How fiendishly clever."

"Thank you, sir." Barnes smiled proudly. "We are having the port properly analyzed. But as we were in a hurry for an answer, this seemed a sensible course of action."

Christmas Day dawned clear and cold. They all went to church in the morning, and then Inspector Witherspoon crossed the gardens to Lady Cannonberry's. He didn't come home until late that night.

The staff had their Christmas dinner in the kitchen, and afterward they exchanged presents, sang songs, and played games. Neighborhood friends dropped by with bottles of sherry, tins of chocolate, and even a fruit basket. Everyone ate too much, drank too much, and thoroughly enjoyed themselves.

On Boxing Day, they received their Christmas boxes from Witherspoon, and then he left to spend another day with Lady Cannonberry. The household was having guests of their own.

Luty and Hatchet, their arms laden with presents, arrived at noon, and Dr. Bosworth, who'd also been invited to share the day with them, had appeared twenty minutes later.

"I understand the Whitfield case has been resolved," he said as he handed Mrs. Jeffries his hat and coat. "You must tell me what happened. No one's been arrested for the murder."

They took turns telling him the details, and by the time they were ready to eat, he'd heard everything. Bosworth stared at them in amazement and then sat down in the chair next to Hatchet. "This was a most unusual case. It's truly a wonder that you solved it at all."

"Thank you," Mrs. Jeffries replied on behalf of all of them. "Would you care to say the blessing?" she asked.

"I would be delighted."

Everyone bowed their heads as he said grace.

When the doctor had finished and they'd all said a hearty "amen," Wiggins exclaimed, "Cor blimey, this is an even bigger feast than yesterday. Look at all this food."

"It's the Feast of St. Stephen," Mrs. Goodge said. "And I think it's only fitting that we're all here together, celebratin'. As the good doctor said, it's truly a wonder we solved this case at all."

"We'd be right miserable if we hadn't," Smythe murmured. He reached for Betsy's hand under the table and was relieved that she didn't pull away from him.

"But we did solve it." Luty raised her glass of beer. "And if you ask me, it's because we're the smartest bunch of detectives on this side of the river."

Everyone laughed and began to help themselves. As they ate, they discussed the case, gossiped, told jokes, and had a rollicking good time. The weather brightened that afternoon, so everyone went out into the garden for some fresh air.

Wiggins tossed sticks, which Fred felt honor bound to chase. Mrs. Goodge decided it was too cold, so she went back inside for a nap. Hatchet declared that Luty had had enough excitement, so they took their leave.

Smythe grabbed Betsy's hand and pulled her toward the kitchen door. "Come on. You promised we could have our talk today."

"But what if someone comes in?" Betsy protested.

"Mrs. Jeffries and Dr. Bosworth are discussing the size of bullet holes." He pointed at the two of them, who were seated on a bench near the big oak. "They'll be talkin' about it for hours."

"Where's Wiggins?"

"He's takin' Fred for a walk." Smythe gently urged her across the terrace and into the house.

The kitchen was very quiet, the only sound the ticking of the clock. Betsy took her usual chair, but Smythe, instead of taking the seat next to her, slipped into the spot directly across from her. He wanted to be able to watch her face.

Neither of them said a word for what seemed a very long time. Finally he cleared his throat and began, "You said you were still willin' to marry me."

"I did."

He was scared to ask the next question, but he had to. "Uh, when would we want to have the wedding?"

Betsy cocked her head to one side and crossed her arms over her chest. She'd thought hard about this matter, and she'd come to a decision. "Well, I'd not like it to be too soon. I'm still a bit raw about what happened."

"Alright, I can understand your feelin's about that," he replied.

"And this time, seein' as our last plans didn't work out the way we'd hoped, I'd like it to be a bit smaller."

He wasn't sure he understood. "What does that mean?"

"It means I want a much smaller wedding." She uncrossed her arms. "I don't want a wedding breakfast, and I don't want a lot of fuss and bother. We can get the banns read and then have a quiet wedding with just the household and a few close friends." She wasn't going to risk being humiliated in front of the whole world again.

A rush of anger surged through him, but as he watched her face, the temper vanished as quickly as it had come. He suddenly understood that she was afraid. Her words had sounded strong and confident, but he could see fear and pain in her eyes.

"Betsy, I love you more than anything in this world, and I'm sorry I hurt you. I'll marry you any way that you want. But know this—I'll never, ever leave you again."

"What if someone from your past shows up and they need you?" she asked. Her eyes misted with tears, but she blinked to keep them back.

"Then I'll take you with me," he replied. "I should have taken you with me to Australia. I should have at least asked and given you the choice. I'll not make that mistake again."

Once more she was silent. She looked away and took a deep breath. When she turned back to him, she was grinning from ear to ear. "That's what I've been waiting to hear ever since you got back. That I come first, that you'll never push me aside again."

"I didn't push you aside before."

"But it felt like you had," she said.

"I'm so sorry, love. I'll never hurt you again," he promised.

"Sure you will." She grinned. "We're going to be man and wife. Even the most devoted couples hurt each other from time to time. But just don't ever put me second again. Don't ever push me aside."

"I'll never push you aside." He leapt up and raced around the table.

Laughing, she got up, and he grabbed her, lifted her up over his head, and whirled her about the kitchen. "You've made me the happiest man in the world," he cried. "When, when are we going to wed?"

"Put me down," she giggled. "Someone will come."

Several of them were already there. Mrs. Jeffries and Dr. Bosworth were hovering in the doorway.

"Tell me when first," he demanded.

She'd thought about that, too. "I think I'd like to marry in the autumn. October is a good month."

"October it is, then," he cried.

"Cor blimey, what's goin' on?" Wiggins pushed past Mrs. Jeffries and the doctor. "Are we dancin', then?"

It was Betsy who answered. "I'm going to be a bride again."

"I like celebrations and parties. We gonna 'ave a big one?"

Smythe lowered her to the floor and waited for her to reply. She looked at the three people in the doorway. "Oh, yes, it's going to be a wonderful wedding. I'm going to invite everyone we know." She reached for his hand. "And this time, if you try to leave me at the altar, I'll hunt you down and skin you alive."

He was humbled by the trust she'd just given him. "I promise you, love—I'll never leave you again."

"And if he does, I'll 'elp ya hunt him down," Wiggins offered.